NEW YORK TIMES
Bestselling Author of
FORGET ME NOT,
A WOMAN WITHOUT LIES,
DESERT RAIN and WINTER FIRE

ELIZABETH LOWELL

IS
"INCOMPARABLE!"
Romantic Times

"A LAW UNTO
HERSELF IN THE WORLD
OF ROMANCE"
Amanda Quick

"NO ONE CAN
STIR THE PASSIONS,
NO ONE CAN
KEEP THE TENSION AT
SUCH A SIZZLING
HIGH, NO ONE CAN GIVE
YOU MORE MEMORABLE
CHARACTERS."
Rendezvous

Avon Books are available at special quantity discounts for bulk purchases for sales promotions, premiums, fund raising or educational use. Special books, or book excerpts, can also be created to fit specific needs.

For details write or telephone the office of the Director of Special Markets, Avon Books, Dept. FP, 1350 Avenue of the Americas, New York, New York 10019, 1-800-238-0658.

ELIZABETH LOWELL

Where the Heart Is

Previously published as
<u>TRAVELING MAN</u>

AVON BOOKS ◆ NEW YORK

Where the Heart Is was previously published in an altered form entitled *Traveling Man* by Silhouette Books in 1985.

AVON BOOKS
A division of
The Hearst Corporation
1350 Avenue of the Americas
New York, New York 10019

Copyright © 1985 by Ann Maxwell; 1997 by Two of a Kind, Inc.
Cover art by Fredericka Ribes
Inside cover author photo by Phillip Stewart Charis
Published by arrangement with the author
Visit our website at **http://AvonBooks.com**
Library of Congress Catalog Card Number: 96-95170
ISBN: 0-380-76763-5

First Avon Books Printing: May 1997

AVON TRADEMARK REG. U.S. PAT. OFF. AND IN OTHER COUNTRIES, MARCA REGISTRADA, HECHO EN U.S.A.

Printed in the U.S.A.

RAI 10 9 8 7 6 5 4 3 2 1

Chapter One

The last thing Shelley Wilde expected to find tucked away in the self-conscious gilt and velvet of her client's house was a man like Cain Remington.

Not that the French antique reproductions were Shelley's fault. She had done everything except hold a gun to JoLynn's stylish head and demand that she have a home that lived up to the spare elegance of its Pacific Palisades setting.

The land was magnificent.

The sky was a cloudless, burning blue. To the west, dry hills marched steeply down to the Pacific Ocean. Bleached by southern California's sun, grass on the hillsides rippled in a tawny echo of the sea's restless waves.

The view of water, wind, and land was untamed even by the expensive homes that stood astride the very crests of the hills.

At least the architect understood the view, Shelley thought. *The house itself has clean lines and a wonderful sense of place.*

What a pity that my client has neither.

The air inside the house was filtered, refrigerated, and carefully odorless. It could have belonged to a hotel anywhere in the world.

Outside the house, the wind was hot and alive, vivid with the scents of chaparral and the secrets of a dry, wild land. She could barely restrain herself from yanking aside the heavy drapes and throwing open the sliding glass doors that led to a redwood deck over-looking the sea.

If she had been given a free hand to decorate the house, the view would have become a living piece of art, a compelling sweep of primary color and primal force.

But Shelley's hands were well and truly tied. The client had insisted on a certain type of decor for her rented house. There must be nothing unusual or unexpected, and absolutely not one thing that wasn't universally applauded and labeled as tasteful.

If an object wasn't labeled, JoLynn didn't know what to think of it.

And despite man's best efforts, Shelley thought humorously, *the Pacific doesn't yet wear a designer label sewn neatly along the seam where land meets sea.*

So instead of the Ellsworth Kelley oils and the Saarinen furniture Shelley would have chosen, her client had required that the formal curves and stilted curlicues of Louis XIV fill the multilevel, ultramodern glass house.

From that choice had followed all the rest. One result was heavy blue velvet draperies shutting out the glorious view. Another was the rented crystal chandelier that looked rather startling against the open-beamed ceiling of the dining room.

Talk about not getting it. I'm surprised JoLynn didn't pout until the landlord let her paint the beams white.

Or gilt.

With a sigh that was also a mild curse, Shelley set aside her notebook. She didn't need to write down obvious or subtle signs of personality and use them to puzzle out the best choice in finishing touches for this house. Whatever individuality JoLynn might have was carefully hidden.

There was excellent taste in the house's interior decor, but no originality. There was great beauty but nothing unusual, nothing to give a clue to the unique combination of education and experience, hopes and fears, dreams and disappointments that made up JoLynn Cummings.

Unhappily, Shelley looked around again, hoping she had missed something.

She hadn't.

If there's anything more compelling than insecurity beneath my client's stunningly well-kept surface, she's not letting on. Everything she rented from my partner could have been taken right out of a catalog of museum knockoffs.

Maybe in the next room, she told herself. *Maybe the Louis Quatorze Fashion Police haven't been there yet.*

And then again, maybe they had.

In room after room, hallway after hallway, nothing was out of place. Even the maid's quarters were all gilt and grace, elegance and gilt. The blue and white and gold fragility was suffocating.

Not that the decor or furniture itself is at fault, Shelley admitted. *The furnishings are exquisite, like everything Brian rents to our wealthy clientele.*

Yet the unrelieved perfection made her itch to put in accents that would subtly remind people that this was a home, not a museum reproduction.

Yawning, she abandoned the fantasy of subtlety and JoLynn. It was obvious that the client didn't have enough confidence in her own taste to survive any ripples in the perfect surface Brian had created for her.

People like that are the easiest and least satisfying kind of client, Shelley thought idly. *Give her a room straight out of the last museum she saw, and she thinks you're brilliant.*

Less individuality and sense of adventure than a clam.

Hope I can stay awake long enough to do my duty. Or at least look like I'm doing it.

She glanced over her shoulder, but saw no one to relieve the boring perfection of the decor.

Brian and JoLynn must still be out in the garden discussing lawn furniture and outdoor marble statuary. White, of course.

Or do they still sell gilded cherubs? Shelley wondered with a shudder.

Part of her was afraid they did.

She skirted the large, flawlessly furnished living room with its velvet-and-chiffon draperies distorting the view of the wild sea. Without much hope, she approached the final wing of the house.

The first door at the end of the hall recently had been repainted white with gilt trim. With a shrug, she opened the door.

The room beyond made her take a quick, surprised breath. Someone in the house was fighting a battle for breathing space amid all the French perfection.

She smiled, then began laughing softly. *Intelligent life*, she thought eagerly. *Finally!*

Louis XIV replicas were almost buried beneath a random assortment of clothes, games, and unidentifiable objects. Posters of barbarians in full sword-and-sorcery costume were tacked to the eggshell walls.

Crookedly.

The hem of the velvet drapes had been ruthlessly stuffed over the top of the curtain rod. Now the spectacular view was part of the living space rather than an enemy at the luxuriously barred gate.

Two inlaid dresser drawers were partially open, allowing folds of socks and T-shirts to creep out into the light. The canopied bed was gloriously unmade. Its powder-blue velvet bedspread had been kicked onto the thick white carpet in a huge pile that was crowned by a pair of battered, grass-stained running shoes.

A turtle as big as a dinner plate was sunning itself in a muddy terrarium perched atop a gilt table. On the floor in a dark corner there was another terrarium with its lid askew.

Excitement quivering in her blood, Shelley looked around the room. She loved finding someone who met life head-on, nothing held back, no need for uniforms or labels or evasions.

This was one room and one personality it would be pure pleasure to work with.

There are so few people like that, she thought almost wistfully, *no matter what their age.*

And I'd guess that the person who "decorated" this room is somewhere between twelve and eighteen.

She approved of the spare yet functionally graceful lines of the computer that overran the dainty desk. Boxes of software were stacked on top of piles of comics and science fiction books. The closet door was jammed open with an ancient *Star Wars* light-sword that had been scratched and bent in cosmic battles. The television sprouted video games in a tangle of wires, cassettes, and joysticks.

But the crowning defiance was a stereo with black speakers powerful enough to speak to God.

Mentally she began a list of the accents she would love to add to the room. Right at the top of the list was a painting now hanging in her own home, a modern painting of St. George and the dragon. It would fit beautifully amid the barbarian posters and science fiction books. The painting radiated power and mystery, good and evil, life and death—all the bloody absolutes that fascinated teenagers.

And the dragon itself was enough to raise the hairs on anyone's neck no matter what the person's age. The beast's powerful muscles rippled and gleamed in a hammered metallic gold, its eyes were as brilliant as diamonds, and its teeth and claws glittered with lethal edges. Clearly, St. George was in for the battle of his life.

It would be a perfect painting for this room, she decided. *But the Louis Quatorze furniture would have to go.*

Period.

The color scheme, though . . . I could accommodate JoLynn there.

Mentally Shelley began working within the restrictions of her client's taste. The blue, white, and gold color scheme could be shifted from French elegance to barbarian splendor by intensifying the colors and giving the gilt a metallic, high-tech finish.

The idea gave her new energy. Hands on hips, she looked around the room again, smiling. Feeling refreshed by the bedroom's vitality, she went back down the short hallway to the living room, ready to face her client's uninteresting needs.

Voices filtered through the silence, telling her that she was no longer alone in the house. She recognized the cultured, drama-school tones of her partner, Brian Harris. The other voice belonged to JoLynn Cummings, recently divorced from more money than Midas ever dreamed of having. Breathy, light, somewhere between a whisper and a sigh, the voice was a perfect match for the Louis Quatorze furnishings.

Without pausing for so much as a glance, Shelley passed by the huge gilt-framed mirror at the end of the hall. At twenty-seven, she had no illusions about her appearance, herself, or other members of the human race, including men.

Especially men.

After her divorce five years ago, she had taken stock

of herself and life. She decided what she wanted from both and got down to work. Now she had a business she had built through her own skill and discipline, owing her success to no one.

Most particularly, to no *man*.

"There you are," Brian said to her. "JoLynn was just telling me about some Grecian statues she saw at the Louvre."

Shelley's junior business partner was taller than she was, almost as slender, and had the natural ash-blond hair that some women spent their lives trying to find at the bottom of various bleach bottles.

Brian also had the classic beauty of a recently fallen angel and business instincts that could easily rule over hell.

She had a good, professional relationship with him, now that he finally had accepted that she was more of an asset as a business partner than a bed partner.

"Sarah Marshall," he said, "convinced JoLynn that you have an absolute genius for matching people with just the right objets d'art for their homes."

"Sorry if I kept you waiting, Mrs. Cummings," Shelley said. "I was taking a brief tour of the house. As usual, Brian has done an excellent job of carrying out his client's wishes."

"Oh, call me JoLynn, please. When I hear 'Mrs. Cummings,' I think of my ex-husband's mother. Awful woman."

"JoLynn," Shelley said.

She held out her hand and shook JoLynn's small, surprisingly strong hand.

But that was the only surprise about the woman. She was exactly what anyone would expect after seeing the decor she had chosen for her rented house.

JoLynn's physical appearance had little relationship to anything except her former husband's bank balance. Her trendy hair, trendy clothes, trendy makeup, trendy nails, hose, and shoes were all of a piece. Unfortunately, they would be out of style as soon as the next fashion newspaper from either coast landed on the front doorstep.

Yet for all that, she was stunningly beautiful. She had red-blond hair, creamy skin, jade-green eyes, and a body that would make a showgirl weep with envy.

"Cain," JoLynn said, turning away, "this is—"

With an exasperated sound, she looked around. Belatedly she realized that there was no one in the room with her but Brian and Shelley.

"Where has that man got to now?" she muttered. Then, loudly, "Cain!"

Shelley stood patiently, waiting to hear an answer from another part of the house.

None came.

Suddenly JoLynn's eyes widened. She looked over Shelley's shoulder.

"There you are," she breathed. "Really, darling. You are the most impossible man to keep track of."

"So I've been told."

The deep voice came from behind Shelley. Startled, she spun around.

Despite the fact that the floor behind her was polished hardwood rather than plush carpet, she had heard no one approach. Even more surprising, the man wasn't wearing soft tennis or running shoes. His big feet were shod in knee-high, lace-up boots of the type used by people who hiked in rough country.

"Cain," JoLynn said, "this is Brian's partner, Shelley Wilde. Shelley, Cain Remington."

Politely Shelley held out her hand to the stranger.

The hand that enveloped hers was as surprising as the man's soundless approach had been. Strong, scarred, callused, the hand belonged to a man who was the opposite of what she had expected to find with the recently divorced JoLynn.

Cain Remington wasn't a too-young Adonis supported by a wealthy older divorcée. Nor was he an overweight, overage businessman supporting a much younger woman. In truth, he didn't fit into any category Shelley could think of.

Though casual, his clothes were excellent. His voice was so deep it was almost rough, yet his accent was neither rural nor overly cultured. Though obviously fit, his body didn't appear to be a product of a Century City personal trainer. He was attractive to her, but except for his mouth, his features were too strong and bluntly cut to be labeled good-looking.

And he was considerably taller than her own five feet seven inches.

Chestnut hair and aloof gray eyes, cleanly sculpted

lips, a mustache that gleams with bronze highlights, and a smile that goes no further than the sharp edges of his teeth, she summed up in the silence of her mind.

He looks on the world with the impersonal interest of a well-fed predator.

With that thought came another that both intrigued and warned her.

If he had been the dragon, St. George would have been lunch.

In all, Cain didn't look shallow enough to be satisfied with JoLynn's obvious but limited assets. On the other hand, Shelley's ex-husband had taught her all about the average male IQ when confronted with a D-cup bra and a breathy, little-girl voice.

"Mrs. Wilde," Cain said. "A pleasure."

He held her hand for an instant longer than necessary, as though he sensed the rather cynical appraisal behind her polite smile.

"Miss," she corrected automatically.

"Not Ms.?"

"If a man cares enough to ask, I make sure to tell him I'm a member of a dying breed."

His glance traveled openly over the gentle curves of her body beneath the finely woven, jewel-toned pantsuit she wore. The anger that flared in her hazel eyes at his unsubtle appraisal passed almost the instant it appeared.

But Cain noticed. He had been looking for it. His mouth shifted into a small, private smile.

"A dying breed?" he said. "Is that another way to say spinster?"

"Define spinster and I'll tell you whether I fit your label."

"A woman who can't hold a man."

"Bingo," she said coolly, but her eyes narrowed against painful memories. "In my case, the spinster is a divorcée who reclaimed her maiden name."

He nodded indifferently.

"I'll bet you're a bachelor," she added.

"A bachelor?"

"A man who can't hold a woman," she explained with a polite smile.

Brian stirred uneasily. "Uh, Shelley, why don't we—"

"Ooooo, Brian," JoLynn interrupted, "you simply must tell me more about that naughty satyr statue you mentioned earlier. I have just the right place for it."

With that JoLynn drew Brian off toward the end of the living room where sunlight struggled to filter through chiffon curtains. Breathlessly she began describing the marble statuary she wanted for the anteroom and side yard.

Neither Cain nor Shelley really noticed that both of them were now alone. They were intent on a moment of mutual anger.

And discovery.

"Actually, I've always considered myself more of a connoisseur," he said.

"Ah, yes," she murmured. "Of women, assuredly."

Before he could say anything, she kept talking in the clipped voice of a fashion-runway announcer.

"Though you aren't a handsome man yourself, you doubtless require that your women be perfectly stunning, objectively superb—a trophy, as it were."

His eyes widened, then narrowed.

She smiled and kept on talking, ticking off items on her fingers.

"Undoubtedly your women have to be more decorative than Greek sculpture and ever so much more flexible in bed. They must also," she added casually, "be blessed with the intelligence and insight of a clam."

"Bright and beautiful, too," Cain said.

His smile was genuine and very male, leaving no doubt that he approved of Shelley.

"To believe that compliment, I'd have to line up with the clams. I have, Mr. Remington, a rather exact appreciation of just how 'beautiful' I am."

He laughed softly. "Call me Cain."

"Wise of you to limit my options."

"In name-calling?"

"Yes."

But she felt her irritation giving way to her own sense of humor and the laughter gleaming in gray eyes that were no longer aloof.

"You're rather a renegade, aren't you?" she asked, smiling despite herself.

"Depends on who you—"

JoLynn's high, piercing scream sliced through Cain's words. As one, he and Shelley turned and raced toward the sound.

Chapter Two

⁓⁓⁓ JoLynn was at the far end of the living room. When Cain and Shelley ran to her, they saw at the same instant a dusty-rose-colored snake curled in a patch of sunlight on the floor.

JoLynn shrieked again.

With a single clean motion, Cain lifted the woman and spun her out of reach of the snake. As soon as he put her down, he straightened and turned to deal with the reptile.

Then he froze in shock.

Shelley was already bending over the slender snake. While he watched in disbelief, she picked the creature up as calmly as though it was a ribbon dropped by a careless child.

Brian made a sound that in a woman would have been described as a tiny shriek.

"Sh-Shelley, what the hell!" he stammered.

JoLynn made meaningless sounds and grabbed at Cain's arms. Without looking, he handed her over to

Brian. When she wouldn't let go of him even then, Cain absently brushed off her hands.

All of his attention was focused on Shelley. She was standing in a cataract of sunlight with the long reptile coiled easily in her hands.

"Relax, Brian," she said without looking up from the snake. "This one's a pet."

"How can you be s-sure?" her partner demanded.

"It didn't faint when JoLynn screamed," Cain offered dryly.

Shelley fought not to smile. In the end, she gave up and bent her head over the snake to hide her amusement.

"It's all right," she managed after a moment. "Really, Brian. This specimen is a lovely, relaxed, well-fed rosy boa constrictor."

JoLynn screamed again.

Casually Cain clapped a large hand over her perfectly painted mouth.

Brian swallowed hard. "A boa? They eat people!"

"Only in bad movies about the Amazon," she said. "This particular species of boa likes dry country and field mice."

Deftly she wrapped the snake around her arm. As she worked, she held the rosy boa's head in a firm yet gentle grasp.

It was obvious to Cain that the snake wasn't going anywhere without her permission. It was equally obvious that the snake was quite at ease.

The boa's dark, forked tongue flicked out repeatedly, "tasting" Shelley's skin with a snake's unusual olfactory equipment. Reassured by her warmth and the matter-of-fact handling, the boa settled in and snuggled itself around her arm like the good pet it was.

"Where did it come from?" Brian asked in a shaken voice.

"The bedroom down the hall would be my guess," she said.

"Why? Was it hungry?"

"All this snake wanted was something warm to snuggle up with."

"Smart snake," Cain said.

She ignored him.

"I'm warmer than a glass cage in a dark corner of a bedroom," she explained to Brian, "so the boa is perfectly happy to curl around my arm. He doesn't have snaky designs on my body."

"Maybe he's not so smart after all," Cain said.

"Maybe he's a reptilian Einstein," she retorted.

Slowly she traced the cool length of the snake with her fingertip. Its whole body was smooth and supple, muscular and resilient.

"Very healthy," she said approvingly. "Whoever owns it knows how to take care of reptiles."

JoLynn made emphatic, muffled sounds.

Warily, Cain removed his hand.

"Billy!" JoLynn rasped.

Nothing was left of her normally wide-eyed, child-like expression. Her skin was unnaturally pale. Her only color was two hot spots of color high on her cheeks.

"I'm going to kill that sneaky son of a bitch! I told him not to bring that thing in my house!"

Shelley tried to think of something tactful to say. All she could think was that if JoLynn was the boy's mother, "son of a bitch" was an apt description.

Not tactful, she thought. *Keep mouth shut. For once.*

"Kill it!" JoLynn demanded, turning toward Cain. "Kill it right now!"

Shelley backed up and put a protective hand between him and the snake.

"That's not necessary," she said. "It's not harming anyone."

The front door slammed.

"Mother, it's Billy," called out a voice. "I'm back from the beach."

As the boy yelled, he rounded the corner into the living room. He was wearing a minimum bathing suit and a maximum coating of sand.

The first thing he saw was his ashen mother.

The second thing he saw was his favorite pet clinging boalike to a strange woman's arm.

His lips formed a word usually reserved for adults.

Cain cleared his throat in time to muffle the boy's curse.

"He won't hurt you," Billy said, hurrying into the room. "Really! He's gentle and clean and he doesn't have any bad habits."

"Must be a female," Shelley said to him, smiling.

"Nope. Male."

"How can you tell?"

"Hates nail polish and hair goop."

She barely managed not to look at the boy's brightly polished and heavily gooped mother. Struggling not to laugh out loud, she stroked the snake again, enjoying the subtle rose patterns of its scales illuminated by the late-afternoon light.

"*He* has lovely manners," she said, emphasizing the gender. "What do you call him?"

"Squeeze, what else?"

Shelley smiled and then laughed out loud. The laugh was like her smile—warm, open, nothing held back.

Cain took an involuntary step toward her, like a cold man walking toward fire. The combination of intelligence, approval, and humor in her expression was more intriguing to him than all of JoLynn's carefully concocted female allure.

"Squeeze," Shelley repeated, snickering. "He certainly does."

Full realization dawned on Billy. He walked over and stared at Shelley. He was exactly at eye level with her, a tanned boy with light brown eyes, dark blond hair, and an expression too serious for someone his age.

"You aren't afraid," he said in disbelief. "Even a little bit."

"Disappointed?"

His brown eyes widened. Then he grinned.

"I'm Billy," he said, holding out his hand. "Who are you?"

"Shelley."

She gave him her left hand because her right was full of contented snake.

"Boy, your kids sure are lucky," he said, pumping her hand. "Can you believe it? A mother who isn't afraid of snakes!"

He shook his head, awed at the possibilities.

"Cain," JoLynn said in a harsh, trembling voice, "kill it!"

"Aw, Mother," the boy said, turning toward her. "You don't mean that."

"The hell I don't."

The words wiped all humor from Billy. He stared at his mother for a stunned moment, then at Cain's unreadable expression. Slowly, almost hopelessly, the boy turned toward Shelley.

She raised an eyebrow and looked right at Cain. Though she said nothing, her entire posture made it clear that he would take the snake from her only if he was ready to drag it from her unwilling hands.

"It's just for two months, Uncle Cain," the boy said.

His words were for Cain and JoLynn, but his eyes pleaded with Shelley.

"I can't take him home because Dad is overseas," Billy explained quickly to her, "and the housekeeper won't allow Squeeze to live there unless I'm there, too, and I'm here, not there, because I'm here."

"I won't allow the snake in my house at all," JoLynn said, her voice harsh. "Evil creatures."

Shelley winced. The other woman's reaction to the snake wasn't just another part of her ultrafeminine appearance. JoLynn's skin was pasty and she was sweating visibly. She was genuinely terrified of snakes.

"I want it *dead*." JoLynn shuddered. "Slimy beast! How can you bear to touch it?"

"Its skin is drier than ours," Shelley pointed out gently.

Her tone made it clear that she was accustomed to snakes and to people who feared them.

JoLynn's lips moved. No words came out.

"Truly," Shelley said. "Have you ever touched a snake?"

Although she hadn't moved, JoLynn made an odd sound and backed up in a rush.

Brian's arm wrapped soothingly around his client.

"Kill it, Cain," JoLynn demanded. "Kill it *now!*"

Billy glanced appealingly at his uncle and started to speak.

"Shelley?" Cain asked.

Then he turned and looked at her.

She stared up at him for a moment, smiled slightly, and nodded. She looked toward Billy again.

"Would you let me keep Squeeze for you until you move back in with your dad?" she asked.

"You wouldn't mind?"

"No."

"Uh, he only eats live mice," Billy said hesitantly, torn between honesty and a desire to save his pet.

"I know."

Her voice was as gentle as the fingertip that stroked the boa's relaxed coils.

"You do?" the boy asked. "How come? Do you have snakes?"

"No, but I grew up with them. My dad is a herpetologist."

As she spoke, she walked slowly toward Billy's room, drawing the boy after her and removing the snake from JoLynn's sight.

Billy fell in step beside Shelley, eager to have his pet out of his mother's reach.

"Do you know what 'herpetologist' means?" Shelley asked.

"Yeah. Someone who studies reptiles."

"Especially snakes."

"Poisonous snakes, too?" Billy asked.

"Mostly, in Dad's case."

Cain followed with a gliding, silent stride, listening intently. He felt as he once had in wild country, when he had been expecting one kind of rock formation and found instead a glittering vein of pure gold. The rush of discovery went through him like an electric current, sharpening every sense.

"Dad is fascinated by what he calls 'sand ecology,'" she said.

"What's that?"

"Shorthand for how reptiles adjust to the very dry places of the earth. As it happens, a lot of desert snakes are poisonous. Really poisonous. They seem to go with deserts the way lack of water does."

"Like in the Mojave Desert?"

"And the Sahara, and the Negev, and the Sonora," she said, walking into Billy's bedroom. "While I was growing up, we lived in most of the great deserts of the world."

"Oh, wow! I've always wanted to live in a desert."

"You've got a leg up on it in southern California. Without our imported water, we wouldn't last a month."

"Really?"

"Really," Cain said, his voice deep, amused.

Shelley whirled around, startled. She hadn't heard him follow her down the hall.

"For a big man, you're very light on your feet," she said tartly.

"You're rather surprising yourself."

She stood on tiptoe and looked over his shoulder. "Where's JoLynn?"

"Mother doesn't come in my room anymore," Billy said. "She hates it."

"Mmm," was all Shelley could think of to say.

The boy began unwrapping the well-named Squeeze from her arm. Or trying to. The snake liked his warm perch.

"My room makes Mom mad," Billy explained. Then he shrugged. "A lot of things make her mad. Especially Daddy. Hey, let go."

He tugged firmly at his pet's warm coils.

Squeeze didn't budge.

"C'mon, loosen up," the boy said. "It's time to go back in the tank."

Squeeze, well, *squeezed,* reluctant to give up his private source of heat.

Cain leaned close and spoke too softly for Billy to overhear. "A snake after my own heart."

"A constrictor?"

Yet even as Shelley said it, she realized that she didn't feel confined by Cain's closeness.

"A connoisseur of warmth," he corrected.

"Squeeze!" Billy said in exasperation. "Let go!"

"Here," Cain said.

He bent even closer to her. Then he took Squeeze's head in one deft, gentle hand and used the other hand to pry off one coil after another.

The snake had absorbed enough of Shelley's body heat to become lively and surprisingly fast. Deprived of one source of warmth, Squeeze looped quickly over and around Cain's hard, bare forearm and began "tasting" his new perch. The reptile's forked tongue looked very dark against the sun-struck bronze of the man's hair.

Cain sighed but didn't object to the intimacy.

"Hey, you're not scared either," Billy said. "Did you study herpetology, too?"

"No, but I was once a boy who liked snakes."

Billy looked up. Way up. "That musta been a long time ago."

"Centuries, at least."

Shelley snickered. Laughter died when Cain switched his glance to her.

His eyes were so close to hers that she could see the tiny flashes of blue and shards of black that gave contrast to the icy gray iris. She could also see the sudden expansion of his pupils as they dilated, and the tiny, sensual flare of his nostrils when he inhaled her perfume.

Though he hadn't touched her, she felt all but

surrounded by him. She felt the warmth of his breath caressing her lips, smelled the clean, sharp male scent of him, and sensed the heat from his body like a promise given in silence.

When his glance shifted to her lips, a shiver of awareness coursed through her.

"Shelley," Brian said from the doorway, "if you're serious about taking that fu—" He stopped abruptly and looked at Billy. "If you really mean to take that, er, creature with you, you'll have to get a cab."

She nodded indifferently.

"I won't have that fu—damned—snake in my car," Brian said flatly.

"No problem," Cain drawled.

The tone of his voice sent something shivering over Shelley's nerves. She licked her lower lip.

His eyes followed the moist pink tip of her tongue.

"You don't even know where she lives," Brian objected.

"It doesn't matter. I'll take Shelley wherever she wants to go."

"That takes in a lot of territory," her partner retorted.

"So do I."

There was a taut silence. Then Brian shrugged with a motion that was more angry than casual.

"Great," he said. "I'll take JoLynn to The Gilded Lily to look over Shelley's stock. Okay, Shelley?"

"Fine."

"Fine, huh?" Brian goaded. "Are you sure about that?"

Reluctantly Shelley tore her attention from the light gleaming in Cain's eyes, making them as deep and mysterious as twilight lakes.

"What's to be unsure about?" she asked.

Brian shrugged again and turned away.

"Don't bother showing JoLynn anything that isn't in high school art history books," Shelley added. "That's her comfort zone."

Her partner's finely curved mouth shifted into a double-edged, frankly sensual smile.

"I'll be very, very soothing," he assured her. "She's had a rough day."

Shelley glanced up quickly at Cain, looking for traces of jealousy.

She didn't find any. Apparently he didn't hesitate to leave JoLynn trembling in Brian's expensively clad, sympathetic arms. Considering her partner's Olympian good looks, either Billy's "uncle" Cain truly wasn't jealous of JoLynn or he was supremely confident of himself.

Or both.

That, along with his casual handling of Squeeze, intrigued Shelley. Despite the conventional wisdom that said only women were afraid of snakes, she hadn't found many men who would approach snakes except to kill them.

"That's nice of you," she said absently to her partner. "We'll meet you at the shop after I get Squeeze set up in my house."

"Don't hurry," he said, searching Cain's face with the same intensity that Shelley had.

"We won't," Cain assured him.

Her partner muttered something and stalked down the hall without saying good-bye.

"Boyfriend?" Cain asked very softly.

"Worse than that. Partner."

"As in bed?"

"As in business."

He hesitated. "Whatever you say."

"If you aren't going to believe me, why bother to ask?" Shelley turned toward Billy. "Is that Squeeze's terrarium in the corner?" she asked.

"Yeah. I must have put the lid on crooked on my way out this morning. I was late," he added.

She had a feeling that being late was a chronic condition with the boy. She didn't blame him. California's hot, burnished summer days gave her a case of wanderlust and waking dreams, reminding her of all the wild winds she had felt as a child, all the distant lands and resilient people.

Automatically she pushed aside the memories and the restless longing that had come to her more and more frequently in the past year.

I made my choice when I was nineteen, she reminded herself. *I chose peace, security.*

A home.

She had needed the certainty that came from knowing if she called out for help, the answer would come in a language she understood. Even more, she had needed to know that there was one place on earth that was hers and hers alone, that her life was her own, to roam or stay in one place as she pleased.

And she pleased to stay and build a home.

"Okay, Billy," she said in a crisp voice. "What's the critter's feeding schedule?"

"He won't need anything to eat for about five days. Better make it six."

"Is he on a diet?"

"No, but if he isn't really hungry, he'll just ignore the poor mouse until I take it out, and then I make a pet of it and have to buy another one when Squeeze finally starts acting hungry."

She made a sympathetic sound. She always felt sorry for the mice, too. But then, she felt sorry for the wildlife that house cats preyed on, and the rabbits and opossums and skunks and domestic pets flattened on the road. Life was incurably messy.

"Right," she said. "I'll be sure Squeeze is hungry. That way it will be quick and clean."

Billy brightened.

"Thanks. I knew you'd understand." He hesitated, then added, "It'd be nice if you let your kids play with him sometimes. He likes to curl around me while I do my homework."

At the word "kids," Cain's eyes narrowed.

"I don't have any kids," she said, "but I'll let Squeeze out to play once in a while. You can visit, too, whenever your mother lets you."

"Can I? Oh, wow! That'd be great!"

With a wide smile, he went to drag Squeeze's terrarium out into the room.

"That's going to be kind of awkward on a motorcycle," Cain said.

"Motorcycle?" The boy straightened eagerly. "Did you bring your motorcycle?"

Cain started to speak, then thought better of it.

Billy's young face assumed blank lines, betraying neither enthusiasm nor longing.

"I have a dirt bike," he said, "but Mother won't let me ride it while I stay with her."

Shelley looked at the hunger and hero worship in Billy's eyes as he watched Cain. She felt sudden, unexpected tears burning behind her eyelids. Her parents had dragged her all over the face of the earth, but they didn't put her through the special hell that came to a child when his parents no longer loved each other enough to live together.

"I know about your bike," Cain said, his voice slightly rough. "That's why I'm here. Dave and I decided that you'd need some company while he's in France."

"You're not here to, uh, see Mother?" Billy asked awkwardly.

"I'm here to see you."

"Does she know that?"

"No."

"Don't tell her. She wouldn't understand. She hates anything to do with Dad."

Cain searched for neutral words to counter the bitter truth in his nephew's young voice. Finally he simply put his hand on the boy's shoulder.

"We'll work out something," he promised. "Until then, can we borrow your helmet?"

"That one?" Billy asked.

He pointed toward a battered motorcycle helmet that was barely visible beneath a sandy beach towel next to the bed.

"Do you have a better one?" Cain asked.

"Nope."

Billy snatched up the helmet, brushed it off, and measured Shelley with a professional eye.

"It will fit her just right if she takes that stupid knot out of her hair," he said.

Cain's left hand moved so quickly that she didn't have time to evade or object. She felt the firm, seeking pressure of his fingers an instant before her hair spilled suddenly down her back. Hidden beneath the heavy fall of hair, his hand caressed her nape, then withdrew, leaving behind a tremor of unexpected pleasure.

Billy fitted the helmet over her head, then lifted it off and stepped back.

"Fits like it was made for you," the boy said.

Shelley nodded absently. She was still feeling the aftershocks of Cain's hidden caress.

"What about Squeeze?" she asked.

"How would you fasten a helmet on a snake?" Cain asked blandly.

The boy snickered. "Scotch tape?"

"That's a thought."

Cain lifted the hand that had been buried beneath Shelley's hair. His nostrils flared slightly as he scented her perfume on his skin. He looked at her intently, wanting to feel the silky weight of her hair again, to taste deeply of her mouth.

Watching her, he wondered if she had felt the same elemental pull he had when he touched her.

And then he knew that she had.

The proof was in the very slight trembling of her lips as she watched him, and the dilation of her pupils as sensual awareness quickened in her.

In that instant it was all he could do not to take her down to the floor and bury himself in her until a lifetime of hunger and loneliness was only a fading memory.

". . . carry Squeeze?" Billy asked.

Cain tried to gather his seething thoughts. He failed. He could think of nothing but the sweet instant when his body would become a part of Shelley's, held tightly within her satin warmth.

"Pillowcase," she said in a strained voice.

Abruptly she closed her eyes, no longer able to bear the intimacy of Cain's look. She forced herself to take a deep breath, trying to calm the frightening storm of sensuality that was electrifying her body.

She had never been aware of a man like this, sensing his every breath, the metallic gleam of light caught in his thick hair, the tawny chestnut mustache curling against the most beautiful male mouth she had ever seen—hard yet full, responsive to laughter, hungry.

Hungry most of all.

"Pillowcase," she repeated, her voice husky, her eyes still closed.

"What about it?" the boy asked.

"I'll carry Squeeze in a pillowcase."

"Oh. Good idea. I hate the darned things. Mother must have told the decorator I was a girl."

With quick motions Shelley turned away from Cain and removed the cover from one of the bed pillows. Immediately she saw why Billy was glad to be rid of it. The powder-blue pillowcase looked more like lingerie than bed linen.

Doubtfully she looked at the lacy froth in her hand and thought of the long coils of snake.

"Maybe we—" she began, turning toward Cain.

There was no time for second thoughts. Boy and man were struggling to unwrap almost four feet of lively, reluctant, stubborn snake. Despite good intentions, Billy was in the way as often as he was helpful.

"Here," Shelley said, shoving the pillowcase at the boy. "Hold it open for me."

Working with both hands, she unwrapped Squeeze from Cain's arm. As she did, she couldn't help feeling the supple texture of his skin and the sliding, muscular strength beneath. But it was his body heat that astonished her. He radiated the vital energy of life.

"It's a wonder you didn't cook Squeeze alive," she muttered.

He bent until he could whisper against her sleek brown hair.

"Funny, I thought the same thing when I pulled him off you," he said. "Hot enough to set fires."

Her hands slipped, then got a better grip on the wriggling reptile. Half of Squeeze's length unwound from Cain's arms. The other half didn't.

"Ready when you are," Billy said.

"I'll get back to you," she retorted.

"Watch that coil," Cain said, laughing. "He's going to—too late."

Triumphantly Squeeze settled a loop around one of Shelley's arms. She unwrapped herself with a quick movement that left three-quarters of the snake without anything to hang on to.

The last quarter was firmly, very firmly, in place around Cain's arm.

"What's a nice girl like you doing with a snake like this?" he asked.

She gave him a disbelieving look, blew hair out of her eyes, and tugged.

Squeeze coiled suddenly around her arm, regaining lost territory.

"It could be worse," he said.

"How?"

"He could be an octopus."

She laughed, lost her grip, and had to start all over again. She had the feeling that Cain and Squeeze enjoyed the game immensely, especially when her hands slipped.

"If you stand any closer," she muttered to him, "you'll be in my pocket."

"Promise?"

His voice was too soft for Billy to hear.

"You sure you don't need help?" the boy asked.

"She's doing fine," Cain said before Shelley could. "Just keep that pillowcase handy. Slide your fingers along my arm under that last coil. Not you, Billy. Shelley. Right. That's good."

"Easy for you to say."

He smiled into her eyes. "Ready?"

"I'm not the problem. The critter is."

"I'll keep it in mind. Hang on to the critter with both hands."

Shelley hung on, Cain shifted his arm rapidly, and Squeeze came undone.

Billy lunged forward with the pillowcase and scooped up all of the snake that was dangling free.

"Got him!" the boy said.

"You could have done that sooner," Shelley said.

"How?"

"Not you. Cain. That trick with your arm."

"Just thought of it," he said blandly.

His eyes gave him away. They were alive with laughter.

She knew she should be angry, but he looked so much like his nephew at the moment that she couldn't be. Shaking her head, she took the pillowcase from Billy and knotted the top so that Squeeze couldn't escape.

"That should do it," she said, smiling.

But Billy wasn't smiling when he looked at his pet thrashing around in the lacy prison.

"We'll take good care of Squeeze," Cain said.

The boy nodded unhappily. "I know. It's just . . . he's company."

The expression on his face said that he was lonely for more than a snake's companionship.

"You're visiting me," Shelley said. "Remember?"

''Yeah, sure.''

The boy's eyes said the same thing his tone did. He thought it was just one more adult promise that would be forgotten by tomorrow.

''I mean it. I'm expecting you.''

Before she could say any more, Cain tilted her chin and strapped on the borrowed helmet with a few practiced motions. He had an angry look about his eyes, but she knew it wasn't for her. He, too, didn't like to think of Billy spending a lonely summer with JoLynn Cummings.

''How does it feel?'' Cain asked. ''Too tight?''

''Just right.''

Billy followed them anxiously down the hall and out of the elegant house.

A stripped-down motorcycle was parked in the driveway.

''Cool,'' the boy said in awe.

Powerful, lean, uncluttered, the bike reminded Shelley of a dark jungle cat crouched to spring.

Cain mounted the bike in a single lithe motion and looked at her. The challenge in his eyes was unmistakable.

She smiled slightly. Bracing her left hand on his shoulder, she stepped on the peg and settled into place behind him as though she had done it a hundred times.

And she had. Motorbikes were more common than cars in most of the countries she had been in.

The bike ripped into life, vibrating with leashed power.

''Keep a tight grip on that pillowcase,'' Billy called.

"And on me," Cain added.

"I'll take care of him," Shelley said to the boy.

"My uncle? He doesn't need anyone to take care—"

"Squeeze," she interrupted.

"Don't bet on it," Cain said, snapping on his helmet.

"I'm in a madhouse."

"No, that's where you were," he said, looking over his shoulder. "I'm taking you away from all that. Ready?"

No.

But Shelley wasn't about to admit it out loud. She put one arm around his hard waist and held on.

"Ready," she said through her teeth.

With a primal roar, man, woman, snake, and lacy blue pillowcase accelerated down the twisting road.

Chapter Three

I need my head examined, Shelley told herself. *A nice tame boa in my house is one thing.*

Cain Remington is something else.

Smoothly he guided the motorcycle into her driveway. A moment later he shut off the powerful engine. All of his movements were both easy and measured.

She couldn't help watching him. He was as coordinated as he was strong. He had controlled the bike skillfully and with complete attention. He was always aware of the heavier cars around him and the unpredictability of drivers who believed they were the only living thing on the road. She approved of his skill, just as she had approved of his handling of the snake.

That was the problem.

I like him too much. Billy calls him "uncle," but I don't think Cain is JoLynn's brother.

A lot of women had their children call their lovers "uncle." It created the illusion of a whole family in a situation where the family was anything but.

The idea of Cain as JoLynn's lover didn't appeal to Shelley at all.

Any man who thinks JoLynn is a good time is the wrong man for me. I made one mistake like that with my ex-husband. Once was more than enough.

Wasn't it?

Uneasiness licked through her again. She was too honest not to know that she wasn't listening to her own good advice. Even as she told herself how wrong Cain was for her, she was deeply aware of him as a man, of the hard warmth of his waist beneath her arm, of the rippling power of his back as he reached for his helmet, of everything about him from the clean golden bronze of his hair to the breadth of his shoulders.

Abruptly she realized that she still had one arm around his waist even though the bike wasn't moving. She yanked back her arm as though she had been burned.

If Cain noticed her sudden retreat from physical contact, he said nothing. With the same easy, clean movements he had used to drive the bike, he got off and hung his helmet over the handlebars.

Feeling awkward by comparison, she climbed stiffly off the motorcycle. The dismount wasn't made easier by Squeeze. The pillowcase bounced and bunched with the boa's muscular protest at being sacked up in lace.

"Settle down," she muttered. "Ready or not, you're home."

Squeeze kept on trying to find an escape hole in the lace. Or make one.

Still holding the lively pillowcase, Shelley struggled with the unfamiliar fastening on her helmet.

Strong, tanned fingers brushed hers aside. The back of Cain's hand caressed her throat as he slowly, very slowly, unfastened the strap. He removed the helmet with equal care, watching her the whole time, holding her eyes in a smoky gaze.

The intimacy of the moment was so great that she felt as though she were being undressed by a lover.

Without looking away, he hung her helmet next to his on the handlebars. When his fingers carefully tucked her tangled brown hair behind her ears, she didn't think to object.

Slowly, he lowered his head to her.

"You don't scream at snakes," he said in a low voice. "You don't curl your lip at motorcycles. What other conventions do you ignore, Shelley Wilde?"

Sanity returned just before his mouth reached hers. She stepped backward.

"I don't kiss strangers, if that's what you're asking," she said curtly.

His gray eyes narrowed. Then he relaxed, though the intensity of his glance didn't change.

"I don't feel like a stranger around you," he said. "And you sure don't *feel* like a stranger to me."

He stroked her cheek with the backs of his fingers.

She took his caressing fingers and wrapped them around the top of the lively pillowcase.

"Pet Squeeze," she said. "He doesn't know strangers from fat shoelaces."

Cain laughed and didn't pursue the kiss he had so clearly wanted. He took the pillowcase in one hand,

Shelley's arm in the other, and walked toward her home.

Not much of the structure was visible from the driveway. Like many California hillside homes, the building was oriented toward the view rather than toward the street. As the view was at the back of the house, the architect had wasted little effort making the front entrance impressive.

From the street, the house looked like a rather long, single-story California version of a weekend retreat—fire-resistant cedar shake shingles on the roof, and walls made of huge panels of thermal glass with natural redwood in between. The narrow yard was landscaped with plants that were well kept and very green against the backdrop of tawny wild grass and chaparral. The privacy of the side yards was guarded by six-foot-high redwood fences.

"Watch your step," she said. "One of the deck boards is loose. I keep meaning to get it repaired, but . . ."

Cain hardly heard her words. The instant he followed her through the front door, he realized that he had only seen the tip of the redwood-and-glass iceberg that was Shelley's house.

Built into the hill, the house dropped down in three levels from the public entertainment area at street height to the privacy and retreat of the bedroom suite more than thirty feet below. There, the architect had taken advantage of a natural outward curve in the hillside and had designed a swimming pool, patio, barbecue pit, and flower garden.

The pool sent up shimmering promises of coolness and pleasure. A faint breeze rising from the bottom of the wild ravine far below picked up the ravishing scent of flowers and spread it throughout the house. Southern California's magnificent light poured through every window in silent golden torrents.

Cain stood in the center of the first level of the house and turned around slowly, trying to take it all in. He had never felt so much at home in any place on earth. Everything from the soft gleam of wooden floors beneath his feet to the smooth, cream-colored walls and open beamed ceilings called out to his senses.

Shelley's home was both civilized and deeply wild. The wildness was there in the view that was a part of the architecture. The hills were so high that they would have been called mountains almost anywhere else in the world. Their stony flanks were thick with chaparral, sandpaper-dry, and so rugged that even the land hunger of metropolitan Los Angeles couldn't wholly conquer them. Nothing walked the steep hillsides and deep ravines except animals that had never been tamed by man.

Cain understood the appeal of that kind of landscape. He had sought it all over the world. The fact that L.A. still had such areas close at hand was one of the reasons it was his home base.

Obviously Shelley had felt the same. A few hundred feet from the road winding up to her house, the land itself hadn't changed since the day a Spanish sea captain mistook a continent for a fabled island and called it California.

Silently he studied the land surrounding her home. Shelley's house and those nearby were a glittering necklace flung in solitary splendor along the crest of steep hills. Far below, the thin ribbon of road leading to the homes was barely visible where chaparral gave way to solid rock.

More shining necklaces of homes stood on the ridgelines of other hills that marched in rising lines from the ocean to the high mountains farther inland. Those hills were broken by occasional long valleys where cities clustered and crowded and consumed the land.

But not here, not on Shelley's hill. Here the land breathed and flexed like the wild, living thing it was.

"Magnificent," he said.

Cain didn't expect an answer. He didn't even know he had spoken his thought aloud. He was focused, intent. He absorbed the elemental harmony of land and house into his very bones.

Gradually other things drew his attention away from the dry, rugged hills. The room itself had groupings of understated furniture whose colors and textures subtly echoed the view. Scattered throughout the huge, light-filled room were various pieces of art.

He smiled and nodded slightly. Unlike JoLynn, Shelley had selected her furnishings and finishings for their harmony of feeling rather than for their perfection of form.

A luminous Kashmir rug glowed like a jeweled pool in one-third of the room. Smaller rugs appeared in the remaining area, anchoring furniture into intimate groups. A superb nineteenth-century Japanese screen featuring eggshell-white cranes angled elegantly off to the right. Other, smaller screens stood throughout the room, dividing what could have been an awkwardly large space into areas that were both comfortable and unconfined.

Silently Shelley watched while Cain walked through the room, the forgotten Squeeze dangling in the pillowcase from his large right hand. Though she said nothing, she wondered what he was thinking while he stood in front of the line drawing of a Balinese dancer suspended timelessly within a golden frame, femininity and strength captured in a few fluid strokes.

Does he see beyond the primitive surface of the Eskimo carving of an old woman to the sheer courage and serenity beneath? she wondered.

Does he look beyond the expensive gloss of the Arabian ivory chess set to the timeless celebration of intelligence and play?

Does he see past the value and antiquity of the Egyptian scarab to the human fear and reverence it embodies?

When he paused, then stood rooted in front of a glass case, she stopped breathing. Inside that case was one of her favorite possessions, a jaguar carved by a German master from a large piece of opal that was still in its native stone. The opal was Australian, a never-ending shimmer of blue and green, blazing orange and shards of gold, a rainbow shattered and then caught forever in a transparent silver-white cloud.

The artist had matched the jaguar's lines to the mixture of native stone and opal in a way that suggested the cat's immense vitality yet acknowledged the animal's deadliness. The stone was a very deep, lustrous gray, almost black, as though jungle shadows were falling over the cat, partially disguising its predatory beauty.

The carving alone was extraordinary, well worth its considerable cost. But what made the piece unique and irresistible to Shelley was the carved ruby butterfly that was perched on one of the cat's solid gold claws. Large wings half spread, their veins a delicate network of pure gold, the butterfly was wholly at ease.

Somehow the artist had given the jaguar an expression of bemused pleasure, as though he didn't know quite how it had happened, but the big cat thoroughly approved of the scrap of beauty that had drifted down to quiver trustingly on his paw.

Cain had worn a similar expression when he saw Shelley pick up the snake that sent JoLynn into hysterics.

A slight motion caught Shelley's eye. Quickly she turned toward the movement.

Gliding, stalking, every muscle poised, a Maine coon cat eased across the polished floor. The cat's predatory gold eyes never looked away from the pillowcase wiggling so intriguingly beneath Cain's large fist.

Shelley took two running steps, snatched the pillowcase from his hand, and hoisted the bouncing lace high above her head. Off-balance, she started to fall into the jaguar's glass case. When Cain grabbed her, keeping her from toppling the display case, she steadied herself by putting her free arm around him.

For an instant it was like being on the motorcycle again, her arm tight around his body. But there was a difference. He was standing, he was facing her, and he was pressed along her soft length.

The difference was devastating to her poise. A flush climbed her cheeks.

"I wouldn't have dropped Squeeze," he said mildly, watching the telltale rise of her color.

Shelley said the first word that came to her mind. "Nudge."

"That was hardly a nudge you gave me," he said, tightening his grip subtly, "but I'm not complaining."

He bent toward her.

"You don't understand," she explained desperately, knowing she couldn't evade his beautiful mouth. It was coming closer with each breath, each instant. "Nudge was stalking Squeeze!"

Firm lips hesitated, then curved into a lazy kind of smile. "Sounds like fun."

"What?"

"Nudge stalking squeeze. Kind of like push coming to shove, only sexier."

She made a strangled sound that was halfway between despair and laughter.

"Nudge is my cat," she said.

"That explains it."

"It does?"

"Either that or you have a third leg that's playing footsie with me."

Shelley's eyes widened. She peered down at the floor. "That's Nudge."

"Claws is more like it."

"If you'll let go of me, I'll—"

"Don't bother," he said, lowering his mouth to hers. "I have nothing against claws."

His kiss was like his smile, sensual and slow, an exploration of the joined possibilities of their mouths. It made her feel like a ruby butterfly held within a jaguar's soft grasp. A quiver of pure pleasure shimmered over her nerves.

She returned the kiss as gently, as thoroughly, as it was given to her. It had been a long time since she had allowed a man to kiss her so intimately.

It had been forever since she had enjoyed a kiss half so much.

A warm, sinuous body wedged itself between their feet. Nudge was trying a different approach to the dancing pillowcase. The cat's familiar pressure along her knees reminded Shelley of where she was, who she was, and the things she wanted from life.

Casual kisses from a stranger weren't among them.

The sudden stiffness of her body was an unmistakable signal. Reluctantly he ended the kiss and released her.

"Cain, I don't—"

"I know," he interrupted in a husky voice. "You don't kiss strangers. I'm not a stranger, Shelley."

"But—"

"I know that you love things that are both beautiful

and wild, civilized and unrestrained. I know you're intelligent, independent, and compassionate. I know that you're very much your own person, yet you will share yourself with a boy you barely know who has just gone through hell.''

Her mouth opened, but not one word came out.

He smiled gently. ''I know you're warmer than my dreams, sweeter, more alive. And you're as elegant as a ruby butterfly trembling on a jungle cat's solid gold claw.''

''Cain,'' she whispered.

His lips brushed over hers.

''Am I a stranger, Shelley?''

''N-no.'' Then, almost fearfully, she added, ''But I don't know you.''

''You will.''

Nudge butted against Cain's knee. Hard.

He glanced down. His eyes widened in surprise as he took in the size of the mottled cat.

''My God, that thing is as big as a lynx!''

''Almost. Coon cats and Himalayans are the biggest of all domestic cats.''

''Domestic?''

He eyed Nudge, who was watching the wiggling pillowcase with frankly carnivorous intent.

''You're sure about that domestic bit?'' he asked dryly.

''Cats are always cats, no matter where they live.''

Nudge stood on her hind feet and reached playfully for the pillowcase.

Shelley was still holding it out of reach, though her arm had begun to tremble with the effort. Squeeze was hardly as light as a shoelace.

"Allow me," Cain said. He took the pillowcase and hoisted it out of danger. "Now, call off your cat."

She bent down, grabbed Nudge firmly, and walked to the front door. With one hand she opened the door. With the other she launched the cat into the yard.

"Good-bye, Nudge. I'll call you for dinner."

After a disgruntled twitch of her body, the cat stalked off to find easier prey.

Shelley turned around and saw that Cain was surveying the room again, his gray eyes intent. She could see that he approved of what he saw. That pleased her as much as the mingled hunger and restraint of his kiss.

"Usually I can tell what a person does for a living by looking at their home," he said.

"And?"

"You've got me."

She bit her tongue against a flip remark. She didn't want to go into who was getting whom, and how.

"What do you mean?" she asked.

"Despite the fact that your furnishings come from all over the world, and despite the fact that some items cost pennies and some cost thousands of dollars, everything is in harmony. The room isn't masculine or feminine. It isn't modern or old-fashioned. It's simply very human."

"Thank you."

"You're welcome."

He turned suddenly, catching the approval in Shelley's tawny-hazel eyes.

"So what do you do for a living?" he asked.

"Gild lilies."

A wry smile changed the line of his mouth. "Care to be more specific?"

"Sure. My clients are the mobile rich, the people who are only in one place for a few months at a time but want that place to be more welcoming and suited to their personalities than an expensive hotel suite."

"If they're that rich, why don't they just buy a place?"

"Then they have to worry about taking care of it. Most of them don't want to buy anything at all, including furniture," she explained. "Come on, let's get Squeeze stashed in a safe place. Follow me."

It was just as well that Shelley couldn't see Cain's very male smile after she turned away. He would have been delighted to follow anywhere the alluring curve of her hips led. But he knew if he said anything, she would retreat again.

"So you rent houses to the restless rich?" he asked.

"No. A realtor rents the houses. I provide the finishing touches."

"An interior decorator, is that it?"

He looked around closely, noting the changes in the house as he followed her.

"Not quite," she said. "I don't do paint and fabrics and such. Most of my clients want to rent everything from the Oriental rug on the floor to the Picassos on the wall to the wall itself. That's Brian's department. Decor. The walls and furniture. The basic lily, as it were.''

"Then you gild the lily."

She nodded. "I have an inventory of various objets d'art, which I use to personalize rented homes, rented furniture, rented lives."

"But you don't live like that yourself."

"No. This is my home."

Her slight emphasis on the word "home" said a great deal about how she felt on the subject.

"Yet," he said slowly, "you understand what it's like to be rootless and still want to live in a place that feels right, even if you can't stay long."

"I spent my childhood wanting a home, a place of my own, the certainty that if I called out in the night—"

She stopped abruptly, realizing what she had almost told him. It was her nightmare, the worst experience of her life. She had been a child, sick and frightened and unable to communicate with anyone in their camp because her mother was also sick and her father was out in the wilderness chasing snakes.

"Yes," Shelley said bleakly, "I understand what it's like to hunger for something more than a rented room."

"Sounds like you've been there."

She turned away without answering the implicit question.

Cain didn't ask any more questions about rented rooms and homes. There was no point. He was certain that she wouldn't answer them.

He didn't like that, but there was nothing he could do about it.

Yet.

Chapter Four

Quietly Cain followed Shelley to the bottom of the first stairway. The second level of the house opened out in front of him. There was a suite on the left that she ignored. She led him past a family room and open kitchen. Both had spectacular views of the hills and distant city.

With an odd hunger to know more about this unexpected woman, he scanned the house carefully, noting each sign of her likes and delights. Cooking was definitely something she enjoyed. Pots of herbs stood three deep on a sunny window ledge. A large white bowl heaped with fresh lemons occupied the center of the counter. Pots and pans hung within easy reach over the stove. Their sides were clean, but showed the patina that came only from long use over heat.

Obviously she preferred to cook in her kitchen rather than to eat out at the multitude of restaurants Los Angeles had to offer. He understood that impulse. There was something satisfying about preparing your own food, whether it was over a campfire, as he often did, or in a well-appointed kitchen like hers.

There was another way in which he and she were alike. Both of them valued privacy. The deeper into the house he went, the more personal the decor became. He sensed that few people ever went below the street level of her home.

There was a hushed quality to the private area of the house that pleased him. Stairs carpeted with a thick, rust-colored wool led down to the third level. Pale, creamy walls displayed paintings that beckoned to him, but Shelley kept walking, giving him no time to linger and learn more about her.

A room pleasantly crowded with overstuffed suede chairs and a huge sectional couch invited Cain to stop and rest, but she never even slowed down. She didn't even pause at the door of what appeared to be a library. The room was filled with racks upon racks of catalogues and art books, as well as novels and a stereo that rivaled Billy's. St. George and a golden dragon fought in deadly silence on the far wall.

Cain stopped. He wasn't going to pass this room with only a look. With long strides he approached the painting, drawn by the gleaming malevolence of the dragon.

When Shelley realized that she had lost him, she turned and looked over her shoulder.

"Cain?"

"In here."

She backtracked to her favorite room—the library.

He was standing in front of St. George, measuring the potent fascination of danger and dragon and immortal combat. She glanced at the pillowcase Cain carried so casually. The lace bulged and bounced energetically.

"Squeeze is getting impatient," she said.

Reluctantly he turned away from the painting.

"I always wanted my own dragon," he explained, catching up with her.

"That particular one is a bit dangerous for a pet."

His smile was lazy and very male. "That's a big part of the fascination."

He saw the flash of her answering smile just before she turned aside to conceal her reaction. The female understanding in the curve of her lips lit up his bloodstream like a shot of neat whiskey.

They returned to the hallway together, walking toward the final suite of rooms. The smell of flowers was stronger here, and with the herbal scents of cured grass and chaparral. The combination of lush summer and desert mystery was irresistible to him. It reminded him of the woman walking beside him, female invitation and wariness at the same time.

"I think it's in here," she said.

He didn't ask what "it" was or where "here" was. He simply enjoyed the tantalizing scents that drifted through the louvered windows of the room she walked into.

It was her bedroom.

For a heartbeat he thought about what it would be like to be invited there for the night. Then he forced himself to think about something else, anything else. He had hardened in a visible, hungry rush, as though he were a teenager instead of a man fully grown.

Concentrate on the room, he told himself sardonically, *not on the woman.*

After a few long breaths, he succeeded.

There was so much glass on the room's western exposure that the effect was like being outside. A wall of mirrored, sliding closet doors reflected the grand view.

Beyond the room, fuchsias in every shade from pale pink to royal purple tumbled out of hanging baskets, making tiny waterfalls of pure color. Lush greenery trailed down the hillside next to a rock stairway. An artificial waterfall fell into a swimming pool that had been designed to resemble a natural body of water. Potted plants, flagstone patios, and multilevel wooden decks surrounded the irregular shape of the pool.

The sound of rushing water was both soothing and sensual. It was a seductive, murmured invitation to let go and float on the warm breast of the water, drifting amid the heady aromas of flowers, mint, and untamed chaparral.

Thinking about swimming with Shelley in that pool beneath a midnight sky shortened Cain's breath. Abruptly he turned away from the view.

The first thing he saw was her bed. It was covered in a vivid bedspread that repeated the colors of the flower garden and pool outside. The bed itself was positioned beneath a transparent skylight.

He would have given a lot to lie tangled with her beneath the stars.

The pillowcase thumped and bounced against his leg, reminding him of why he was in the bedroom of the most intriguing woman he had met in a long, long time.

Wrong reason, he told himself curtly.

Right place, right woman. Like they say, two out of three ain't bad.

Think about something else. Anything else.

Shelley brushed past Cain on the way to the closet. She flinched as though she was startled to find anyone else in the room but her.

"Sorry," she said automatically.

I'm not, he thought. *You feel good.*

But all he said aloud was, "No problem."

Through narrowed eyes he watched her slide open one of the big mirrored closet doors. She shoved hangers to one side and bent over, tugging at a huge aquarium that was in the bottom of her closet. The glass rectangle was as stubborn as it was heavy.

Cain checked the knot on the lacy pillowcase and set it on the bed.

"Stay there," he muttered to the lively snake.

The lace jerked and seethed.

With a final wary glance at the pillowcase, he went to the closet.

"Excuse me," he said.

"What?"

Instead of answering, he lifted the aquarium past her and set it on the rug.

"Planning to raise sharks?" he asked mildly.

"That's about all that could survive Nudge."

"Likes sushi, huh?"

"Only if it's still wiggling. This aquarium was full of the most beautiful fish . . ." She sighed.

"What happened?"

"Nudge went swimming."

He snickered.

"The fish that survived were never the same," she said. "I gave them to a neighborhood kid, siphoned out the aquarium, and dragged it into the closet."

"Is that where you're going to keep Squeeze?"

"Aquarium, yes. Closet, no. Too cold."

Thoughtfully she looked around the room. Then she pointed to the north corner, where a deep bookcase held art books.

"Over there, " she said. "It's warm enough but not too warm. Wouldn't want to cook the poor devil."

"Nudge?"

"Squeeze."

"My pleasure."

He brought Shelley close and hugged her gently.

"Cain—"

"But you agreed we weren't strangers."

"That doesn't mean we're kissing cousins."

"You're sure?" he asked, brushing against her lips. "Let's explore our family trees."

Just before she would have objected more forcefully, he released her. As though nothing had happened, he picked up the awkward, heavy aquarium and walked toward the bookcase.

"Wait," she said.

She rushed past him and began pulling out books until she had cleared a space as long as the aquarium.

"There. See if it fits."

He lifted the aquarium and slid it onto the middle shelf of the tall bookcase. There was just enough room at the top for Shelley to have access to the aquarium, but not enough for Nudge to go swimming. Or hiking.

"Perfect," she announced. "Now for the sand and rocks."

She opened one of the sliding glass doors and vanished around the side of the house.

Curious, Cain tucked the aquarium under his arm looked around the corner of the house. There was a potting shed. In addition to the usual peat moss and dirt, there were bags of sand. Shelley was scooping sand into a one-gallon pail.

He set the aquarium down on the patio and watched, wondering why she wanted to fill the big glass container a bucket at a time instead of just pouring sand straight from the bag.

When she finished filling the bucket, she braced her feet and lifted. Abruptly he understood. His arm shot past her. His hand wrapped around the bucket's wire handle.

"I'm the beast of burden, remember?" he asked. "You're the beauty who thinks up new ways to work me."

"Huh?"

"I knew you'd understand."

Cain returned to the patio and dumped the bucket of

sand into the waiting aquarium. Then he went back and grabbed the bag of sand.

"Wait," she said.

He looked at her.

"Once it's filled with sand, won't it be too heavy?" she asked.

"For the bookcase?"

"To lift."

"You really are used to living alone, aren't you?" he said.

"What do you mean?"

"You think in terms of what you can do by yourself."

He almost smiled at the intent line her eyebrows made as she tried to understand what he was thinking.

"Take this aquarium," he said.

"I'd rather not."

"That's my point exactly."

"What is?" she asked.

"Empty, you could have dragged the aquarium into place on the bookshelf somehow."

She nodded.

"Full, it would be too heavy for you," he said. "But for me, no problem."

"Your point is that you're stronger than I am? Now there's a bulletin."

"My point is that you didn't think about using any strength but your own."

"So?"

"So you aren't used to having a man around."

Shelley hesitated, looked into his clear gray eyes,

then turned away without saying anything. She was unsettled by his insight into her life.

Into her.

She wasn't accustomed to being around people who saw beyond their own needs. She wasn't sure she liked it. Cain brought an uncontrolled element into the comfortable arrangement of her life.

Comfortable? she thought. *Or predictable. Maybe a bit too predictable.*

Maybe "dull" is the word I'm looking for. God knows Brian has used it to describe my life more than once.

But then, Brian's idea of interesting was something like JoLynn.

While Cain finished adding sand to the aquarium, Shelley went out into the garden and gathered several smooth, flat, fist-sized ornamental rocks. Without a word to him, she arranged the rocks on top of the sand.

A quick trip to the kitchen produced a pottery saucer. She sank it flush with the sand and added some water.

"Ready," she said. "Need help hoisting it into the bookcase?"

"Let's find out."

He bent, scooped up the aquarium, and carried it into the bedroom.

"So far, so good," he said.

"You're laughing at me."

"Me? I don't have the breath. This is soooo heavy."

"I'll get even."

"Promise?" he asked.

She took one look at his lazy smile and bit her tongue, ruffled by his deadpan teasing.

It wasn't an unpleasant feeling. It was rather like sipping good champagne, dry and fizzy and sweetly biting all at once.

Maybe Brian was right, she thought. *Maybe my life is just a wee bit boring.*

Or was. Nothing about Cain Remington is boring.

On the other hand, St. George probably felt the same way about the dragon.

From the corner of her eye, she watched as Cain fitted the aquarium into the bookcase. The strength in his arms and back was apparent with each smooth shift of muscle and tendon. He had rolled up the sleeves of his blue chambray shirt. The power of his forearms was softened by a shimmer of hair bleached gold from the sun.

She remembered how easily he had controlled the heavy, powerful bike, and how gently he had held her. His combination of strength and restraint was as compelling to her senses as the combined scents of chaparral and flowers.

The temptation to run her fingertips over the shifting gleam of male hair and tanned skin was almost overwhelming.

Not a good idea, she told herself.

She didn't believe it.

Not a safe idea.

She believed that. But it didn't worry her as much as it should have.

Hurriedly she switched her attention to the bed. A blue pillowcase rippled and bulged as though alive.

"Snake, don't get your knickers in a twist," she said. "Freedom is at hand. Sort of."

She untied the pillowcase, opened it wide, and grabbed Squeeze just behind his darting, rosy-beige head.

"Gotcha. Now hold still."

The snake wasn't having any of it. He wasn't a happy reptile. He had been stuffed into a lace sack, driven through traffic, dumped on a bed, and ignored. He was looking for something to chew on.

Shelley knew it. She was careful not to provide Squeeze with a target.

"If you would just hold still," she said.

He didn't.

"Have it your way."

She lifted the snake higher and let him thrash free of the dainty pillowcase all by himself.

"I'll take the middle," Cain said.

"Is the aquarium ready?" she asked.

"I hope so."

"On three. One. Two. *Three*."

Together they gently stuffed Squeeze into his new home.

For a time Cain watched the snake glide swiftly around the inside of the glass cage, testing everything within reach of its dark, forked tongue.

"What's to keep him from crawling out?" he asked.

"The lid."

"What lid?"

She made a startled sound and raced to the closet.

While he watched, two pairs of hiking boots and a yellow rain slicker tumbled out into the bedroom, followed by a sleeping bag and a lightweight aluminum mess kit. All that was visible of Shelley was her nicely rounded bottom as she burrowed into the contents of her closet floor.

He leaned against the bookcase, crossed his arms, and enjoyed the view.

And he wondered if she felt half as good as she looked.

With any other woman, he simply would have walked across the room and run his palms over the feminine curves. Shelley, however, was not any other woman. She was a woman who had chosen to live very much alone. There was no sign that any man had been in her home long enough to leave a shaving ring around the sink, much less spent enough time for her to count on a man's strong arm for help.

Why? he thought curiously.

It wasn't that she lacked passion. She had responded to his kiss in a way that made blood gather heavily in his body. Yet she also had retreated in the next breath, shock and surprise clear in her hazel eyes.

The contradictions that were Shelley Wilde tantalized him. Like the house, she had a civilized exterior that was sophisticated and pleasing. Beneath that was an elemental wildness that called to Cain's male senses like nothing he had ever encountered in his life. He got hard just looking at her.

If she doesn't stand up straight soon, I won't be able to, he thought wryly. *Damn, but that woman has a fine ass.*

She crawled backward out of the closet, face flushed. Then she dragged a rectangle of thick glass triumphantly from the closet and turned toward him.

"Found it," she said.

He smiled, watching her supple movements as she came to her feet. He thought about what it would be like to be in a glass cage with her, those long legs wrapped around him and his body locked deeply with hers.

The thought did nothing to cool the heat of his blood. Nor did the realization that her bedroom was very much like a glass cage, but instead of sand, there was a thick rug to ease the sensual impact of flesh meeting flesh.

His pants began to feel distinctly tight.

Cursing silently, he thought about what it was like to prospect for minerals fifteen thousand feet up the side of the Andes. Cold. Very, very cold.

He didn't offer to help her fit the big glass lid to the aquarium. He didn't trust himself to be that close to her just yet. She fiddled with the heavy top until it lay just off center, allowing air to circulate.

"How did Nudge ever get to the fish?" he asked finally. "Did you forget to cover the aquarium?"

"Nope. See that hinge going down the middle?"

"Yes."

"She flipped up the hinged part, hooked her claws under the rest, and dumped the lid onto the floor."

His eyebrows climbed in silent admiration. "Strong cat. Smart, too."

"Carnivorous most of all."

He laughed. "Well, she won't be able to get to Squeeze in the bookcase."

"That's the whole idea."

Shelley replaced a few of the art books around the aquarium, wedging it snugly in place. The rest she stacked on the floor to one side. She stepped back to look at the aquarium, cocked her head, and began laughing softly.

The sound went through Cain like silver lightning.

"Can you believe it?" she asked. "A rosy boa sandwiched between *Netsuke Through the Ages* and *Shades of Tiffany: A Study of Glass Art*."

"Having met you, I can believe anything."

She started to ask what he meant, then thought better of it. She wasn't sure she was ready for the answer.

And she was sure he would give it to her if she asked.

"We'd better get back down the hill," she said, turning away. "JoLynn will be wondering what I've done with you."

"Brian looked like he could answer any questions JoLynn might have, and then she could give him a few answers of her own."

"I doubt it."

Shelley's voice was wry, but beneath it was the certainty that when it came to sex, Brian had asked all the questions and gotten all the answers long ago.

"Then Brian and JoLynn are well matched," Cain said. "Like us."

She looked away from the sensual certainty in his smoky eyes.

"Right," she said, "the only two snake-handlers in L.A."

"That wasn't what I meant."

"Cain—"

"Don't look so wary," he interrupted, smiling crookedly. "I'm not going to wrap myself around you and squeeze until you can't say no. Remember?"

She remembered the gentleness of his kiss, the restraint that had held the male power of his body in check despite his obvious hunger.

And the hunger that was still obvious.

Flushing, she looked away from his all-too-masculine body.

"A perfect match," he continued smoothly. "I'm in need of gilding, and you're the best gilder around."

"You don't look like a lily."

"You noticed," he said, pushing away from the bookcase.

Instantly she retreated.

He didn't come any closer. He simply stood and waited for her to realize that she was safe with him.

She let out a long breath and relaxed.

"See?" he said. "Harmless."

She looked at Cain's six-foot-three-inch height, the width of his shoulders, the flex and shift of muscle beneath his shirt, the blunt strength of his large hands, and the lean, powerful length of his legs.

"Harmless," she repeated. Without meaning to, she smiled. "Cain, if you could only see yourself. *Harmless.*"

"I don't look harmless?" he asked wistfully.

"No."

"How about trustworthy?"

She started to say no, then realized it wasn't true. Despite being alone in her bedroom with a large, not-quite-strange man, she wasn't afraid. Her instincts told her that although Cain had a primitive male interest in her, he would pursue that interest in a civilized fashion.

"Yes," she said huskily.

"Good. People who do business together should trust each other."

She blinked. "Business?"

"Of course. You're gilding my lily, remember?"

"Er, no."

"I'll tell you about it while I make some fresh lemonade for us. Those big yellow things I saw in that bowl upstairs were lemons, weren't they?"

She stared at him. "Lemonade?"

"Unless they're grapefruit." He held out his hand. "Ready?"

She looked at his hand, remembering its strength and callused warmth. The scars on his knuckles showed as a lighter shade of brown beneath the gleaming sun-bleached hair.

"No," she said, her voice low and distinct.

Gray eyes narrowed in the instant before Cain's face relaxed. "Is it all men or just me?"

She watched him, her eyes wide. "I'm not—that is, I don't—"

"You don't do business with men?" he interrupted. "Funny, I could have sworn Brian was a man beneath all those designer labels."

"Business, yes. The rest, no."

He smiled slowly. "Whatever you say."

She closed her eyes. She knew, she just *knew*, that he was remembering the kiss they had shared.

And it had been a sharing. She hadn't been passive in his arms, waiting for an unwanted embrace to end.

That was what frightened her. She hadn't felt anything for a man in years. Nor did she want to. She had fought a long time for the security she had. She didn't need some hard stranger sweeping in and turning her home and her heart upside down.

The sooner Cain Remington was out of her life, the better.

She opened her eyes to tell him so, but found herself staring at his retreating back. He was climbing the stairs two at a time, his strides long and easy. His voice came floating back down to her.

"When life gives you lemons, you make lemonade. Didn't your daddy ever tell you that?"

"Only when life gives you sugar, too!" she retorted in exasperation.

He stopped. There was a moment of silence,

followed by rich, male laughter. Then he looked over his shoulder at her.

"As long as you're around, sugar will be no problem at all."

Chapter Five

⟨⟨⟨ "Let me," Cain said.

Automatically Shelley started to refuse, but then thought better of it. After the lush coolness of her house, a long motorcycle ride in the hot sun had made the safety helmet an oven. Even worse, the chin buckle was as stubborn as cement.

As soon as she lowered her hands, he went to work. She stood patiently while his long fingers coaxed the stiff leather free of the buckle. The clean fragrance of lemon oil drifted up from his hands, filling her nostrils. She barely stilled a quiver of pure sensual pleasure.

He hadn't bothered to use a juicer on the fresh lemon. He had simply squeezed liquid out of the fruit with a speed and power that had startled her. She didn't consider herself a weakling by any means, but his strength kept taking her by surprise.

So did his smile.

"Almost done," he said.

"I wasn't complaining."

"I know. That's another thing I like about you."

He eased the helmet from her head, brushing aside silky strands of her hair as he went. He could have done the job more quickly, but he enjoyed the texture and warmth of her hair sliding over his hands.

He inhaled deeply. Mixed with her understated perfume was a haunting drift of lemon fragrance. The lemonade she had drunk so eagerly had left a pale line along her upper lip.

He smiled, knowing that if he licked the silver residue, it would be sweet. Sugar-sweet, and tasting of woman.

A glitter of sensation went over Shelley when she saw Cain's smile.

I've got to put a stop to this, she thought. *I'm letting him come too close too fast*.

Yet a deep part of her only wanted to be closer and then closer still, as close as a man and a woman could be.

Abruptly she stepped away and rummaged in her purse for a hairbrush. When she glanced up once more, he was hanging her helmet next to his on the handlebars.

For a moment she stared, struck by how out of place the black bike looked parked next to Brian's silver Mercedes 450 and the scarlet Ferrari that belonged to JoLynn. There was nothing sleek or polished about the motorcycle. Its tires were large and rough, designed for off-road as well as highway use. Cutaway fenders and the absence of chrome added to the outlaw effect.

Like the man, the bike was honed down to basics. Its power, endurance, and speed didn't need any flashy decorations.

Cain turned away from the bike and stretched. Then he looked around curiously. He rarely came to Beverly Hills. Overpriced goods and overdressed women didn't appeal to him.

He glanced from the elegant storefront of The Gilded Lily to the equally elegant woman whose hair was as dark and satiny as melted bittersweet chocolate. He envied the brush that was sliding through the gleaming strands.

"Is this where you gild my lily?" he asked.

"A bike like that doesn't need gilding. It is what it does—beautifully."

For the space of a breath he was too surprised to speak. When he did, his words startled both of them.

"I've been looking for you for a long time."

"You should have tried *Architectural Digest*," she said, putting away her brush. "I'm a regular advertiser."

He laughed, enjoying her quick tongue. Instinct told him that his frankly male interest made her uneasy. Instinct also told him that there was nothing specifically personal in her wariness of him. In fact, he suspected that he had gotten inside her defenses more than any man in a long time.

What happened to you, Shelley Wilde? he thought. *Who taught you to mistrust yourself and men?*

But the questions went no further than the silence of Cain's mind. He sensed that he had pushed her as far as she was going to go at the moment. If he pushed any more, she would simply smile professionally and slide through his fingers like sunlight, leaving only darkness behind.

He followed her to the glass-fronted shop that looked more like an art gallery than a store. She put in the key and began working the stiff lock.

"I should have thought of that sooner," he said.

"What?"

"Checking the ads in *Architectural Digest*. I would have enjoyed L.A. a lot more."

She concentrated on the lock.

He looked away from her clean, naked fingers to the electronic burglar system that protected the shop. The windows had a nearly invisible border of hair-fine wires and glass thick enough to survive a determined hammer. Elegant calligraphic script announced the name of the shop. Beneath the name was the discreet warning: By Appointment Only.

The lock gave way with a faint, definite click.

He followed the gentle swing of Shelley's hips into The Gilded Lily. Inside, various pieces of fine and decorative art were displayed throughout the area much as they would have been in a private home. The furniture, too, suggested a residence rather than a commercial establishment, with casual conversational groupings that invited relaxation.

When she turned to say something, she saw that Cain was looking at the shop with the same intensity he had her home. Silently he went from one display to another, pausing over soapstone carvings of birds from Baffin Island and a Landsat photo of the Sahara.

The photo showed the desert reduced to its essence, a purity of line and light and shadow that was almost surreal. He studied it for a long time.

Other displays received little more than a glance from him. Minimalist art didn't hold his interest, nor did the more avant-garde experiments in mixed media or warring colors. Such works drew little more than a cool glance from him.

Just when she had decided that he didn't like abstract art, he stopped in front of a large, free-form wood sculpture. The surface of the wood was intensely smooth. It had a soft satin gleam rather than a hard lacquer finish. The grain showed in a series of long, darkly curving lines.

The shape of the sculpture was utterly abstract, resembling nothing in the real world. Yet the flowing curves and satin texture somehow cried out to be touched.

For several moments Cain did just that, running his fingertips from one fluid curve to the next. Finally he let his palms smooth lightly down the sculpture's satin sides.

The sheer sensuality of his reaction made Shelley's breath catch. She had seen many people stroke the sculpture. This was the first time she envied the sleek wood.

After another slow tracing with his hands, he looked down and saw the title of the sculpture: ''I

Love You, Too.'' He threw back his head and laughed with delight.

The sound of his laughter pleased her as much as his appreciation of the sculpture. The piece was one of her personal favorites, a combination of sensuality and humor.

''Is this for rent?'' he asked.

She hesitated, for the sculpture was very useful to her in assessing clients' reactions. Many of her people had specifically requested it. She had always refused and substituted another touchable sculpture. Yet she was reluctant to disappoint Cain.

''I usually keep it here,'' she said. ''It requires a lot of petting. That's the source of its special glow.''

The corners of his mouth turned up in a slow smile. His sun-streaked chestnut hair gleamed as he bent closer to the inviting, polished curves.

''Like a woman,'' he said, smoothing his palms over the sculpture again.

''Are you saying men don't like to be petted?'' she retorted.

''You're a woman, you tell me.''

She bit her tongue and didn't say the words that were choking her.

My former husband didn't want to be petted. At least not by me. Busty barflies were a different matter entirely.

With the ease of long experience, Shelley concealed the painful memories beneath an expression of cool indifference and an equally cool tone.

''You're asking the wrong woman, remember? I'm the one who can't hold a man.''

His head snapped up. He stared at her as intently as though she was a sensual sculpture waiting to be appreciated.

At the moment, she looked more like ice than warm flesh. Her hazel eyes were distant, as watchful as a cat that has known more curses than kindness.

Not for the first time, Cain regretted the cutting remark he had made to Shelley when they met at JoLynn's house. Unfortunately, his temper had been tested past its limits already that day. Several times.

Damn JoLynn anyway. That female would try the patience of twelve saints.

"And I'm the man who can't hold a woman, remember?" he asked.

"I doubt that you ever wanted to."

She turned away, dismissing the subject.

And him.

With a long step he closed the distance she was trying to put between them.

"Have you?" he asked.

"What?"

"Ever wanted to keep a man."

"Once. The cure was quite effective."

"What cure?"

"Growing up."

There was an edge of savagery in her voice and in the metallic gleam of gold in her eyes.

"What does that mean?" he asked.

She turned sharply and faced him. "It means that I am my own person now. I have furnished my home and my life to suit myself."

"And there's no room in it for anyone else, even on a temporary basis?"

"Especially on a temporary basis. Rented rooms, rented people, rented lives. No thank you, Cain Remington. I'm not for rent."

"Are you for sale, then?" he asked politely.

"What?"

"Marriage. An outright purchase until death do you part."

"Or divorce, whichever comes sooner. And we both know which comes sooner, don't we?"

"So that's it. Your husband dumped you."

"Tactful to the core, aren't you?" she asked.

"Did he?"

"Did he what?"

"Dump you."

"Like a handful of dirt. Satisfied?"

"No."

Cain's expression changed as he looked at the taut, angry lines of Shelley's face and the curving feminine lines of her body, a living sculpture crying out to be stroked.

"I'm not satisfied at all," he said.

"I'll find JoLynn. I'm sure she comes with a money-back guarantee."

A large hand wrapped around Shelley's wrist, holding her in place. "I don't want JoLynn. I want you."

"You can't afford me," she said in a clipped voice.

"Name a price."

She listened to the cold, confident tone and felt

anger uncurl hotly. Her former husband had been confident, too.

And he, too, had been wrong.

"Love, not money, Mr. Remington."

Emotion showed for an instant on his hard face. Then all expression faded into a polite mask.

"Love is an elusive commodity," he said.

"So that's it," she said mockingly, echoing his earlier words. "You loved a woman and she dumped you."

"Tactful, aren't you?"

"To the core."

Pointedly, she looked down at the large hand wrapped around her wrist.

"Excuse me," she murmured. "I have a lot of work to do."

"So do I. Your husband burned you but good, didn't he?"

As Cain spoke, he caressed her inner wrist with the ball of his thumb.

The combination of his hard fingers and gently caressing thumb took the heat out of her anger, leaving only the hurt beneath. She swallowed and wanted to look away from his too-knowing eyes. Pride wouldn't let her.

"My ex-husband taught me the price of sharing my dreams."

"Disillusionment?"

"Was that what happened to you?"

"You could say that I was disillusioned." Cain's voice was mild, but his eyes were the color of winter ice. "You could also say that I was mad enough to kill."

Her eyes widened. She had the distinct feeling that she wouldn't want to be on the receiving end of this man's unbridled rage.

"Did you?" she asked before she could stop herself.

"I was mad at myself, not her. She wasn't worth killing for."

Another question came to Shelley's lips, but she said nothing aloud. Beneath his anger she had seen a flash of old pain that reminded her all too much of her own.

"Neither was my husband," she admitted.

She touched Cain's arm where sun-bleached hair gleamed over tanned skin.

"I'm sorry," she said simply. "I had no right to pry."

He gave her a wry smile.

"I had it coming," he said. "I've been chipping away at your civilized veneer ever since I saw your cynical little smile when you looked from JoLynn's cleavage to me."

"Was I that obvious?"

"Only to a man watching you very closely."

"The way you are now?"

He smiled and her heart hesitated. His thumb moved over the inside of her wrist with slow, gently searching strokes.

"The way I am now," he agreed.

"Why?" she asked, curious. "I'm not the sexy kind of woman who makes men stop and stare."

"Like JoLynn?"

"Yes. She's drop-dead gorgeous."

"She's drop-dead boring."

"But—"

"When I saw you pick up that snake and hold it as carefully as a kitten, I wanted to know you. I wanted to know how a woman who spends her life surrounded by the finest products of civilization had learned to handle snakes and lonely children."

Shelley didn't know what to say. Even if she had, she wouldn't have been able to talk. The sensations radiating up from Cain's caressing thumb had stolen her voice.

His smiled widened and became even more gentle.

"And then you calmly stepped onto my bike in your silks and stylish shoes, carrying a pissed-off boa constrictor in a Spanish lace pillowcase."

His warm thumb kept up its slow, hypnotic rhythm against the pulse beating beneath her soft skin.

"When I walked into your house, your civilized and deeply wild home, I realized that I *had* to know you. But you kept retreating."

"Cain, I—"

"You're still retreating. Don't. Please. I don't want to hurt you or frighten you. I just want to know you." His clear gray eyes searched her face. "Truce?"

She felt the tug of his words on her mind as deeply as she felt the lure of his sensuality on her body. She had no doubt that he was telling the truth. Hurting her was the last thing on his mind.

"Truce," she agreed softly.

He lifted her wrist and pressed his mouth against the soft skin his thumb had been caressing. The feel of his lips and the silken brush of his mustache awakened every nerve ending in her body. She discovered nerves that had slept for a long time. Nerves that she had forgotten.

Nerves that she had never suspected existed.

He caressed her wrist again. The soft, startled parting of her lips and her pulse accelerating beneath his mouth sent a shaft of pure hunger through him.

"What do you want to eat for dinner tonight?" he asked. "Seafood or French food? Portuguese? Thai? Indian? Mexican? Chinese?"

"Cain, I don't—"

"Eat?" he interrupted smoothly. "Don't be ridiculous. Of course you eat."

"But—"

"Besides, how else are you going to find out how to gild my lily? I'll tell you right now, I won't tolerate the museum crap that JoLynn has. I want something that suits me, not some decorator's idea of ancient or modern home fashions."

"Do you really have a house that you want me to work on?"

"Of course. What did you think I meant when I said I wanted you to gild my lily?"

Shelley caught herself just before she would have apologized for mistaking Cain's business proposal for a very different kind of proposition.

There he stands, calmly kissing my wrist and at the

same time acting indignant over having his intentions misunderstood.

The man is lethal.

The fact that he had almost gotten away with it told her just how easily his particular brand of charm slid past her defenses. He was indeed what she had called him. A renegade.

A very seductive one.

Cain's expression of injured innocence gave way to a wickedly appealing smile as he saw the flush climbing beneath her skin.

She tried to ignore him. It was impossible. She gave up and laughed out loud.

"Then you'll do it?" he asked.

"How can I resist gilding a renegade lily?"

Like her eyes, her voice was vibrant with laughter and challenge and the feel of his lips against her skin.

His smile changed, more intimate now, as warm as the slow pressure of his mouth sliding over her pulse.

"I'm usually quite well behaved," he said. "You and your half-civilized smile have a disastrous effect on my temper."

"You and your sharp tongue have a similar effect on mine," she retorted.

"Sharp? Are you sure?"

Delicately he ran the tip of his tongue over the veins of her wrist. Then he lifted his head to see her response.

The intimacy of the moment and the gesture disturbed her more than she wanted to admit to anyone, even herself. Especially herself.

"Cain, if you don't stop, the truce is off and so is the lily gilding."

He saw the determination and fear that lay beneath her quiet words. His long fingers opened, letting her hand slide through his in a release that was also another kind of caress.

"Have you decided where you want to have dinner yet?" he asked calmly.

"It isn't necessary."

"You're wrong."

The flat statement surprised Shelley into silence.

"I meant what I said," he continued. "You'll have to know me better before you can make an accurate assessment of what will or won't please me. Making a home is an . . . intimate . . . process."

"Not *that* intimate."

He smiled slightly. "I'll behave, mink. I promise. It will be business and only business, unless you say otherwise."

"Mink?"

"Soft and wild," he explained. "Mink."

"Is this your idea of business?"

"Am I touching you?"

"No, but you're reaching me!"

His laughter was no comfort to her ruffled nerves.

"And you're learning about me, aren't you?" he asked. "That's business." His grin was a clean curve of white beneath his golden-brown mustache. "I'll pick you up at seven."

Bemused, she stood and watched him walk out of The Gilded Lily and mount the black bike. Even through the thick glass of the store windows, the motorcycle's primal roar made her shiver.

Not with distaste, she admitted silently. *Like the man, the motorcycle doesn't try to conceal what it is and is not.*

It definitely isn't civilized.

The insight didn't worry her nearly as much as it should have. Cain's gentle caresses were still fizzing through her blood.

"Awful machine," said JoLynn's breathy voice next to Shelley's ear. "But the man is something else."

"They're one and the same. Uncivilized."

"Like you, Shelley," Brian said, coming up behind them.

"Me?" She glanced in surprise toward her partner.

"Darling," JoLynn drawled, "no civilized woman would hold a slimy snake."

"Darling," Shelley said, "fish are slimy. Snakes are not."

JoLynn shuddered.

Shelley smiled. It wasn't a friendly gesture.

Brian cleared his throat.

"Uh, Shelley, why don't you have JoLynn show you what she found in the catalogs?" he suggested.

"Only if she has washed her hands since she touched that snake," JoLynn said harshly.

Shelley looked down at her clean hands and counted to ten.

It wasn't high enough.

"I haven't washed my hands since I touched Cain,"

she said very clearly, "and he felt just like Squeeze. Strong and warm and hard. Very, very hard." She looked at JoLynn with wide, innocent eyes. "Do you think I should wash after touching Cain?"

The other woman made a strangled sound.

"You're right," Shelley said agreeably. "I should. Few men are as clean as a snake."

Chapter Six

Even hours later, as she dressed for dinner with Cain, the memory of JoLynn's expression made Shelley's mouth curve in a smile that wasn't a bit civilized. It had taken Brian a few minutes to soothe the beautiful client into a businesslike frame of mind. By the time Shelley returned from the wash-room—vigorously drying her hands on a paper towel—JoLynn had been calmed down enough to point out the items in the shop that she wanted to rent for her own house.

Predictably, she chose nothing that hadn't been displayed in a famous museum somewhere in the world.

Shaking her head at the limited tastes of some clients, Shelley went to her closet. While she looked at various clothes, she stuffed camping gear back into place. She soon discovered that bringing a small amount of order to her bedroom was easier than deciding what she should wear.

"You would think that he'd tell me where we're going to eat," she complained to Nudge.

The cat flicked an ear toward Shelley, but didn't look away from Squeeze's glass house high in the bookcase.

"Or whether we're taking the motorcycle again. But no, that would make things too easy on me, right?"

This time Nudge didn't even twitch an ear.

"Well, I guess this calls for my all-purpose, what-in-hell-am-I-going-to-wear slacks."

She pulled out a pair of black slacks and looked them over critically. The roughly woven silk was strong enough to take a motorcycle ride, understated enough to eat hamburgers in, and elegant enough for a fancy restaurant if it came to that.

"They're even clean—as long as I stay away from shedding cats that are the size of a small pony."

Nudge looked at Squeeze.

Shelley pulled out a summer-weight wine silk sweater that met the same all-purpose requirements as the pants. Ditto for a necklace of tiny carved jet and amethyst beads. Black high-heeled sandals completed her outfit.

After she dressed, she automatically began pulling her hair into a smooth knot at the base of her neck. Then she remembered the motorcycle.

"If I have to wear the helmet, the knot won't work. Why didn't you remind me, Nudge?"

The cat ignored her.

After a moment of hesitation, she sectioned off her

hair for a sleek French braid. Instead of wearing the beads around her neck, she wove the glittering jewelry into her hair. When she was finished, her hairstyle matched her clothes, understated yet elegant enough for anything short of a black-tie dinner.

The sound of chimes drifted down from the upper level. Nudge sprang to her feet and darted out the door toward the front of the house.

"Some guard cat you are," Shelley muttered. "An army could camp on the steps and you wouldn't look away from Squeeze until they blew reveille in your hairy ear."

She crossed the room to the intercom and pressed a button. "Yes?"

"Glad to find you in such an agreeable mood."

"Dream on."

But she was smiling. Cain's deep voice was unmistakable even after being filtered through the intercom. She pushed another button, releasing the electronic lock on the front door.

"Come on in. I'll be right up."

She grabbed a deep maroon summer jacket and ran lightly up the two flights of stairs. She found him only a step or two inside the front door. He was squatting on his heels, rubbing strong fingers down Nudge's back.

The cat arched and preened in the manner of all felines no matter what their size. Her purr sounded like a very large hummingbird on overdrive.

Smiling, he stood up after a final lingering stroke. Nudge bumped her head against his knee, demanding more petting. He laughed softly.

"If you say 'Just like a woman,' " Shelley warned, "I'm going to sic Squeeze on you."

His mustache shifted slightly as he tried not to smile.

She watched each subtle movement of his mouth, realizing all over again what beautifully formed lips he had. Neither too blunt nor too thin, the shape of his mouth would have done credit to Michelangelo.

The elemental temptation of Cain's mouth shouldn't have fit with the unyielding planes of his face or the thick, uncompromising pelt of his hair, yet it did. She decided it was the lively intelligence in his gray eyes that drew everything together, balancing the sensuality of his lips with the angular lines of his face.

"Is my mustache on crooked?" he asked with a lazy smile.

Abruptly Shelley realized that she had been staring at him as though he were a piece of art she was considering acquiring.

"Sorry," she said. "You have an unusual face."

"Unusual?" He laughed briefly. "Is that a polite way of saying ugly?"

Startled, she said the first thing that came to her mind. "Good God, the last word I'd use to describe you is ugly. You have the most beautiful mouth I've ever seen on anyone, man or woman."

It was Cain's turn to be startled. His eyes widened as he realized that she wasn't being coy or flattering. She had told him the truth as she saw it.

"Thank you," he said simply.

Then he smiled again. It was a slow, dangerous

invitation that sent warnings down to Shelley's very feminine core.

"I'd tell you what I thought of your mouth," he said, "but you'd accuse me of being unbusinesslike."

She didn't disagree.

"So I'll show you instead."

With no more warning than that, he gathered her into his arms and lowered his mouth over hers. He fitted his lips to hers exactly, gently, and then the tip of his tongue traced her mouth in a caress that told her more about the beauty of her lips than any compliment could have.

She felt the tremor of desire that went through him, heard the deep sound of hunger he made when his tongue probed the moist warmth of her inner lips. She forgot all the bitter lessons she had learned from her ex-husband, forgot how little she had to offer a man sexually, forgot everything but the glittering wonder of wanting a man and being wanted in turn.

Dangerous, she reminded herself even as her heartbeat quickened. *So dangerous.*

And so tempting.

"Cain—"

Her voice was more husky than protesting, though she hadn't meant it to sound that way. He heard the difference and took advantage of her parted lips to slide his tongue inside, expanding the kiss.

Slowly he sampled every texture in her mouth from the tiny, sharp serration of her teeth to the slight, sensual roughness of her tongue and the creamy softness of her inner lips. Though he knew he should stop before he frightened her, the taste and feel of her were too good to give up.

The kiss deepened until he filled her mouth completely. The world shrank to the slow, rhythmic movements of his tongue sliding over hers, the heat of her body flowing over his, her softness fitting against his strength as perfectly as his mouth fit over hers.

He felt the tremor that took her, heard a sound come from deep in her throat, a cry that was balanced on the razor edge of fear and desire. Reluctantly he lifted his mouth. Yet even as he spoke, he dipped his head between words for small, brushing tastes of her mouth.

"Before you yell at me for being unbusinesslike," he said, "think how much you just learned about me."

Shelley took a ragged breath and tried to put the world back in its proper, safe place. It wasn't easy. Her thoughts kept scattering with each caress. The taste and feel and scent of him filled her senses.

And he was right. The kiss had told her a lot about him. He was a man of shattering sensuality.

Physically, kissing Cain was more intimate and exciting than anything she had discovered in or out of marriage. Mentally, kissing him was a kind of sharing that was like nothing in her experience.

He had given himself to the kiss with a completeness that first surprised and then set fire to her. Yet he had been so restrained in his demands on her that she hadn't felt either crowded or angry at the intimacy.

And despite his gentleness, he was more than strong

enough to support her weight when her body had decided to turn into warm honey and flow all over him.

"We better get out of here before I forget my manners," he said huskily.

She heard the question lying just beneath his words. Sanity returned.

"Will I need the helmet?" she asked.

Her voice was as husky as his. The sound of it visibly tightened his body.

"No. I brought my car."

"I'll get my purse."

In silence she followed him to the classic black Jaguar parked in the driveway. The car's sinuous lines appealed to her in much the way the man himself did. Both were restrained without being at all tame.

Though decades old, the engine started at the first turn of the key. The sound the car made was a well-tuned, throaty growl. She climbed in, ran appreciative fingertips over the leather-covered seat, and clicked the safety belt into place.

Under the guidance of his big hands, the car devoured the twisting, narrow hillside road with the gliding ease of a jungle cat.

"Have you been keeping this in a time capsule?" she asked.

"Close. When I'm out of the country, I leave the Jag in storage with a classic-car nut."

Out of the country.

The words echoed and reechoed in Shelley's head.

I should have expected it, she told herself. *Nothing about Cain says that he's a stay-at-home kind of guy.*

"You're a traveling man," she said flatly.

He looked over briefly, searching her expression. Then he focused on the road again.

Her face was like her voice had been—withdrawn, remote, shut down. She was sitting within arm's reach but she was light-years away, retreating farther from him with each breath, each instant of time.

When Cain spoke, his tone was soft, yet it couldn't conceal the surprise and anger he felt at her retreat. "You say that like a curse."

"It's a fact. Like death."

"Life is also a fact."

She shrugged, pulling her composure around herself like armor. She needed a shield against this man's potent appeal to her mind and body.

I watched Mom grow old trying to make a home for a traveling man, Shelley reminded herself savagely. *That should have been enough.*

But it hadn't been. She had married a traveling man herself. She had believed if she provided an inviting enough home, her husband would no longer wander.

She had been wrong.

Traveling men aren't capable of appreciating homes or the women who make those homes and wait, hoping and hoping and hoping, until hope finally dies.

How many times do I have to learn the same lesson before it sticks?

Grimly she dug into her oversized leather purse, giving herself plenty of time to listen to her own good advice. Finally she pulled out a notebook and a slim gold pen. Composed again, she settled back in the comfortable seat. In quick, neat strokes she wrote "Cain Remington" across the top of one page.

"How long are you usually in the country?" she asked.

Her voice was completely professional, utterly neutral. It was not the voice of a woman who had just melted and run like honey beneath the sensual heat of a man's kiss.

With a smothered curse, Cain downshifted suddenly. The Jaguar roared. It was a deep, almost angry noise.

She looked up from her notebook, but not with alarm. He handled the powerful car the same way he had handled the bike—ease, skill, and control combined.

To the right of the pavement there was only brush climbing up the old, abandoned road cut. To the left there was more brush, a thick growth of chaparral that dropped steeply away into a canyon that had no name.

The tires made a high, wild sound as he took the car through a tight curve. At that moment she realized just how angry he was. Somehow he had sensed the finality of her retreat.

He reads me like a book, she thought unhappily. *That will make the job harder for both of us.*

And that's all this is. A job. He wants to rent some personal touches to gild his temporary residence.

Shelley was damned if she would be one of the items he rented.

Chaparral went by in a brown-and-gold blur.

"What do you have against traveling men?" Cain's voice was as hard as the steel color of his eyes.

"Not a thing," she said evenly. "Without them, I'd be out of business."

Rented homes, rented people, rented lives.

"How long will you be in the country this time?" she asked.

Her tone of voice said more clearly than any words that she was inquiring for business rather than for personal reasons.

His mouth thinned.

For long minutes the silence stretched. The black Jaguar consumed the twisting, narrow road.

Evening light poured into the interior of the car, turning Cain's features into a tawny study of planes and angles softened by velvet shadows. Gold burned in his hair and mustache, but none of the warmth reached his eyes when he glanced at her. Like ice, his eyes took the rich light and transformed it into translucent shades of blue and gray, colors as still and deep as an Arctic twilight.

Without warning, the Jaguar swooped into a turnout at the edge of the road. In front of the car the brush-choked canyon was another shade of darkness. He turned off the engine and faced her.

"I'm not a mercenary," he snarled.

Startled, she half turned in the seat toward him. "I didn't think you were."

He paused as though examining her words for truth. Finally he nodded. But his impatience showed in the tightening of his hands on the wheel and the curtness of his words.

"All right. What *do* you think I am?"

"A traveling man, that's all."

"A lot of men travel in their work. What's so dishonorable about that?"

"I didn't say it was dishon—"

"The hell you didn't," he interrupted. "When you heard that I traveled, you shut down completely. No warning, no explanation, just good-bye, Cain Remington, and don't bother to write."

Damn! she raged silently. *Why does he have to be so perceptive? Most men wouldn't have noticed my withdrawal or have confronted me with it if they did.*

"Since when do good-byes bother traveling men?" she asked. "Tonight, tomorrow, or two months from now, it's all the same. Good-bye, so long, see you around."

She heard her own voice, cool and very calm.

Too calm.

But if she let her control slide just one fraction of an inch, she would be yelling at Cain. Neither one of them deserved that. It wasn't his fault that he was so very attractive to her and at the same time the worst possible man for her. Traveling man.

A man who would be here today and gone tomorrow. But her emotions wouldn't go away. They would stay with her, eating her alive.

"Good-byes can't be new to you," she said. "Or is it just that you're not the one saying it this time?"

He took a long breath and a better grip on his temper. What she was saying was reasonable. He was accustomed to good-byes.

And, he admitted to himself, *I'm used to being the one to say good-bye.*

Score one for sweet reason.

But he was not ready to say good-bye to Shelley Wilde.

After a few moments Cain forced himself to relax. He had excellent instincts about people, and right now every instinct he had was telling him to walk very carefully with her, business and business only.

No more wild honey of her kiss. No more of her womanly softness flowing over him and teaching him how hungry and alone he had been. No more heat and thick need gathering inside him, tightening his body until he ached in time with the heavy beating of his heart.

Sweet reason can take a flying leap into the canyon, he thought bitterly.

Then he took a second long breath and started the Jaguar again. Its powerful, subdued sound was almost soothing.

Almost.

"You're right," he said, his voice an uncanny echo of the car's primal purr. "I'm used to good-byes. Let's go eat."

Smoothly he let out the clutch and turned back onto the road.

Guided by hard, skilled hands, the Jaguar resumed prowling through the tawny evening.

The restaurant was the intimate French type that L.A.'s West Side did so well. It wasn't one of the tiresome watering holes like the Polo Lounge, where rude tourists demanded autographs and Hollywood hustlers paid the maitre d' to page them for nonexistent phone calls from important people.

La Chanson served nouvelle cuisine, aged wines, and haute checks. The civilized gleam of linen, silver, and crystal provided a perfect backdrop for the equally civilized murmur of patrons who discussed books and art and the theater as often as they discussed the Dow Jones, real estate, and the IRS.

But then, books and art and the theater were also businesses, ones in which La Chanson's patrons invested income as well as intellect.

"Do you live in L.A. often?" Shelley asked as she opened her menu.

Cain gave her a sharp look, but she hadn't taken out her notebook again.

Thank God for small favors, he thought grimly. *If I see that damned thing anytime soon, I'll burn it over the table candle.*

It had been a long time since anyone had made him quite so angry as she had by withdrawing behind her seamless business facade. The reappearance of her notebook would have been the death of his uncertain hold on his temper.

"I live in L.A. whenever I can," he said.

"Do you like it?"

He began to feel hope. There was real curiosity in her voice instead of the relentlessly neutral tone she had used since she had discovered he was a traveling man.

His mouth turned up slightly beneath the tawny brown of his mustache.

"I like it," he said. "Unfashionable of me, isn't it?"

She couldn't help smiling in return. Getting people to admit that they liked L.A. was almost impossible. It was a social obligation to hate Los Angeles. All the trendy folks did, and were proud of it.

But a man like Cain wouldn't give a damn about trendy or not, in or out, up or down, she reminded herself. She had known it the instant he had called her a spinster and then pigeonholed her as a woman who couldn't hold a man.

Rude, yes, Cain was that.

And accurate.

"What do you like about L.A.?" she asked.

"Freedom. Technology. Fine food. Bookstores. The ocean. The endless rivers of cars."

"What don't you like about the city?"

"The usual things. Traffic jams when I'm in a hurry. Smog when I want to see the mountains. People when I'd rather be alone. Noise when I'd rather hear silence."

"And then you leave."

It was more of an accusation than a question.

"Some people run away by staying in one place," he said, looking pointedly at her. "It's called hiding."

"I'm not working for 'some people.' I'm working for you. You run away in the usual manner."

Shelley heard the echo of her own words in her mind. Not very businesslike at all.

"I'm sorry," she said, smiling her best professional smile. "That came out rather badly. Everyone needs variety. Men more than women, I'm told."

With that she set aside her menu and reached for her leather-bound notebook.

Cain reached for his temper.

The click of her slim ballpoint pen seemed very loud in the silence.

His teeth came together with a small, feral snap that went no further than his lips.

"What are you doing?" he asked in a deceptively mild voice.

"Writing down your likes and dislikes," she said without looking up. "It will help refresh my memory when I go through my catalogs."

"I see." Then, savagely. "Here's something to work on. I despise leather-bound notebooks and little gold pens that go *click*."

Shelley's hand paused and her head snapped up. Her hazel eyes were wide, startled, almost gold with the reflected gleam of candlelight. Very carefully she put the notebook and pen back in her purse.

"Perhaps," she said, "I'm not the person you need to add warmth to your temporary home."

Cain laughed harshly. Need? Right now he needed her so badly it hurt. But he didn't say it aloud. He didn't want to see her give him another meaningless smile, then stand up and walk out of his life. And he knew that would happen as surely as he had known she was angry when he called her a woman who couldn't hold a man.

If she kissed her ex-husband with half the passion she did me, her ex must have been a brass-bound jackass to go looking for the "variety" she mentioned.

He cleared his throat, managed not to drum his fingers on the table, and picked up his own menu.

"Sorry if I was out of line," he said, smoothing the savage edges off his voice. "I'm never in my best temper when I'm hungry."

"Then we should order."

Cain looked at the menu. No matter how hard he searched, he could find no entree called "Shelley Wilde." With a sigh he condemned himself to an undetermined time of hunger.

"Appetizer?" he asked.

"I can't decide between stuffed mushrooms and oysters on the half shell."

She licked her lips in anticipation of the food.

He watched the pink tip of her tongue leave a sheen of moisture over her lips. He remembered how warm and sweet her mouth had been. With a silent curse, he forced his attention back to the menu.

By the time the server appeared, he had decided on his dinner. So had she. They both chose the same one.

"Baby salmon stuffed with bay shrimp," she said to the server.

"What was your second choice?" Cain asked. "Gulf shrimp in lemon butter with herbs?"

"How did you guess?"

"It was mine, too," he said dryly. He looked at the server. "One baby salmon for her and one Gulf shrimp for me. We'll have the Kentucky lettuce salad and the New England chowder. For appetizers, bring an order of stuffed mushrooms and one of oysters."

"I can't eat that much," she protested.

"I can."

She looked at his hard, wide-shouldered body and decided he could eat his dinner, and hers, and then look around for dessert.

"I'm assuming you prefer dry wines to sweet," he said.

She nodded.

"Chardonnay?" he asked.

"Please."

"French or California?"

She remembered that a "touch" of garlic and a "whisper" of shallots had been mentioned in the description of both entrees.

"California, if you don't mind," she said. "Some of the French Chardonnays are so light they can't stand up to any garlic at all."

He ordered the wine, handed the menus to the server, and turned back to her with a smile.

"You can gild my dinners anytime. It's like listening to myself order."

"Sounds boring."

"Not at all. Sometimes I surprise the hell out of myself." He looked caressingly at her mouth. "And I think you do, too."

Shelley glanced down. Her near-black lashes shielded the reckless response in her eyes, but Cain sensed it. He was watching her very closely. With each movement she made, the amethyst beads woven through her dark hair gleamed like a distant constellation shimmering through midnight.

"What do you do for a living?" she asked quickly.

Her voice was ragged. She felt the intensity of his glance like a caress, shattering her careful control. She licked her lips once, a gesture of nervousness that didn't help calm her.

She still tasted of him. Slightly sweet, slightly salt, completely unique.

A single kiss and I can't lick my lips without tasting him all over again, she thought almost frantically. *I've got to stop this.*

"What do you think I do?" he asked.

The edge of hostility in his voice surprised her. She looked at his hands, hard and scarred and strong, clean and gentle and sensitive.

"I don't know," she said. "Whatever it is, I'm sure you do it better than anyone else."

It was his turn to be surprised. "Why do you say that?"

"You aren't the kind of man who does things by halves."

Even a simple kiss, she added silently.

The server returned with the wine before Cain could think of any response. He tasted it without expression, then defied convention by handing the glass to Shelley and waiting for her judgment.

She sipped, savoring the expanding flavor of the wine and the realization that his lips had touched it just an instant before hers. When she handed the glass back to him, her hand trembled almost invisibly.

He saw it. His pale eyes missed nothing that she did, not even the slightest hesitation in her breath. He accepted the glass from her and drained it with a quick movement that was quintessentially masculine. Then he nodded to the patient server, who poured wine and vanished.

"The wine tasted even better the second time," he said. "Warmer."

Shelley knew he was referring to the fact that her lips had touched the wine, rather than to a good Chardonnay's trait of improving in flavor with slight warming. But she could hardly accuse him of being unbusinesslike in his conversation without betraying the direction of her own thoughts.

Unfortunately, too much of what Cain said could be taken two ways—one utterly normal, one richly sensual.

Maybe it's just me, she thought. *Maybe I'm too sensitive*.

He sipped again and smiled at her. The smile was like his conversation, filled with levels of meaning and invitation.

After another sip he settled more comfortably in his chair. He had the air of a man who had made a decision and was going to follow it through to the end, whatever that end might be.

"I'm a geologist."

"Oil?" she asked.

"Everything but."

Shelley nodded as though he had confirmed a private guess.

"What does that little nod mean?" he asked.

"Most petrologists work for very large companies. You're too independent to do well working with a corporation." She smiled slightly. "Unless you owned it, of course."

"I do. It's called Basic Resources. We do mineral surveys, Landsat interpretations, and mining consulting, as well as resource planning, projections, and conservation." His pale gray eyes narrowed. "And despite what dear JoLynn might have hinted, I'm not a mercenary or some kind of covert government agent."

Surprise showed for an instant on Shelley's face. It wouldn't have shocked her if Cain had been "some kind of covert government agent." He had the self-confidence, intelligence, and physical hardness to survive very well as a lone wolf.

"All JoLynn told me about you was that the bike was awful but the man was something else."

His smile was reluctant, and real. His tawny chestnut mustache shifted, making candlelight gleam in it like molten gold.

"Be grateful she didn't elaborate," he said.

"Why?"

"She can be a real bitch."

"Somehow I hadn't expected you to notice."

His eyes narrowed until little was visible but a slice of metallic silver.

"It's hard to miss," he said. "When I went back to her house this afternoon and asked her permission to take Billy for a run with his dirt bike, she told me a picnic was more what she had in mind. A picnic for two, neither of whom was her son."

"I . . . see."

"I suppose I could have finessed it, but I didn't feel up to a polite fencing match. So I reminded her that I was Dave's stepbrother and that if I had to, I'd get a court order appointing me Billy's guardian as long as Dave was in Europe."

"Are you—" Shelley began, but Cain was still talking, getting rid of words as though they left a bad taste in his mouth.

"I assured her that I'd get custody in such a way as to cause her the maximum embarrassment, and in the process scare off whatever wealthy sugar daddy is paying her rent."

His smile was as feral as the gleam in his eyes.

"She saw the light real quick," he drawled. "I'd rather not use the courts to enforce a boy's needs, but I will if I have to. With her track record, JoLynn would lose. And she knows it."

Shelley felt off-balance, almost battered by the leashed violence she sensed just beneath his smile.

"Dave Cummings?" she asked. "Billy's father? Are you really Billy's uncle?"

Chapter Seven

⌒⌒⌒⌒⌒⌒Cain stared across the restaurant table at Shelley.

"Of course I'm his uncle. Why would I—" Realization came. "Hell, I suppose Billy does call Jo-Lynn's men 'uncle.' "

"It's not uncommon."

"Well, I'm a certified uncle, even though I haven't seen Billy for a long time. And Dave's a certified fool."

"Because he let JoLynn go?"

"Because he believed JoLynn's heart was as soft as his head."

"Did you know her before, um, well . . ."

"Before Dave?"

She nodded.

"I met JoLynn twelve years ago, took one look, and told Dave that if he wanted a piece of that action, fine, take it—but for God's sake, don't marry it. Cheap shoes never wear well, especially when somebody else has already rounded off the heels."

Cain's casual, brutal summation of a woman who obviously wanted him shocked Shelley.

Is that what he thinks of all women? If you want it, take it, but for God's sake, don't marry it? Is he one of those insecure males who won't marry anything but a virgin for fear she might compare him unfavorably with other lovers?

"Don't look so horrified," he said. "JoLynn deserves every word I say."

"Because she wasn't a virgin when she married your brother?"

"Hell, no. Because since she married him she's had more men than a public toilet."

"Cain!"

"Sorry. No, I'm not. I'm sorry it's true. JoLynn is a real, cast-iron—"

Abruptly he stopped talking. He ran a hand through his thick, sun-streaked hair and moved his shoulders impatiently.

"How would you describe a female who offered to trade me a few hours of her son's time for a few hours of mine—in bed?" he asked sardonically.

Shelley couldn't hide her shock. Or her disgust. She thought of Billy pleading with his mother not to kill his pet. She remembered the boy's vividly individual room, his casual expertise as he fitted the helmet on her head, his open smile and warmth.

"JoLynn must have the maternal instincts of a scorpion," she said without thinking.

"You slander scorpions."

"I'm sorry," she said quickly. "I have no right to judge JoLynn."

"Why not? You gave Billy more kindness in an

afternoon than she's given him in a year. He loves her anyway, though.''

''Of course. She's his mother.''

''I could forgive her the men, but not the boy.'' With a bitter laugh, Cain said, ''But who am I to talk about fools? I married a bitch just like JoLynn. If she didn't have a man on top of her, *any* man, even a stranger, she didn't know she was alive. Thank God we didn't have children to grind up between us.''

Shelley swallowed hard. When she spoke, her voice was barely a whisper. ''Your wife must have been very unhappy.''

''I hope so. She sure as hell passed misery around. Like JoLynn.''

''If it's a feeling of being loved JoLynn needs, she should look at her son.''

''Why? She's got him. Wait until he gets old enough to walk away from her. Then she'll chase him all over creation until she's the center of his universe again.''

Shelley thought of Billy and shook her head sadly. ''What a waste. What a damned waste.''

A big hand smoothed over her hair.

''Soft little mink,'' Cain said gently. ''Don't look so unhappy. JoLynn isn't your problem. She's mine. That's why I left God's own mess in the Yukon and came back to L.A.''

''But Billy . . .'' she said helplessly.

''In a few months, JoLynn won't be Billy's problem, either. Dave has found a wonderful French woman. He's bringing her to America in time for

Thanksgiving. Soon Billy will have a real home, one that's full of love. Until then, I'll be here to do what I can for him.''

Tears burned behind Shelley's eyes at hearing her dream spoken out loud—*a home full of love*.

"I'm glad," she said. "Otherwise I would steal Billy for myself and end up in jail."

"I'd break you out. Then I'd throw you over my shoulder and show you the world."

Reality returned like a cold wind.

"No, thanks," she said bitterly. "I've seen the world."

"All of it?"

"Everywhere they had a snake."

"And you didn't like it."

"The snakes? They were fine."

"Then what didn't you like?"

"Never having a home."

The words were all the more forceful for the softness of Shelley's voice.

"But the whole world was your home," he pointed out. "Every wonderful bit of it."

"And none of it."

Her tone said that the subject was closed.

Period.

Cain's teeth clicked shut with a sound rather like that of her gold pen. For a moment he was tempted to push her on the subject of what did or did not make a home. But a quick look at her told him that a frontal attack would end the conversation. And the date.

He picked up his glass and swirled the golden wine until its heady fragrance caressed his nostrils.

"Did your parents have a good marriage?" he asked.

"What an odd question."

He shrugged. "Is it?"

"They had a wonderful marriage. It wouldn't have survived otherwise."

"What was wrong?"

"We were always moving. Mom worked so hard making every place we were in a home, but we never stayed there long. When I was old enough to understand that no place was home, I used to watch her fixing up our rented houses and I'd feel like crying."

"Did she?"

"Cry?"

"Yes."

Shelley tried to remember whether her mother had ever cried when they pulled out the moving cartons and went to work packing up.

"I don't remember," she said finally. "I cried, though. For a while."

"Then what happened?"

"I learned that we'd always leave, so I stopped putting down roots. Or I tried to." She shrugged. "It took me a long time to get the knack of existing in a place without *living* there. I never was very good at it."

Cain sipped wine and considered his next question very carefully.

"How old were you when you stopped living with your parents?"

"Eighteen," she said.

"Young."

"Maybe. But I knew what I wanted."

"A home."

"Exactly. I decided if I was ever going to have one, I'd have to make it for myself."

"Did you?"

"You were in it today."

"That's not what I meant," he said. "What did you do for a home in the years between eighteen and . . . what are you now . . . twenty-three?"

"Twenty-seven. Well into spinsterhood."

He winced. "I'm going to be a long time living down that crack, aren't I?"

"It's the truth. Not very flattering, perhaps, but true just the same."

"You prefer 'bachelorette'?"

"God, no. Awful word. Conjures up visions of a shiny-faced swinger who's still paying off the orthodontist. I'd rather be a spinster any day."

He grinned and started to ask more questions about her past, specifically about the man she had married. Before he could choose the right words, the server brought plates of stuffed mushrooms and oysters on the half shell.

For a time the only sound at the table was the slight crunch of cracked ice shifting beneath shells as Shelley and Cain ate the succulent oysters. Fork poised between two equally tempting oysters, she looked up at him.

"What about your childhood?" she asked. "Settled? Unsettled? Happy? Sad?"

"Yes."

"So helpful. I have to warn you, if you persist in one-word answers, I'll gild your home with chrome mannequins and heavy-metal rock posters."

"You wouldn't."

She smiled, showing a lot of teeth.

"You would." His mouth turned up in a reluctant smile. "I just wanted to keep my answers short, so you wouldn't have to take notes."

Shelley stabbed the fork into an oyster with enough force to grate against the shell. The notebook was her shield against taking him too personally. Somehow he knew it.

Silently she ate her oyster and cursed his uncanny insight into her. Even her parents hadn't understood her that well. She had always been a mystery to them with her longing for settled places, predictable days, lifetime friends.

"I'll try to restrain myself from taking notes," she said coolly, putting distance between them with her voice instead of her notebook.

Cain heard the tone, understood it, and bit back any comment. Instead, he did something that he almost never did. He talked about himself. He did it as a way to touch Shelley, the only kind of touch that she would allow.

"I lived in one place, in New Mexico. My days were as ordered and predictable as the course of the planets."

She muffled a startled sound at the unsettling parallel between his thoughts and her own.

"I had the same friends going through the same schools and the same experiences," he said. "Until I was twelve."

He stopped talking.

"What happened?" she asked.

"The usual."

"You moved?"

"My parents divorced."

Her hazel eyes darkened as her pupils expanded. She made a soft sound of sympathy.

He smiled, but not from amusement.

"It was a relief," he said bluntly. "Mom and Dad fought like a house on fire. No time-outs and no rules. Despite what you think, staying in one place with the same people, the same house, the same schools— none of that means one damn thing about having a *home*."

Silently she shook her head.

"Two people in love are a home wherever they are," he continued, pinning her with steel-gray eyes, "no matter how often they move. Two people without love aren't a home even if they stay in the same house until hell freezes solid. You don't want to believe me, but it's true."

With great attention she selected a stuffed mushroom, avoiding his eyes.

"I learned what a home really was when my mother married again," Cain said. "Seth, my stepfather, taught me what a difference the right man can make in a woman's life. Mom laughed instead of crying, loved instead of withdrawing, smiled even when she thought she was alone in a room."

Shelley's fork hesitated halfway to her mouth.

"Later, from Seth," Cain said, "I learned that a woman can make a hell of a difference for a man, too. My mother and stepfather brought out the best in each other, not the worst."

Unwillingly she looked up, caught by the intensity of Cain's voice. His eyes were fixed on her, their cold gray color warmed by the flare of candlelight. For a moment she was lost in their clear depths, hearing nothing, tasting nothing, knowing only the hunger and yearning of the man who sat so close to her. Then his deep, rough-edged voice surrounded her again, claiming her whole attention.

"Seth was an engineer. He worked on projects all over the world. And he took us with him."

She held her breath.

"Dave was four years younger than I was, Seth's son from an earlier marriage. Mom and Seth had two more kids. Girls. Pretty and bright and sassy as they come. They're married now, both of them. I'm looking forward to some sassy little nieces."

Cain's smile was something Shelley had never seen from him before, whimsical and indulgent and loving, like a man watching kittens cuff and tumble over each other. The smile did odd things to her, sending shivery feelings of warmth and pleasure chasing over her nerve endings.

Then the smile vanished, leaving only haunting memories. His mouth became a grim line.

"Wish Dave had been half as bright as the girls," Cain said. "But JoLynn was the sexiest thing he'd ever seen. He had to have her. Well, he had her, all right. And vice versa." Then he added under his breath, "More vice than versa."

Shelley watched his strong white teeth crunch into a mushroom and sensed that he would like to have crushed JoLynn as thoroughly. He was a man who was protective of those he loved. He clearly loved both his stepbrother and his nephew.

Cain made a curt gesture with his fork, dismissing JoLynn. He concentrated only on Shelley, wanting to see the effect of his words on her.

"My stepfather was what you call a traveling man."

She flinched.

"That traveling man," he said softly, "taught me more about love and family and home than twelve years of staying in the same unhappy house did. Coming or going, staying or leaving, Seth was a man who knew how to love. That's what makes a house a home. Love."

"Don't tell anyone else," she said distantly, toying with a mushroom. "I'll be out of work."

"No, you won't."

His voice was so deep and certain that she had to meet his glance. His eyes were smoky with intensity.

"Your work is an expression of your ability to

love," he said. "You understand your clients' hunger for an environment that reflects their individuality. It's their home when you're finished, not yours."

Without knowing it, she nodded.

"Even poor, silly, sad JoLynn," Cain said roughly. "You're going to leave her house as perfectly sterile as you found it, because you know that's the only way she'll feel comfortable. You'll give her as much of a home as she can accept, and your only regret will be that she's too shallow to accept more."

Eyes wide, Shelley stared at the man who somehow knew more about her than she knew about herself.

It had taken her years to fully understand why she had chosen the work she had. Cain had known her less than a day—and he had seen through to her core. If she hadn't experienced his gentleness, it would have been frightening to be that transparent to him.

Even so, she was shaken.

"You're unnervingly perceptive," she said finally. "It must be very useful to you in business."

His eyes narrowed briefly as he heard the trace of fear in her voice.

"Being able to judge the amount of truth and violence in people has saved my ass a few times," he said. "It's also ruined what could have been relaxing interludes between business problems. There are some people you don't want to know a whole lot about, like temporary bed partners."

"Amen."

Despite the softness of Shelley's voice, there was no doubt that her agreement was emphatic. He smiled.

"Same problem for you, too?" he asked.

"I was never into temporary, whether it was bed or business. But you're right. Because I could see beneath the surface, I had to pass up a lot of otherwise attractive men."

"Like Brian Harris?"

"Brian is civilized, polished, wealthy, bright, handsome as the devil."

"And?"

"He's just not my kind of man. No one woman will ever satisfy him. A lot of men are like that."

"Boys."

"What?"

"Boys are like that. Men know enough about themselves, life, and women to get beyond hormones."

One of her sleek, dark eyebrows cocked questioningly. "An unusual point of view."

He shrugged. "It's common to all the *men* I know."

She opened her mouth to respond just as the server arrived with dinner.

For a time the conversation was confined to food.

When Cain casually offered Shelley a bite of his shrimp, she took it from his fork before she realized the unthinking intimacy of the gesture. It recalled times from her childhood, when her father and mother used to laughingly share tidbits from their separate plates. Even in desert campsites when they had exactly the same dinner of dates, figs, and bread, they still would exchange bites.

"Where are you thinking about?" he asked softly.

"Tinrhert Hamada, the Great Eastern Erg of the Sahara."

"Algeria."

"Yes." She smiled slightly. "I'm used to thinking in geographical rather than geopolitical terms. Comes of being raised by a scientist, I guess."

"What made you think of the Sea of Sand?"

"Eating from your fork. Mom and Dad used to do that all the time."

"Share their food with each other?"

She nodded. Her eyes were unfocused, looking at the past. She could still see the incredibly vast sweep of country known as the Sea of Sand, where only the toughest and most wary survived. The stark magnificence of the land still haunted her memory at odd moments.

The Sea of Sand rolling golden to the horizon, wind-rippled dunes tiger-striped with velvet shadows. Silence as vast as the desert itself, an unearthly stillness where only the wind spoke in a husky whisper of sand sliding down the slipface of a dune. . . .

In the long silence he studied her, watching memories like elusive cloud shadows change the appearance of her expressive face. He sensed a buried yearning in her, a longing for the wild places of the earth. He was very familiar with that yearning. It had drawn him to some remote, dangerous, and incredibly beautiful places.

Shelley blinked and focused on her dinner once more.

"Did you like the Sahara?" he asked quietly.

"Yes. It has a beauty that's just . . ."

Her voice died. She spread one hand in a gesture of helplessness. She had no words to explain her response to the Sahara.

"Yes," he said softly. "Landscapes of the soul."

Caught again by the accuracy of Cain's insight, she could do no more than stare at him. Then she realized that her fingertips were resting on his palm. Even when she had been lost in her memories, she had reached out to him as though she had a right to share his warmth, his life.

Landscapes of the soul.

Hastily she pulled back her hand, frightened by the depth of her sharing with him.

He's a traveling man. He'll be happy to take whatever I have to give. Then he'll leave.

He wouldn't mean to hurt me, but he would end up destroying everything I've worked so long to build. Traveling men and homes just don't mix.

And a home was all Shelley had.

She gathered herself, picked up her fork, and changed the subject.

"How old were you when you began to travel alone?" she asked neutrally.

He looked at the hand she had touched. Slowly his fingers curled over as though to shelter the warmth they had known. But when he spoke, his voice was like hers, matter-of-fact and unemotional despite the soul-deep hunger prowling through him with unsheathed claws.

"I hit the road right after college," he said. "I worked for a mineral-survey outfit until I was married. She didn't want to travel, so I stayed home."

"And you didn't like it."

"It was damned educational."

"Really?"

"Yeah. I learned that being away doesn't make a wife cheat any more than staying at home makes her faithful."

Shelley didn't know what to say.

"But the time wasn't a total loss," he said. "I started my own business."

She opened her mouth to ask about the business. What came out was entirely different.

"Did you love her?"

"I was too young to know the difference between lust and love. Did you love him?"

"Who?"

"The one who taught you to hate traveling men."

Carefully, thoroughly, she chewed a bite of salmon. She wished she had never brought up the subject of love and marriage and traveling men. Yet she couldn't duck the question.

He hadn't ducked hers.

"I thought I loved him," she said.

"And now?"

"Now I realize that it takes two people to make a home. He thought I'd be happy with a house to play in and meals to make and babies to dress up."

"You had children?"

"No. At the time, I told myself it was because I wanted to finish college."

"You didn't trust him," Cain said bluntly.

"You're very quick. And very right."

"Then you didn't love him. Without trust, love just isn't possible. How old were you?"

"Twenty."

"How old was he?"

"Twenty-nine. He was a sales rep for a large company."

What she didn't say, what she didn't need to say, was that her ex-husband had traveled a lot.

Cain took a sip of wine, set it aside, and began to eat.

Just when Shelley thought she had escaped, he asked another casual question.

"How long had you been away from your parents when you got married?"

"Two years."

"Lonely?"

"As hell," she said, her voice tight.

"Living in rented rooms, watching other lives, wanting a home of your own."

Her fork struck the china plate with a clear, ringing sound.

"Why ask questions when you already know all the answers?" she said curtly.

Long, hard fingers stroked lightly over her clenched hand.

"I was lonely when I got married, like you," he said. "I wanted a home, like you. And like you, I mistook one thing for another. It wasn't the kind of love you build a life on."

Then, in the same quiet voice, he asked, "May I have a bite of that salmon?"

Automatically she offered him the piece of fish she had just slipped her fork under. His mouth opened, then his lips closed neatly over the tines. She felt the slight, sensual tug of resistance as she removed the fork from his mouth. The silver was gleaming, clean, and his eyes were watching her.

"Your dad was right," he said, his voice husky.

"What?"

"Food tastes better from a woman's fork."

"Cain—"

"That's a very businesslike observation. It tells you that your dad and I have something in common. Do you want to write that down in your notebook?"

Suddenly she felt trapped, frightened, angry. "I haven't agreed to work on your house. I have more than enough work as it is."

His pupils dilated until his eyes were more dark than light, more steel than silver.

"But you have to do my house," he said flatly.

"Why?"

"Because I'm a man who needs a home, and you're a woman who needs to make a home for me."

She couldn't look away from his changing gray eyes—now clear, now smoky, now silver, now almost black. Slowly, unwillingly, she realized just how much she wanted to work on his home. He was too complex, too different, to summarize in a few standard pieces of sculpture and a framed oil. He offered a professional challenge that excited her.

He's bent on seduction, not homemaking, she reminded herself roughly. *But he won't be the first client to think I should be for rent along with the bed. I've been chased by experts, men like Brian and my ex-husband, men who think that sex makes the world go round.*

Like Cain said, the time wasn't an entire waste. It was educational.

And what Shelley had learned was that she would rather curl up with a Sotheby's catalog than a sweaty man.

Abruptly she decided that she could keep Cain at bay long enough to meet the most fascinating challenge of her professional career—to make a civilized, emotionally satisfying home for the kind of man who found satisfaction only in seeing what was beyond the curve of the earth.

"I'll do it," she said.

His smile had such savage pleasure in it that she regretted her decision. She was on the point of changing her mind when pride and common sense stepped in.

I can't go back on my word. Besides, I'm safe. Cain is a traveling man to the soles of his feet. He won't be around long enough to break my heart.

Somehow the thought didn't comfort her.

Chapter Eight

The following day Shelley looked over the battleground. Cain's residence was a large penthouse atop a Century City condominium high-rise. The view was limited only by the curve of the earth or smog, whichever came first.

Today the Santa Ana winds were blowing, bringing a desert clarity to the Los Angeles basin's often murky air. Viewed from Cain's residence, the city was a gently rumpled green-and-white tapestry thrown between the pale blue shimmer of the ocean and the cinnamon thrust of the San Gabriel Mountains.

The view was the only thing compelling about the penthouse. The interior was expensively finished and not at all individual. Obviously it had been done by a decorator who was competent and uninspired in equal parts. Stark white, dusty black, and an odd, dull red dominated the living room.

"Did you choose the color scheme?" she asked.

"No. I just told the decorator if there were any pastels I'd cut his fee in half."

"Yet you liked my house."

"You didn't have any pastels."

"Cream, buff, wheat, toast, sand, eggshell," she said, ticking off colors quickly. "I have all of them in one room or another."

"Those aren't pastels."

She turned quickly. He was watching her with a patient look on his face.

"When you say pastel, what do you mean?" she asked.

"Pink, baby blue, lavender, that sort of thing."

"Easter-egg colors."

"Yeah."

She smiled. "You're right. They wouldn't suit you at all."

"Thank you."

"Does this?" She waved her hand at the living room.

"What do you think?"

"I think if you ever stayed here for more than a few weeks at a time, you'd have the whole thing redone."

He smiled crookedly. "Know any good decorators? I can't stand the place after jet lag wears off."

Frowning, she thought of all the decorators she knew. Every one of them was excellent in his or her own way . . . and not one of them would be right for Cain. She sighed and broke her rule about never becoming involved in paint chips and carpet samples.

"Me," she said. "That is, if you'd trust me. I don't have any formal training."

"I'd trust you with anything I have."

The quiet statement startled her. She focused on him instead of the room. As always, she was caught by the changeable color of his gray eyes. Against the bleak blacks and whites of the room, his eyes were alive with light, like fog just before the sun breaks through.

He is too damned attractive to me, she realized again.

Cain smiled gently, as though sensing her sudden uneasiness, and its cause.

"Want to see the rest?" he asked.

She accepted the change of subject gratefully. "Lead the way."

As she followed him through the penthouse, she mentally tried out different color schemes. By the time he led her back to the living room, she had decided on subdued background colors in a variety of textures; a natural setting for the art she would add to bring focus and individuality to the rooms.

"You're frowning," he said. "Is it that bad?"

"I was just thinking about the odd-colored turquoise tiles in the bathroom. The Jacuzzi is beautiful, and the sunken tub is big enough to swim in. I'd hate for you to go through the inconvenience and expense of replacing it all just for the sake of color . . ."

"Do it. That particular shade of turquoise isn't one of my favorites. All I ask is that you get the contractor to do the work while I'm gone."

She looked away before Cain could see the sudden downward turn of her mouth.

"When will you be going?" she asked evenly.

"I'm not sure. I left a real mess up in the Yukon."

"What happened?"

"Two of my mining engineers are arguing over Landsat interpretations, maps, and ore samples. Both of them drink too much, and there's a woman, too," he added, raking his fingers through his hair.

"A woman who drinks too much?"

"No. A woman they're fighting over. Hell, Lulu drinks too much, too, now that I think of it."

"Sounds, um, interesting."

"That's one way of putting it."

He sighed and raked his fingers through his hair again.

"Compared to Lulu, JoLynn looked like a piece of cake," he admitted. "Besides, Billy needed someone to look after him. In the past, Dave always took the brunt of JoLynn's behavior, protecting Billy. But he's in France, so I came back. I'll stay here as long as I can."

"And then?" she asked, walking over to the west-facing windows.

"I'll come back as fast as I can."

She looked out the windows without really noticing the magnificent view.

"Seen enough?" he asked after a moment.

"Yes."

He had the distinct feeling that she wasn't referring to the view, but to his lifestyle.

"Shelley—"

"Call me before you fly out," she said professionally, cutting across his words. "If you feel comfortable leaving me a key, I'll oversee the work here while
you're gone."

"What if I don't leave? May I call you anyway?" he
asked with biting politeness.

"Of course."

"You're too kind."

"Kindness has nothing to do with it."

She pulled her notebook out of her purse and began
writing.

"You'll have to approve the paint and carpet samples," she said as she made notes. "Then there's the
question of furniture."

His hand moved in a savage, cutting gesture.
"Whatever works is fine with me. Just so it's big
enough for me to be comfortable while I'm here."

She looked up from her notebook. Her expression
was that of an attentive professional listening to a
client. Her eyes were very dark beneath the dense
shadow of her lashes.

" 'Whatever works'?" she repeated. Then she
shrugged elegantly. "Whatever you say. It's your
home, after all."

"It's my *house*. A home is built with love, not paint
and carpet samples."

The slender gold pen gleamed as she waved her
hand in a vague circle that included the penthouse.

"A home is lived in," she said. "This isn't."

In the silence that followed Shelley's statement, the
click of her retractable ballpoint pen was very distinct.
She returned pen and notebook to her purse and
walked to the door.

"I'll call you when I have a selection of samples for you to look over."

"Not so fast, Miss Wilde."

She hesitated. Then she turned around. One mink-brown eyebrow formed a questioning arch.

"Yes, Mr. Remington?"

"I'm going to be with you every step of the way. Paint chips, carpet samples, panels of wallpaper, pieces of tile, the whole tortilla."

"I thought you trusted me."

"Oh, I do," he retorted, gliding toward her with his soundless stride. "I trust you to show me all the things this penthouse has been missing. Starting now."

For an instant she was certain that Cain was going to fold his arms around her and teach her again how unnerving a man's kiss could be. But he didn't. He simply smiled and held out his arm for her to take.

The extent of her disappointment dismayed her.

"Shall we?" he murmured.

She thought of endless rows of color wheels and swatches of cloth and carpet. Smiling rather savagely, she put her arm through his.

"This," she said distinctly, "will bore the pants off you."

"I can't imagine that having my pants off around you would ever be boring."

A pale wash of rose heightened her color. She knew that she had to do something to cool off his sensual heat—and her own futile response to it.

"Trust me," she said, her voice utterly neutral. "It would be boring. Ask my ex-husband."

Cain's arm tightened beneath her hand until his flesh felt as though it had been carved from wood.

"Are you trying to tell me something?" he asked.

"Think of it as a friendly warning. I'll gild your house, but if you're expecting fireworks in the bedroom, you came to the wrong woman. Is that clear enough, or should I set it in tile and put it in your hall entrance?"

"Did your ex-husband bore you with his pants off?"

Shelley shrugged and didn't answer.

"Can't remember?" he suggested.

Suddenly she remembered too much, too vividly. None of her usual defenses against the past were working. The pain and humiliation were surprisingly intense.

"What I do or do not remember about my marriage is none of your damned business."

"In short, you were bored."

She closed her eyes and tried to think of another way to describe how she had felt about her former husband's infrequent attempts to make love to her. From the start of their marriage, his cutting comments about her small breasts and lack of sexiness in general had made her so self-conscious that passion had been all but impossible. Later, the marriage counselor told her that her husband's belittling of her body was simply his way of dealing with his own feelings of inadequacy as a man.

Maybe, Shelley thought unhappily. *Maybe, maybe, maybe. And maybe he was right. Maybe I'm just not much of a woman.*

After the divorce, she hadn't been eager to test the counselor's theory or her ex-husband's opinion. She had stayed well away from men in any but a business capacity.

Until Cain came along, tempting her. And then frightening her with his temptations.

What if my husband was right? What if I give myself to Cain and he's disappointed?

Or worse. Scornful.

As her husband had been.

"Did I bore you, Shelley?"

Her eyes flew open.

Cain was only inches away.

The heat of his body radiated out to her in a tantalizing, teasing caress. His eyes were heavy-lidded, intent, almost silver with suppressed emotion. The immense male vitality of him made her hunger for things she couldn't name.

"It would be impossible for you to ever bore a woman," she said, her voice husky and sad.

"Tell that to my ex-wife."

She looked from his thick chestnut hair down the hard length of his body to his feet.

"At least," she said tightly, "your ex couldn't complain about the basic equipment. Unless she was as blind as she was neurotic."

He looked startled, then speculative. "Was your husband?"

"Neurotic? In a man it's called something else. A need for variety."

"Was he blind, too?"

She didn't bother to evade or to ask if Cain meant what she thought he did. She knew he meant exactly that.

And she knew that she was going to tell the truth. As her husband had taught her, there was nothing quite like a cold splash of truth to drain the heat from passion.

"He complained about the basic equipment." With an immense effort, she shrugged casually. "He had cause. I'm not Playmate of this or any other month."

"Is that what it took to turn him on? Big tits?"

The blunt question made Shelley wince. It sounded so much worse spoken aloud, even more harsh than her memories.

Truth like ice water, chilling her.

"Yes," she said.

"Did *he* measure up?"

She didn't know how to answer.

Callused fingertips traced the line of her cheekbone. She made a helpless gesture, regretting her idea of using truth like a weapon to defeat his sensuality.

"Did he measure up?" Cain repeated softly.

"Not with me." There was no color left in her face now, only memories, cold and white and bloodless. "But I'm told he was an upstanding regular on the meat-market circuit."

Cain's smile was almost cruel.

"I wonder if he ever met my wife. God, I hope so. They were meant for each other. Makes me wonder if

Fate didn't mix up the cards a bit, dealing us exactly the wrong partners at the wrong time. We were both vulnerable as hell when we married, weren't we?''

"And dumber than a roomful of ratted hair," she added bitingly, remembering her own naive dreams.

There was an instant of silence. Then he exploded into laughter. He gathered her against his chest and rocked slowly, laughing.

She could no more resist his gentle, undemanding embrace than she could his deep laughter. Both surrounded her, sinking through protective layers that had been built over the lonely years. Laughter and gentleness and the sheer heat of his body reached into her, finding the woman buried beneath the shame and disappointment and fear. She hung on to him and laughed until she cried.

Then she simply hung onto him and cried.

"Even your tears are sweet," he whispered.

With catlike neatness, his lips and the tip of his tongue took silver drops from her cheeks.

"Oh, Cain—what am I going—to do with you?" she asked between broken breaths, defenseless against the man who rocked her in his arms, a stranger no more.

"I have a few suggestions that would shock you."

He looked down at her with an utterly male smile that made her want to bawl again. Her laugh was as soft and broken as her crying had been.

"Cain, Cain," she whispered, holding him tightly, rocking him as he had rocked her. "I'll only disappoint you."

And then, she added silently, *you'll disappoint me. Traveling man, we're all wrong for each other*.

"Kissing you was the first thing in years that hasn't disappointed me," he said.

He rubbed his lips lightly, slowly, across hers. His tongue flicked out, tasting and adding to the moisture of her tears.

"If I make you mad, will you stick out your tongue at me?" he asked hopefully.

The last of her tears vanished in quiet laughter. She rubbed her cheek against the resilient muscles of his chest.

"You're a renegade," she said. "But a very gentle, very intelligent one."

His hand fitted around her throat with exquisite care. Slowly, he tilted her face upward.

"I've never been accused of being gentle before. I like it."

His lips moved softly over her mouth, the hollow beneath her cheeks, the gleaming darkness of her eyelashes still wet with tears.

"And I love the taste of you," he whispered.

His arms slid down and tightened around her, holding her hips against his. There was no mistaking his intent or the extent of his arousal.

"I want to take off your clothes and taste all of you," he said. "I've never wanted to do that to a woman before."

He looked down into the wide, dazed hazel eyes that were watching him with a combination of wariness and the beginning of desire.

"I know," he said simply. "You think it's too soon. But I want you to know what you do to me. I want you to think about it. I want you to know beyond any doubt how hungry you make me. You're the most exciting woman I've ever touched. Whatever lies that bastard ex-husband told you are in the past. We live in the present. And this isn't a lie."

Cain lowered his head. Slowly, inevitably, he took Shelley's mouth with slow strokes of his tongue. The sensual rhythm was reinforced by the equally slow movement of his hips against hers.

After the first instant of shock, she returned the kiss hesitantly, almost shyly. She felt the tiny tremor that ripped through his body when her tongue moved against his. Knowing that she had an effect on him was more heady than breathing heated cognac. Her arms crept around his neck and she stood on tiptoe, instinctively straining to match the soft fulfillment of her body to the hard need of his.

He felt the change in her, felt the womanly promise of her caressing mouth and body. With a thick sound, he lifted one hand from her hip to her breast.

Instantly she froze.

"No," she said, her voice raw as she tried to twist away.

"I'm not going to drag you into the bedroom," he said, moving his hand soothingly down her ribs to her waist, then slowly back up again. "I just want to touch you."

Her hand intercepted his. *"No."*

There was no mistaking the desperation and panic in her voice.

"What's wrong?" he asked.

"What I have in that department isn't worth fighting over. Take my word for it."

Her voice was as flat as the line of her mouth.

"I think," he said grimly, "that I'm hearing echoes of the past."

"Think what you like. The answer is still no."

She stepped back and freed herself.

Cain could have held on to her, but he didn't. He opened his mouth as though to argue, then thought better of it. His teeth clicked shut. He looked at her tight expression, saw her uneven breathing, and remembered the exciting softness of her breast against his palm in the instant before she had twisted away from his touch.

"Am I likely to meet your former husband any time soon?" Cain asked almost absently.

"Not unless you have business in Florida."

"I don't." He flexed his hands. "It's just as well. Likely I would probably lose my temper and hurt him."

The matter-of-fact statement shook Shelley as deeply as his kiss had. His predatory smile while he looked at his strong hands did nothing to make her feel more at ease.

"Cain?" she asked hesitantly, almost afraid.

Silence, then a long sigh.

"It's all right, mink. Wanton cruelty makes me angry, that's all."

"I didn't mean to be cruel."

His gray eyes widened in surprise. Then his expression changed, as gentle now as it had been savage a moment before. His fingertip traced the line of her mouth. He smiled when he felt her lips soften beneath the caress.

"Not you," he said. "That bastard you were married to. He did his best to ruin you, didn't he? And you know why?"

Numbly, she shook her head, listening to Cain ask the question that had tormented her for a long, long time.

"Because you're all woman and your husband wasn't even half a man."

Tears magnified her luminous eyes. She knew that she was on the edge of crying again, yet before today she had not cried since her husband's last, humiliating attempt to have sex with her.

"I think," Cain said, his voice husky, "it's time we look at paint chips. Either that, or I'll forget my good intentions."

She blinked back tears and tried to smile. "You mean if I don't take you up on it right now, you'll wiggle out of having to look at all the boring samples?"

Slowly, he shook his head. "I mean that if I don't get you out of here right now, I'm going to take you down on this ugly carpet and teach you things about yourself and me that you just aren't ready to accept."

She started to say again that he would be disappointed, then realized that her words would sound like a challenge or an invitation or both at once. She didn't want that, despite the heat uncurling in her core.

He's right. I'm not ready to accept him—us—right now. And then she remembered that he was a traveling man. *I'm not ready for anything more with Cain.*

Ever.

Quickly she opened the door and walked out of the penthouse she was going to transform into a home.

"We'll take my car," she said distinctly. "I parked just across the street."

"I don't mind driving."

"Your Jaguar shouldn't be trusted to public parking lots. Your bike isn't big enough for carpet, paint, and tile samples. Besides, I know my way around. I've lived in the city for years. You've only visited it."

Cain shut up and followed her to her car. He wasn't surprised to find that she handled L.A. traffic with the same quiet skill she had handled Squeeze.

"Do you want to rent furniture?" she asked as she drove.

"No. Rented things are for houses. This will be a home for me."

"Whenever you're here."

She tried to keep the edge out of her voice. She wasn't very successful.

"Whenever I'm here," he agreed, watching her intently. "I own the company, Shelley. I can be wherever I please a whole lot of the time."

"And you please to roam," she said, her voice relentlessly casual, her eyes on the traffic. "I understand that. There are some beautiful places way off out there."

He listened to the unconscious softening of her voice when she talked about "out there," and smiled with satisfaction.

"You love them, too, don't you?" he asked.

"What?" she asked, throwing a quick glance in his direction.

"The wild places of the earth. The Sea of Sand and the pampas, the outback and the Tibetan plateau, mountain ranges as tall as God and abandoned cities as old as time."

She heard the resonance in his voice, memories thickly layered, beauty haunting him, calling to him, making him roam.

Traveling man.

"I love my home more," she said.

Her tone was a complex mixture of despair and fear, longing and desire, loneliness and hunger; and more, emotions as thickly layered in her voice as memories had been in his.

Different emotions. Different needs.

"This is the only place I've ever really belonged," she said. "This is my home."

He heard the accusation in her words, and the defiance.

"Who told you that you can't have both a home and the world?" he asked.

"Life," she said succinctly.

With that she downshifted and came to a smooth stop at a red light.

"Not everything you learn is true," he pointed out. "Look at what your husband taught you—a load of bullshit if there ever was one."

"You can't be sure about that," she said, feeling cornered again, not wanting to talk about it.

"My wife tried to teach me the same thing."

"What?"

"That I was worthless as a lover."

Shelley turned and stared at him, her mouth half open, disbelief clear in her expression.

"It's a miracle you stopped laughing long enough to sign the divorce papers," she said finally.

It was Cain's turn to be startled. Then he smiled slowly. "I take that as one hell of a compliment."

She flushed and looked away.

"It's the truth and you know it," she said, sticking to her point.

"I didn't know it then. I went through a lot of women, finding out what was true and what wasn't. You didn't do that, though."

"Go through women?" she said flippantly. "No. I'm hopelessly old-fashioned in some ways."

He smiled but refused to be distracted from his pursuit of her past. "You didn't go through men, looking for your own truth."

It was a statement rather than a question, but she answered anyway.

"No."

"Old-fashioned or afraid?"

"Try finicky."

"And just a bit afraid of what you might find out?"

"Yes, damn you!" she said tightly, angry again. "Are you satisfied now?"

"Far from it," he said, smiling slightly.

She remembered the deep, rhythmic kiss they had shared and the hardness of his body moving against her belly. Her mouth flattened and she looked away.

"That's the problem with me and sex," she said bitterly. "No satisfaction for anyone involved."

"Wrong. Your husband didn't have the first idea of what to do with a real woman."

Cain's voice softened as he ran his fingertip down the tight line of her jaw, down her neck, to the soft hollow where her life beat visibly, quickly.

"And I'm glad you're finicky, mink. Very glad. I've been that way for a long time. It's part of growing up."

A horn honked, telling Shelley that the light had turned green. She went through the intersection with unusual speed and a high flush on her cheeks.

Determined to give him no more openings for too-personal conversation, she drove quickly to the Design Center, talking about colors and textures and tiles every block of the way.

He listened politely, commenting from time to time.

As long as she didn't look at him, she could keep the illusion of having a businesslike exchange of views with a client. But when she looked at him, his eyes and his mouth reminded her of all the shimmering, treacherous feelings she was trying to forget.

She was relieved when she drove into the acres of parking lots surrounding the Design Center. The Center itself was a huge, long, glass-walled building that held a boggling variety of furniture. Every designer who had aspirations to national and international celebrity had a showroom in the Center. A few of the designers did retail business out of their showrooms. Most did not. That wasn't a problem for Shelley, who had a wholesale license.

"We're off," she said, locking up the car.

Cain didn't look nearly as delighted at the prospect as she did.

Two hours later, he dug in his heels and refused to look at one more piece of furniture. He had seen hundreds of things, each distinctive, each demanding attention, each asserting a completely different set of aesthetic values.

"I feel like I've been on one of those European economy tours of the great churches," he said. "If you show me one more chair, I'll turn into a babbling idiot."

She grinned. "Perfect! Now you're ready to do some serious shopping."

"Didn't you hear me? I'm burned out."

"Oh, I heard you, all right. Did you hear me?"

"Is this some unsubtle form of torture?"

"Nope. It's some unsubtle way to get past the surface and down to what really suits you. The way you feel right now, if anything catches your eye, that will mean it really speaks to you."

He muttered something she chose not to hear. Then he sighed and followed her into the next showroom.

By late afternoon they had been through every display at least once. Some they had gone through several times. Shelley's notebook and pen had been out all the time, but Cain hadn't objected. He knew that there had to be some way to keep track of designers and colors and delivery dates.

And he had to admit that her shopping technique was effective, if ruthless. After hours and hours of looking, he knew instantly whether a piece of furniture could hold his interest. He also knew which decorating effects were merely spectacular and which had staying power for him.

It was the same for colors and textures. Some combinations that at first had appealed to him tended to bore him on the third or fourth or fifth look. Other combinations became more attractive each time he saw them.

His responses became reflexive, a gut-deep yes or no that had nothing to do with anything except his unique, personal taste.

"Mercy," he pleaded at last.

"You're in luck. They're closing up the building." She frowned. "I wish I'd taken time to measure the rooms in your penthouse."

"Do you need it to the inch?"

"No. But I can't decide between two or three groupings for your living room, and the bedroom might be too big for—"

"Twenty by thirty-eight feet," he interrupted, yawning.

"What?"

"The living room. The bedroom is fifteen by thirty. You want the rest?"

"Whatever you have."

"Is that a promise?"

"Behave yourself, or I'll use my influence for an after-hours tour of every furniture showroom we've already seen."

Cain began reciting the dimensions of his penthouse. Quickly. She wrote it all down with her own brand of shorthand. When he was finished, she looked up.

"You're sure?" she asked.

"I'm an engineer. I've got an eye for measurements." He smiled, looking at her from head to toe.

Her pen jerked as she remembered just how cruel some kind of measurements were.

"You wear a size ten dress," he said, "except in the more expensive lines. Then it would be an eight. Same for your shoe size. Eight, that is."

"About the shower alcove in your penthouse," she began.

He talked right over her. "You're thirty-four, twenty-four, thirty-five, give or take some fractions. And," he continued, holding his hand out, looking at it, remembering, "you fit perfectly in my palm. That means a nicely filled B-cup."

"Stop it."

"Why? You're learning something, aren't you?"

"I know my own measurements."

"And now you know that you can trust my room measurements." His smile was challenging. "Right?"

She closed her notebook so hard that the pages

snapped together. "I have some furniture to order. Why don't you settle in over there and wait for me?"

He looked over his shoulder and saw replicas of a medieval rack, a stock, an iron maiden, and a bed of nails. Some whimsical furniture designer was using the ancient torture devices to show what should be avoided in the name of human comfort.

"I confess," Cain said, throwing up his hands. "Whatever it is, I'll confess to anything." His hands dropped to her shoulders and he drew her close. "Except lying. I never lie, mink. You fit perfectly in my palm."

His kiss was both gentle and hot, as were the hands sliding down her back to her waist. He released her so quickly that she didn't have time to object.

"Don't be long," he said. "We have reservations for dinner."

"Dinner?" she asked.

She was off-balance, caught between objection and response, unable to express either one.

"At the beach. With Billy. Don't worry," he added, yawning. "JoLynn won't be around."

"I can hold my own with her."

"I don't doubt it."

He waited until Shelley had turned and walked away several steps before he spoke.

"I'm glad you think I feel like Squeeze—strong and warm and very hard."

Her steps hesitated as she realized JoLynn must have told Cain about being compared to a snake. Quickly she turned and glanced back at him.

He was smiling a remembering kind of smile.

She turned away with a rush. Her heels made a distinct, determined clicking sound in the hallway. Like her heartbeat, her steps accelerated.

Even though nothing followed her but the memory of his smile, she felt pursued.

Chapter Nine

The sea rolled toward sand that had been turned a deep gold by the slowly descending sun. The light at the beach was magical, shimmering with mystery, touching even the most ordinary things with myth and majesty. A child's forgotten, half-buried plastic bucket became a wide crescent of precious lapis lazuli set in rough gold. Tiny stranded jellyfish became moonstones gleaming with time and riches. Rocks became ebony sculptures whose shadowed faces appeared and disappeared with each breaking wave, each shift of light.

During the heat of the day, the sand had been churned by thousands of feet. The sun worshippers were gone now, but the footsteps they left behind were miniature dunes and velvet shadows that recalled the epic sand mountains of the Sahara. The sea itself was an iridescent blue that was almost tropical in its intensity.

Shelley looked over the tips of her sandy toes and watched Billy and Cain bodysurf. Though it had been years since Cain had played with Pacific waves, it was obvious that he was holding his own against his agile nephew.

With deceptive ease, Cain caught wave after wave, riding the foaming water with little more than his powerful shoulders showing above the creamy surf. Billy stayed right beside his uncle, his slender body making up in determination and skill what it lacked in power.

Smiling lazily, she watched the males at play. She was outmatched in the big waves and had no problem admitting it. After an hour of being tumbled around by the surf, she had been ready to lie on the beach and let the thunder of waves lull her to sleep.

Now she was awake again. And hungry. Dinnertime was at hand, but the surfers were reluctant to give up their play.

A few feet beyond her, the bonfire she had just built crackled within a ring of stones. Everything was ready for roasting hotdogs.

Except the men.

She stretched and listened to her stomach rumble, but didn't get up and do anything about it. The low, rhythmic voice of the surf was unraveling her all over again.

After a few minutes, all she wanted to do was burrow into the warm, silky sand and watch golden light flow over Cain. When he rose from the creamy remains of a wave, he looked like a god cast in pure gold. Muscles in his calves and thighs flexed rhythmically, carrying his body with a grace that made her stare without knowing it.

He radiated vitality as surely as the sun radiated heat. Water ran like golden tears down his body, burnishing every line of muscle and sinew, outlining him with liquid fire. For a long time she watched him with a complex yearning that was both sensual and something more complex.

And she tried to imagine how it would feel to flow like water over his body, to know him as intimately as the sea did, touching all of him.

The thought made her breath hesitate, then quicken in time with her own heartbeat. She had never wanted to know a man's body like that, completely, curiosity and passion rising equally within her.

Would he like to be touched that way? she wondered. *Would he allow my fingertips and palms and lips, my teeth and tongue, all of me to discover all of him?*

Would his inner thighs be as sensitive as mine? Would his nipples harden beneath my lips? Would he enjoy being stroked, arching into my touch like a great cat?

And beneath all those questions, the fear that held her sensuality in a cold prison.

Would I be able to arouse him to the height of need— and then be woman enough to answer that need?

Fear and sensual hunger warred within Shelley. She closed her eyes, but still she saw Cain walking toward her, each movement of his body a separate seduction. She had known other men who were better-looking or more socially polished, bigger or smaller or more physically perfect. None had been more intelligent, more perceptive, quicker of mind.

No man had ever called to her own mind and body as Cain Remington did.

No man but Cain had made her want to abandon fear and memories of humiliation and give herself to him. No man but Cain had made a satin flower begin to bloom inside her body, petal after soft petal unfolding . . .

She shivered invisibly. *What will happen if I give in to the sensations that both frighten and fascinate me? What if Cain is right? What if I'm able to please him?*

Dear God, what if he's wrong?

"Wake up, mink. It's time for dinner, and you promised to be the cook."

She opened her eyes. Instantly she wished that she had kept them closed. Cain was standing so close to her that she could have turned her head and licked golden drops of water from his leg. The temptation to do just that shocked her.

When she tried to look away from the water-darkened hair and well-defined muscles of his calf, her glance simply went higher. She remembered the hardness of his thighs as he had pressed against her. And another, more urgent hardness.

Almost desperately, she looked away from his tight navy swim trunks. But the curling line of dark hair that appeared above the top of his trunks and then fanned into a wedge-shaped mat across his chest did nothing to cool her thoughts. She wanted to rub her cheek against his chest, to seek the skin beneath the male pelt with nails and tongue, touching him.

Then she realized that she had been staring at his body far too long. She looked up and saw the sensuality darkening his eyes.

"Do you know what I'd like to do?" he asked.

She shook her head, unable to speak because her heart was crowding into her throat, blocking it.

He sank slowly to his knees in the sand, but he didn't touch her. He didn't trust himself to. He had seen her hunger and approval as she looked at him. Now he wanted nothing more than to run his fingers beneath the maddening French cut of her bathing suit and caress her deeply, discovering if her body was half as ready as her eyes had been.

"I'd like to show you how beautiful you are," he said.

"But I'm not."

"You are to me."

One of his hands wrapped around both of her wrists. Slowly he raised her arms over her head and bent down to her.

"Billy will—" she began.

"He's playing in the waves. Even if he looked this way, he couldn't see through me."

Cain's glance moved from her face to her slender neck to the gentle swell of her breasts. His free hand followed the line of his gaze, approaching her breasts.

Suddenly she understood that he was going to touch her and this time she wouldn't be able to prevent it.

"But—you can't!"

"Oh, but I can."

"I'll scream."

"I'll tell Billy how ticklish you are."

Lightly he ran his fingernails over the smooth garnet

fabric where it was drawn tightly over her ribs. His hand stopped just short of intimacy.

"Unless you'd rather explain to me why you don't like having your breasts touched," he offered.

Her cheeks flamed with a combination of embarrassment and anger. "You know why."

"All men aren't like your ex-husband."

Cain's fingers moved in a light, maddening circle around her breast, just avoiding the soft flesh. But with each word he spoke, the circle became smaller, and then smaller still.

"Some of us prefer quality to quantity." He smiled at her gently. "If you don't believe me, ask a baby. Any more than a mouthful is wasted."

His hand closed around her breast caressingly.

She could have twisted away. He would have let her. She knew it, and so did he.

She didn't move. She was held by the hunger and approval in his eyes, his voice, his touch.

"Definitely more than a mouthful," he said. Then, almost roughly, "God, how I would love to prove it!"

She felt the desire that went through him like an electric current, shaking him. He closed his eyes and turned away for a moment, but his hand still caressed her.

An involuntary tremor took her, arching her into his touch. When he felt her nipple tighten, he made a deep sound of pleasure and need. His fingers slipped beneath the fabric of her swimsuit.

"Cain, you—I—shouldn't—Billy—" She gave up trying to speak.

"It's all right." He captured the tip of her breast with his fingertips. "Billy is out there waiting for a wave and everybody else has gone home."

"But—"

"Hush, mink. Let me show you how little size counts between a man and a woman."

Shelley gasped when she felt her breast released from the garnet cloth. Abruptly she felt helpless, wholly vulnerable, afraid. She turned her face away, certain she would see only disappointment in his.

"Now do you believe me?" she asked through her teeth.

"I believe you're a fool."

Her head whipped around. He was looking at her naked breast with the kind of pleasure she had never expected to see in a man's eyes.

"You're beautiful," he said huskily. "Can't you see how perfect you are?"

She looked down at herself and saw only what she had always seen. Breast too small to interest a man.

Then Cain bent down to her and taught her how to see herself as he did.

Beautiful.

She quivered at the delicious brush of his mustache against her nipple. She heard him whispering against her skin and savored the heat of his breath caressing her.

But most arousing of all was the desire that had drawn his body like a bow. He had meant every word he said about finding her beautiful. His body was proving it in the most unmistakable way.

A hot flower began unfolding deep inside her, melting her inhibitions.

"I shouldn't," he said, lifting his head slightly. His eyes fastened on her ruby-tinted nipple. "But I have to. Just one taste. Please . . ."

She shivered again, watching his mouth.

His hand closed more tightly around her wrists, yet it was more from passion than from any thought of restraining her. She hadn't fought him before.

She wasn't fighting him now.

Hungrily he bent down to her again.

Shelley gasped as the tip of his tongue traced a circle where the smooth skin of her breast became the textured darkness of her nipple. Unknowingly she made a small, pleading sound, but it wasn't freedom she asked for. She wanted a greater intimacy, a deeper holding.

He answered by imprisoning her within the changing pressures of tongue and teeth. Then he drew her deeply, repeatedly, into the caressing heat of his mouth until she arched beneath him and cried out her pleasure.

After a few sweet moments, Cain forced himself to release her breast. The peak glistened with moisture, a ruby hardness that flaunted her arousal. His teeth closed over her erect nipple with a fiercely restrained sensuality that made her twist against him, increasing the pressure of his touch.

Groaning in frustration at having to stop, he turned

his head aside and pulled her bathing suit back into place with fingers that shook. Then he gathered her against his body, letting her feel the evidence of his own arousal.

"Any more questions about what it takes to turn this man on?" he asked raggedly

"N-no." Like her body, her voice trembled with surprise and passion.

"Good, because I'm about an inch from taking you right here, right now, and answering a few questions of my own."

He rolled aside and onto his feet in a single motion. Without looking at her again, he ran down to the sea and threw himself into the waves in a long, low dive.

Shelley lay motionless, too weak to move, passion like a drug in her body, outlining her nerves with fire. The breast that he had kissed ached sweetly, still hungry for his knowing mouth.

With a small sound she rolled over, fighting for control of her own body. She had so little experience with passion that she felt like a stranger caught inside a network of fire, her own nerves burning her alive.

A few minutes later, the trembling finally stopped and the hungry flower inside her folded in upon itself once more, hiding its satin heat deep within her. Taking a long, ragged breath, she stood up and went to work on dinner.

By the time Billy and Cain came in from the water, she had set out relishes, soft drinks, and potato chips, and was turning a long-handled fork loaded with hotdogs over the dancing yellow flames. Buns were balanced on the fire ring so that they would be warm.

Except for an occasional tremor whenever she remembered what it had been like to be caressed by his beautiful mouth, she was in control of herself again.

But the fire was cooler than her memories and much cooler than Cain's eyes as he watched her bend over the flames.

"You should have stayed in the ocean," Billy said, scattering sand and cold drops of water with equal enthusiasm. "The waves were perfect and the water was really warm. At least seventy, I'll bet."

"Not as warm as my pool," she said, putting a hotdog into a toasted bun. "Here you are."

"You have a pool?" the boy asked.

"Complete with its own waterfall."

Billy slathered mustard and catsup over the innocent hotdog.

"Waves, too?" he asked.

"Only when I do a cannonball."

He looked at Shelley's slender body and shook his head forcefully.

"You need more weight to do a good cannonball. You're too, uh . . ."

"Skinny?" she suggested with a wry twist to her mouth.

"You're just right for you. Any more and you'd droop around the edges, like Mother before she goes on another diet."

Cain made a heroic effort not to laugh.

It wasn't quite enough.

He concentrated on rummaging in the ice chest for beer while his shoulders shook. When he glanced up, Shelley couldn't evade his brilliant gray eyes and the silent, laughing message.

Any more than a mouthful is wasted.

Color climbed her cheeks. Her mouth twitched as she fought against secret amusement. Finally she gave up and laughed out loud.

Billy looked up from eating his incredibly messy hotdog, smiled, and attacked the oozing remains. Then, without a pause, he consumed three more hotdogs, a whole bag of potato chips, and three soft drinks.

In stunned surprise Shelley watched the lanky boy power through food. She looked away from the sight only when Cain offered her a third hotdog for herself.

"No, thanks," she said, smiling. "I wouldn't want to, um, droop."

He snickered, ate the hotdog himself, and then pulled a Frisbee out from under his beach towel. He faced his dinner companions with a challenging smile.

Billy jumped up immediately, his face alight with anticipation. Shelley was slower, but still game. The three of them fanned out over the sand in an unequal triangle. Without warning, Cain bent his arm across his body at waist level, then quickly straightened it and snapped his hand forward.

The white Frisbee sailed fast and clean to Billy, who scooped it up and sent it flying toward Shelley. She surprised them by snatching it out of the air and sending it in a flat, sizzling curve back to Cain.

Billy gave a whoop of admiration and a thumbs-up

signal. Then the three of them settled in and ran one another ragged. She laughed and jumped and sprinted, feeling like a child herself.

But Shelley remembered she was a woman when Cain leaped high to catch the elusive Frisbee. For an instant his sun-burnished body defied gravity. Then, he landed lightly on the sand, his body coiled around the plastic saucer, and he released it in a powerful surge that made her mouth go dry.

For a while the Frisbee flew like a wild moon orbiting between three planets. Around them, surrounding them with light and color, southern California's huge summer sun drifted slowly toward the water.

Finally it was too dark to judge the saucer's flight any longer. Cain leaped high into the air, rescuing the toy from certain drowning in the rushing indigo sea.

Shelley knew she would remember that moment for the rest of her life, his body suspended against the radiant twilight like a wave before the instant of breaking, and then the inevitable descent, as smooth and powerful as the ocean itself.

"Great catch, Uncle Cain!"

He waved the Frisbee, but didn't send it toward his nephew. Instead, he walked toward Shelley, watching her with eyes the color of twilight. When he held out his hand, she took it without hesitation. The warmth of his fingers threading between hers made her whole body tighten with pleasure. He gave her a look of approval that was a caress in itself.

"Graceful as a mink, too," he said.

"Flattery will get you a toasted marshmallow."

"I can think of something sweeter."

She met his eyes for an instant, then looked away. The sensual teasing both pleased and unsettled her.

"Uncle Cain?" called Billy. "Just a few more?"

"Nope. It's marshmallow time." Cain's voice carried clearly across the twilight.

His look told Shelley that he wanted her more than any dessert.

"Here," he said, handing the fork and bag of marshmallows to Billy. "You be the chef."

"I'll set them on fire."

"I'm counting on it."

Grinning, the boy stuffed marshmallows onto the fork and held it in the heart of the fire. Everyone ate the charred results without a whimper. Shelley wouldn't have cared if she were eating sand. All she could really taste was the memory of Cain's tongue moving over hers. The heat radiating from him was a temptation and a revelation, like sitting close to a gently burning sun.

"Cold?" he asked, seeing her tiny shiver.

"With you right next to me? Impossible."

He touched her cheek in a brief caress. She looked at his eyes and knew that he wanted to wrap his warmth around her and hold her close.

Just hold her.

When he put his arm across her shoulders and cradled her against his body, she felt an irresistible sense of homecoming. Putting her cheek against his chest, she relaxed with a sigh.

"More?" Billy asked, looking up from the ash-covered marshmallow fork.

"No, thanks," she said.

"Uncle Cain?"

"No way," he said, laughing quietly. "My mustache will never come unstuck as it is."

"Try lighter fluid," the boy suggested. "It works on bubble gum, anyway."

"Yuck. How can you stand the taste of that stuff?"

"Lighter fluid?"

"Bubble gum."

Billy laughed at his uncle, then looked down at the half-filled bag of marshmallows. "You guys sure you don't want any more?"

"We're sure," Cain and Shelley said together.

"Okay."

Calmly, Billy began cramming marshmallows onto the fork. For every one that was squeezed on, another went down his throat. Obviously he didn't intend to stop eating the sticky sweets until he reached the bottom of the bag.

Shelley made an involuntary sound of dismay.

"Don't worry," Cain said. "I used to do the same thing when I was his age. I survived."

"Who held your head while you threw up?"

She felt the vibration of his silent laughter beneath her cheek.

"No one. Seth always made it clear that damn fools cleaned up after themselves."

"Have you told your nephew?"

Though her voice was deliberately soft, Billy heard. He looked up from the fire and grinned.

"The first thing Uncle Cain said when he asked me on the picnic was that he wouldn't tell me what to eat if I wouldn't expect him to play nurse afterward."

"Was your mother in on the bargain?" Shelley asked.

Instantly she wished that she had bitten her tongue before she said anything about JoLynn. Relaxation and pleasure vanished from Billy's face, replaced by a mask that was too old and too emotionless to belong to a boy.

"Mother has a party in San Francisco. She won't be back tonight."

"Billy agreed to baby-sit me," Cain said easily. "He knows I'm not used to big-city life. In exchange, I'm going to take him out on his dirt bike as soon as I find a good place."

"There are some rough dirt roads near my home," Shelley said, seizing the change of subject. "Old fuel breaks and such. I've heard trail bikes out there before. Is that the kind of thing you're looking for?"

The mask fell away as Billy looked eagerly toward his uncle.

Cain smiled. She felt his approval in the subtle, hidden caress of his fingers along the inside of her arm.

"Sounds good to me," he said.

"Oh, boy! Tomorrow?"

Cain nodded.

"Just be sure you have spark guards on," Shelley

said, "or whatever they call them. You know—the gizmo that keeps exhaust sparks from setting fires. The brush is really dry at this time of year."

"Billy?" Cain asked.

"Dad wouldn't let me out of the garage without a spark arrester. And a regulation muffler, too," he grumbled, "even though it cuts down on the power."

"Then all we need is another bike for Shelley."

"Wrong," she said quickly. "I'm strictly passenger material, and on city streets at that. You'll be better off without me."

Long fingers tightened on her arm. Cain's head bent until his lips brushed her ear. He spoke too softly for Billy to hear above the crackle of flames.

"There's no way I'd be better off without you."

"Your nephew needs a little undivided 'man' time," she whispered, rubbing her cheek lightly against his chest. Then she added in a normal tone, "I'll be glad to feed the conquering heroes. What's your favorite dinner, Billy?"

"Fried chicken, mashed potatoes, gravy, and choc- olate cake. Uh, if it isn't too much trouble?"

She tried not to smile at his hopeful expression. "Not at all. How about you, Cain? Any additions?"

"Fresh lemonade."

She gave him a startled look.

"There aren't many lemon trees in the Yukon," he explained.

There was a sudden flare of light. Billy's forgotten marshmallows were burning like a cascade of falling stars.

After a few futile attempts to blow out the fire, he jumped up and ran down to the water, waving the marshmallow fork around like a sword. The accidental torch burned brightly against the black sea. Sounds of a fierce battle floated back as the boy slew dragon after dragon until his marshmallow weapon burned out.

Shelley laughed softly, remembering what it was like to be young and have a world full of safely exciting demons to tame.

"That's quite a nephew you have."

"Yes," Cain said simply, bending to brush his lips over her hair. "And you're quite a woman. Can you ride a dirt bike?"

"It's been a long time. When I first came here, I couldn't afford a car, so I bought a motorcycle. Sometimes I kind of miss it. Especially when it isn't raining and I don't have to show up looking like a fashion plate for an appointment."

"Billy wouldn't mind if you came along tomorrow."

She shook her head, sending a fall of silky hair over Cain's arm.

"I don't know anything about off-road biking except that it takes more skill and strength than city streets," she said.

"I'll bet you're up to it."

"I'll find out some other time. Billy is enjoying a chance to be with his uncle. You're a hero to him. You can see it in his eyes when he watches you."

A long finger caressed her jawline before settling under her chin, tilting her face up to his lips. The kiss was gentle, a butterfly touch of warmth and sweetness.

"Normally," he said in a husky voice, "I'd be delighted to have my nephew around. He's good company. But I was hoping to take you home tonight. And keep you."

Her breath stopped at the sensual promise in his voice.

"But," he said, "I knew that wouldn't happen when JoLynn told me it didn't matter what time I brought Billy back after the picnic. She'd be gone, and the maid would let him in."

Cain's mouth hovered just above Shelley's. His lips touched hers lightly between words.

"I keep telling myself that it's just as well," he said. "I know it's too soon for you to accept me as a lover. But I feel like I've always known you, always laughed with you, always missed you, always cared for you, always wanted you."

Without hesitation she kissed him as he had kissed her, moving her lips lightly around the edges of his beautifully shaped mouth. She felt a need to give warmth to him that had nothing to do with passion or desire. She wanted to touch him with her mind, but couldn't, so she gave him back the exquisitely tender caresses he had given to her.

She had never kissed a man like that before, a gentle sharing of self that was as deeply moving in its own way as passion had been earlier.

It was the same when Cain walked Shelley to her front door. He held her as though she were more fragile than a butterfly's wing. His lips were very gentle over hers.

"Tomorrow," he said.

"Come early." She ran a fingertip over his soft mustache. "You can go swimming before dinner."

"I feel as though I'm drowning now. Will you save me?"

"Cain . . ."

"Thank you."

He took her mouth as gently as he had taken her lips. Slowly he touched the tip of his tongue to hers, felt her tremble at the caress, tasted her sweetness as she touched him in return. Warm and soft, trembling in his arms, she made him want to worship and ravish her at the same time, to protect her from any harm and to crush her body to his with every bit of strength he had. There was paradox in his feelings, but no conflict.

He wanted her in every way it was possible for a man to want a woman.

And he knew that she didn't want him in the same way. Not yet. At some level she was still afraid of herself and of him.

Traveling man.

Reluctantly Cain let go of her.

"Tomorrow," he promised.

Silently Shelley watched him walk back to the car, where Billy waited.

Tomorrow had never seemed farther away.

Chapter Ten

Normally Shelley spent Saturdays attending auctions or rummaging among the new catalogs that poured into The Gilded Lily during the week. But this week there were no auctions to amuse her. Business was entering its fall decline. The lowest point would be in December. Then, around the second week in January, everyone would realize that the fun was over and it was time to get back to planning for the next year.

Restlessly Shelley went through the house, wondering how to fill the hours. There was no point in vacuuming, for the cleaners had come yesterday. There was no point in shopping, for there was nothing new to add to her home. It was finished, perfect, complete within itself.

Too soon to go swimming and too late to fiddle around in the garden, she thought, looking at her surroundings.

The art catalogs she had been itching to read a few days ago looked uninteresting now. She picked up one of the glossy magazines and flipped through it with a feeling that she had seen all of its treasures many times before.

What's wrong with me? she wondered irritably. *I've always enjoyed time to myself. Until recently.*

When the telephone rang, she reached for it with a sense of relief. She didn't like the way her thoughts were being pulled to Cain and his laughter, to Billy and his quick smile, to the echoing emptiness of her home.

"Hello," she said.

"It's Cain. I've got to talk fast before Billy comes back. Dave called this morning. It's Billy's birthday. Could you surprise him and add ice cream and candles to tonight's menu?"

Eagerness went through her for the first time that day.

"Sure. Does he need anything else? What time will you be here? Does he have any friends he'd like to invite?"

"We'll keep it simple this time. Oops, here he comes. I miss you, mink."

The phone went dead before she could answer.

She stared at the receiver for a moment, hearing the echoes of his deep voice in her mind.

Mink. Soft and wild.

The idea of a man like Cain thinking she was sexy made Shelley grin. Then, laughing at herself and the world, she started organizing her day around a birthday celebration for Billy.

Her first stop was at his house. The housekeeper

recognized The Gilded Lily's business card, let Shelley in, and went back to cleaning ornate silver candlesticks.

For the sake of business appearances, Shelley made a lightning tour of the house before she concentrated on Billy's room. A quick look at his overflowing closet told her that clothes wouldn't be on his birthday list.

His CD collection was equally intimidating. If quantity alone hadn't warned her off, the boggling covers would have. After reading the names and looking at the photos, she couldn't imagine what the music would sound like.

Elephants mating, she decided. *During a volcanic eruption.*

Out of her depth and knowing it, she turned toward the software stacked on top of the comics. She felt more at home with the computer materials. She had just finished gilding the home of an electronics nut, using everything from framed "first editions" of software to modern sculpture made of recycled circuit boards.

Notebook in hand, she flipped through the software pile, writing down the titles of games. Then she turned toward the bookcase that supported the dozing turtle's home. She had read enough science fiction herself to recognize many of the authors. Not surprisingly, Billy showed a distinct preference for sword-and-sorcery epics. He also leaned toward the better writers within that specialty.

Shelley wrote down the gaps in his collection of

favorite authors. She was surprised to find that he had only one of the many science fiction art books that were available.

"Doesn't he like them?" she asked the turtle. "Or are they just too expensive?"

Without waiting for an answer, she took down the lone art book. It had been thumbed through so often that the gloss had worn off some of the page corners.

"Yes!" Shelley said softly. "He likes them."

Humming "Happy Birthday," she let herself out of the house and drove to her favorite science fiction bookstore, which also carried a large selection of fantasy games. The store had a window display of gleaming lead miniatures. Dragons, knights, trolls, and assorted monsters guaranteed to delight an amiably bloodthirsty imagination were all locked in battle beneath the clear southern California sun.

The centerpiece of the display was eighteen inches of shining silver dragon. The creature looked both graceful and deadly. Unlike the miniatures, the dragon had been cast with a loving attention to detail that showed in the intricate patterns of each scale and the polished, deadly curve of tooth and claw. The artist who created the dragon had a considerable knowledge of art as well as anatomy and myth. Light shimmered over the creature in rhythmic patterns, as though the dragon were slowly breathing.

"Lovely," she said. "Just the thing to focus his bedroom."

Smiling, she went inside. The bookstore had everything Billy might want, and more. She picked out several of the irresistible art books, an illustrated collection of his favorite science fiction author, and a few other paperbacks.

Then she bought the gleaming silver dragon.

Just as she was getting ready to leave, she spotted an unusual painting tucked away in the corner. Vivid, almost surreal in its clarity, the painting showed the universe as it would look if seen from the center of the Milky Way.

Shelley walked back into the store and stood in front of the painting. A sea of stars swirled in cosmic currents across the sky, pulled by tides undreamed of by man. Vague faces and alien places seemed to condense out of the ancient star sea, endless possibilities turning and returning with each shift of her attention, each blink of her eyes.

Exhilaration swept through her as it had when she first saw Billy's rumpled, defiantly individual room. Whoever had created this painting understood the mystery and beauty of the unknown, unknowable universe. The painting was a window looking into a limitless, extraordinary future, challenging and seducing at the same time, demanding that she look up from her comfortable life and admit to an infinite universe of possibilities.

Shelley went and found the store owner. She was determined to buy the painting, despite the fact that it bore no particular resemblance to anything in her home.

Dragon under one arm, fantasy books under the

other, and a universe clutched in both hands, she walked back to the parking lot. Then she stood next to her car, blinking in the bright sun, somehow surprised to find herself in a world that looked the same as when she had left it less than an hour ago.

Several hours later, the presents were safely wrapped and hidden in Shelley's bedroom, waiting for the surprise party she had planned. Only a few details remained undone. She was taking care of them in her own way, at her own speed.

At the moment, she was stretched out on a comfortable chaise longue by the pool. A bowl of fresh string beans rested on her stomach. Lazily she pulled the string, snapped off the top and bottom of each bean, and tossed the rejected bits back into the metal bowl. Then she snapped the rest of the beans into bite-size pieces and dropped them into a pot beside the chaise on the flagstone patio.

She was half asleep. The waterfall at the end of the pool spoke in rushing, husky, tumbling syllables, promising relief from the heat that welled up out of the ravine below her house. There was a summer's worth of intense sunlight radiating back through the tangled chaparral.

Squinting against the sun, she watched Cain and Billy chase each other through the clear depths of the pool, leaving silver trails of bubbles behind. Each time the boy surfaced, his cupped hand sent a fountain of water arcing to the point where he thought his uncle would come up. Then, shouting with glee at the watery ambush, Billy would dive again, somehow eluding the quick, powerful man who always seemed just on the point of catching him.

Shelley knew that Cain could have grabbed his nephew any time he cared to. But it was more fun to pretend to be outdone by the eager, laughing boy.

Her eyelids lowered all the way. Smiling, drifting in a warm kind of twilight punctuated by Billy's laughter, she fished in the bowl of unsnapped beans. She chose a bean by touch, prepared it, and dropped the pieces in the pot.

After a time, she sensed as much as felt the slight sinking of her cushion. Something had settled ever so lightly next to the bowl of beans that rested on her stomach.

"Nudge?"

The cat did. Twice. A paw, claws politely sheathed, rested on her thigh in a silent plea. Or warning.

Sighing, eyes still closed, Shelley searched for a U-shaped bean. Nudge liked the curvy ones best.

The cat bumped its head against her hand, urging her to choose a bean quickly.

"Patience, cat. I'm working on it. Ah, here we go."

She held out a curled bean on her palm.

Nudge scooped the bean up in her mouth, jumped lightly to the ground, and began to bat the defenseless vegetable around the flagstones.

Without opening her eyes, Shelley smiled, knowing

what the cat was doing. As a kitten, Nudge had developed an odd passion for string beans. She hadn't outgrown it.

The cushion gave slightly again. The bowl of green beans on Shelley's stomach shifted under another gentle nudge. She didn't bother to open her eyes.

"Back so soon? What happened? Did you knock the poor bean into the pool and drown it?"

The bowl slid to one side.

"Nudge! Watch it!"

"Not Nudge. Squeeze."

Her eyes flew open.

Cool, wet arms wrapped around her and lifted her from the chaise. The metal bowl tipped upside down onto the flagstones with a clear, ringing sound.

She barely noticed. She felt the heat of Cain beneath the evaporating water as he squeezed gently, pulling her against his chest. Sunlight glittered in the drops caught in the burnished golds and browns of the wet hair on his chest. She wondered if the drops would taste warm or cool, sweet or saline.

Slowly, almost helplessly, she turned her head and licked up a single drop of water from his chest. She felt the tightening of muscles that went through his whole body.

"I wish to God," he said huskily, "that we were alone."

"I'm sorry. I didn't stop to think."

"I know. That's what made it so damned sexy."

Startled, she looked into the face that was so close to hers. The subtle tones of blue in his eyes were more pronounced beneath the open sky, making his irises a pale, silvery azure that shifted color with each movement of his head. Now almost blue, now nearly transparent, now silver, now darkening to steel gray as the pupils expanded, his eyes fascinated her.

"Your eyes are as beautiful as your mouth," she said.

Then she realized that she had done it again, acted without thinking. She closed her eyes.

"Sorry," she muttered. "You have a drastic effect on my self-control."

"I think we both need a cold bath."

"The pool is eighty-two."

"That's a hell of a lot colder than either one of us right now."

In three strides he was at the edge of the pool. The fourth stride took him into the deep end near the waterfall, still firmly holding her.

While the initial burst of bubbles still shielded them from Billy's sight, Cain took Shelley's mouth in a hard, quick kiss. Then he pushed up from the bottom of the pool in a powerful surge that brought both of them shooting back into the air.

The first thing she saw was Billy's anxious face as he leaned toward her from the side of the pool.

"I told him not to get your hair wet! You aren't mad, are you?"

His expression said a lot more than his words. He was afraid that the day had been spoiled.

For an instant she didn't think why he would be so certain she was angry. Then she realized that JoLynn would have been furious if her carefully applied paint and hair spray were ruined by a casual dunking in the pool.

Stupid woman, Shelley thought. *Doesn't she know how much a child's laughter is worth?*

She smiled up at Billy, slung dripping strands of hair out of her eyes, and swam lazily to his side of the pool.

"I don't get mad," she said. "I get even."

She grabbed Billy's wrist and yanked him into the pool. Moments later he surfaced with a delighted grin.

A wild, three-cornered game of tag started. The shouts and laughs, splashes and thrashing limbs attracted Nudge's predatory interest. She paced around the pool, following the action eagerly, ducking her head when random jets of water came her way.

When no one had breath left for tag, Billy suggested a few rounds of blindman's bluff. He even volunteered to be It.

Shelley and Cain kept away from Billy for a while, until the older man winked at her and "accidentally" splashed noisily. The boy lunged and managed to grab his uncle's arm.

"You're It!"

After a decent interval of floundering and splashing, Cain caught a giggling Billy, who caught a giggling Shelley. They traded being It until Billy finally began to get bored. Then Cain allowed himself to be caught. He and Billy whispered for a minute.

Cain closed his eyes, counted to ten very slowly, and began to search for victims.

Squinting against the late-afternoon sun, Shelley

watched him. Arms spread wide to sweep as much of the pool as possible, he moved silently in the water.

Making no noise, Billy submerged, swam underwater toward the deep end of the pool, and then slipped out onto the flagstones under cover of the waterfall's gentle splashing. He put his fingers over his lips and tiptoed toward the house. With great stealth he opened and closed the door, leaving her alone in the pool with Cain.

She tried to be as quiet as the boy had been, but she was in the middle of the pool, which meant she had a lot of water to cover before she could slip away. As she eased over to the side, Cain turned swiftly toward her, sensing the currents she made when she kicked her legs underwater. She moved aside, letting herself drift.

As though he had sonar, he turned when she did, pursuing her in slow motion. There was an eerie silence and a predatory grace to his movements as he herded her toward a corner of the pool.

Her heart began to beat faster in a combination of anticipation and vague, instinctive fear. He looked unreasonably large, impossible to escape from, smooth and very powerful.

She dropped beneath the surface and fled toward the waterfall. A large hand fastened around her ankle just as she came up for air behind the waterfall's liquid veil.

Cain surfaced very close to her, shaking water out of his eyes with a toss of his head.

"Guess I'm It," she said, suddenly breathless.

"Guess again."

He used his body to crowd her against the edge of the pool. Then he braced his arms on either side of her, caging her. His eyes were smoky with desire.

"Billy will—" she began.

"Billy's making lemonade for his poor, worn-out uncle."

Cain looked at the sleek, water-polished woman in front of him. Her hair was smooth and dark, her eyes almost green in the pale radiance that filled the grotto behind the waterfall. Water gleamed on her skin, made black stars of her eyelashes, and transformed her hair into a dark veil floating against him, touching him.

"Mink," he said thickly. "I want you."

His lips opened as his head bent to hers.

She had plenty of time to turn aside. She didn't. She wanted his kiss with an intensity that shook her.

His mouth was warm over hers, and his tongue was hot enough to burn. He thrust slowly, deeply into her mouth, silently telling her that he would be both hard and gentle when he became a part of her, that he wanted to fill her with himself and be fulfilled in return.

When the kiss finally ended, he was trembling with a bittersweet combination of pleasure and raw hunger.

"Do you want me?" he asked, his voice hoarse. "Tell me you want me just a little bit. Tell me I'm not the only one who is aching."

She made a sound deep in her throat and flowed against him, wrapping her arms around his neck, opening her mouth beneath his, denying him nothing of her response.

He took what she offered with a hunger that was just short of uncontrolled. His mouth bit into hers as though he were starved for the taste of her, the feel of her, the heat of her tongue sliding over his.

And he was.

She returned the bruising kiss with every bit of her strength, her nails clinging to his shoulders, her body straining against his, her teeth nipping him. The violence of her hunger should have shocked her, but all she could feel was the burning of his flesh against hers.

Even so, the instant his hand moved toward her breast she stiffened in automatic withdrawal. But when he tore his mouth away from hers, she whimpered in protest.

"I didn't mean it," she said.

The sound went through him like a knife, tightening every muscle in his body. He didn't want to let go of her, but he knew he must. If he didn't, he would forget about Billy, forget about her harsh experiences with her ex-husband, forget about everything but the raw need clawing at his body.

He didn't want to take Shelley that way. He didn't want to be as selfish as the man who had humiliated her years ago, making her bury her sensuality beneath layers of fear.

Tenderly Cain brushed his lips over her flushed face, murmuring reassurances. As he felt the tension begin to leave her, he hugged her gently.

"I—I'm sorry," she said raggedly. "I don't know what got into me."

His eyes widened as he realized that she was telling the exact truth. She didn't know what it was like to be aroused, hungry, demanding of her lover.

"I'm not a damned bit sorry," he said.

Still embarrassed, she refused to meet his eyes.

"Look at me, mink."

Slowly she raised her head. Her eyes were still darkened by the storm of passion that had shaken her.

"That's the way a woman is supposed to be in the arms of a man she wants," he said. "Soft and wild."

"But I—I attacked you."

"I enjoyed it. Every bit. Teeth and nails and all."

She looked startled, then disbelieving.

His head bent. His teeth closed on the skin where her neck curved into her shoulder. Gently, firmly, he caressed her smooth flesh with his teeth.

He heard her breath catch with surprise. And then he felt the shudder of her response. Her nails dug into his shoulders again, asking for more.

Demanding it.

With a soft laugh he kissed away the small marks his teeth had left on her skin.

"Now do you believe me?" he asked. "You can touch me any way you want to, any time you feel like it. I'm as hungry for it as you are."

The outside screen door banged, announcing Billy's return.

Cain looked at Shelley's mouth and saw the passion that trembled visibly in her.

"We'll be alone soon," he said. "I promise you."

With that he dropped beneath the surface of the water and pushed off from the side. He shot out from behind the waterfall with a speed and power that reminded her of how much strength he had held in check despite his own raw hunger and her heedless, passionate demands.

Billy headed for the pool, carefully balancing a tray. Plastic glasses full of lemonade slopped a bit with each step he took.

"Did you catch her?" he asked Cain.

"Yeah, but I cheated."

"You peeked?"

"Nope." Cain smiled wickedly. "I used my teeth."

The boy looked startled, then he laughed. "Everybody out. It's lemonade time."

"I'll drink mine in the pool," Cain said.

He hooked one elbow over the sun-warmed flagstones and reached for a glass of lemonade.

Shelley knew why he was staying in the pool. But she didn't have to. Her arousal showed only in a flush that could have come from the sun. She was free to get out of the concealing water and enjoy her lemonade while sitting in a chair.

Sometimes, she decided with silent amusement, *the female of the species definitely has an advantage over the male.*

Billy drained his glass in a few gigantic swallows and looked over at Shelley.

"It sure smelled good in the kitchen," he said.

"Did you notice what time it was?" she asked.

"Five-thirty. There was a timer buzzing on the stove."

"The potatoes!"

She leaped to her feet and ran toward the house.

Cain laughed aloud, but his laughter died as he watched Shelley's graceful, long-legged flight. The garnet two-piece suit she wore fit her like wet satin spray paint, showing every curve, every swell, the taut rise of nipples hardened by evaporating water and a desire that was far from evaporating.

It was a few minutes before he felt cool enough to get out of the pool. He wrapped a towel around his hips, scooped up all the empty glasses, and began leaving wet tracks on the rock stairs that skirted the waterfall on the way to the second-level kitchen entrance.

"Pick up the green beans," he called over his shoulder to Billy. "And then it's time you learned how to set a table. You won't always have a maid to do your work."

"Aw, Uncle Cain."

"Aw, Nephew Billy," he said, exactly imitating the boy's plaintive tones.

Glumly Billy squatted down on his heels beside the spilled green beans and began picking them up.

Nudge glided over, intent on more vegetable prey.

Cain saw what was going to happen, started to warn his nephew, then shrugged and decided to let nature take its course.

As he opened the kitchen door, Billy let out a startled yelp.

Shelley looked up from the potatoes she had just rescued. "What was that?"

"Nudge nudging."

"Sure it wasn't Squeeze squeezing?"

He wrapped his arms around her from behind and pulled her against his body with a gradual force that made muscles stand out along his arms.

"This," he said, "is a squeeze."

She didn't have enough breath left to do more than nod agreement. He kissed her shoulder and then released her with a reluctance that was another kind of caress.

"Anything I can do?" he asked.

She gave him a sidelong glance and a raised eyebrow that made him smile.

"Anything that we won't mind doing in public," he amended.

"How are you on squeezing potatoes?"

"Terrible. I mash the poor devils every time."

She winced. "I should have drowned you when I had the chance."

"Oh? When did you have the chance?"

He lifted her damp hair and nibbled on her neck. The potato masher slipped out of her fingers and hit the counter with a metallic ring. He caught the tool before it hit the floor.

"Did anyone ever tell you that you're a distracting man?" she muttered.

"You. Just now. Do I really distract you, mink?"

"Yes!"

"Good. God knows that you play hell with my concentration."

He lifted her, pivoted, and put her down. With quick, efficient motions, he reduced the steaming potatoes to a thick, smooth mass.

Shelley stood on her tiptoes and peered around his broad back.

"Now I know what women did before electric mixers," she said.

He gave her a sidelong look.

She poured in hot milk and melted butter. When he flexed his arm to resume mashing, she delicately bit his biceps.

He froze.

"Shelley—" he began, his voice husky, warning.

Billy came up to the kitchen door, carrying various bowls of green beans. He levered the screen door open with an elbow.

"Lucky for you," Cain said under his breath to Shelley.

"Luck? It was superior timing."

She proved it by stepping just out of his reach.

"What was timing?" Billy asked her as he came into the kitchen.

"Watch the cat," she said.

He looked down, stuck his foot out, and held the screen door open while Nudge slipped inside. Shelley took the beans from him before they had another fall.

"What's timing?" the boy asked her again.

"The secret of making good mashed potatoes."

"Real potatoes?"

There was a touching combination of hope and disbelief in his young voice.

"As real as I can make them," Cain said.

The rhythmic, heavy thump of the masher against the pot underlined his words.

"Cool!" Billy said. "I was afraid we'd have mashed potatoes out of a box."

"Ugh," she said. "Wallpaper paste."

"What?" Billy asked.

"Library glue," offered Cain.

She snickered. "Papier-mâché."

"Concrete."

Billy looked from side to side like a spectator at a tennis match. Then he grinned as understanding came.

"You don't like instant mashed potatoes any better than I do," he said.

"Oh, they're not bad if you're hiking in the wilderness," Cain said.

"And you've already walked fifty miles," she added.

"Without eating."

"For five days."

"And there's no other food around."

"For a hundred miles."

"And your leg is broken."

"And you need to make a cast!" she said triumphantly.

Billy waited, but his uncle was laughing too hard to respond to Shelley's topper.

Smiling, she went back to sorting out beans.

Nudge landed on the countertop with a muscular, graceful leap. Intently she watched the vegetables.

"She likes beans," Billy said.

"Really?" Shelley asked dryly. "What was your first clue?"

"Her cold nose in my—"

"Billy," Cain interrupted warningly.

"Er, rear."

"Set the table," Cain told his nephew.

"Yes, sir."

Cain handed the potatoes over to Shelley. "How long until dinner?"

"As soon as I cook the beans."

"Is there enough time for me to check my answering machine?"

"Still worried about Lulu?"

"Does whiskey still have alcohol in it?"

"There's a phone just inside the door in the next room."

"Thanks."

While Billy worked on the table, Cain called his apartment. After a minute Shelley heard him curse. He hung up hard, then punched in a long series of numbers. He talked with someone for several minutes, but she could make out only the tone, not the words.

Cain was furious.

Numbly she wondered what else had gone wrong in the Yukon, when he would leave to fix it, and how long he would be gone.

Traveling man, never in one place long enough to have a home.

He likes it that way, remember? she asked herself harshly.

But she hadn't remembered.

She didn't want to remember even now. Each time she came up against his rootless ways, she was dismayed. Each time it sliced deeper into her.

There was no longer a question if he would hurt her. The only question was when.

And how badly.

Chapter Eleven

By the time Cain came back into the kitchen, the table was set and dinner was ready to be served.

He didn't look ready to enjoy it.

Instead of the relaxed, lazy smile she had become used to seeing, he was thin-lipped and frowning. Then he made a visible effort to throw off whatever he had learned about his project in the Yukon.

She started to ask what had happened up north, then decided against it. If he wanted to talk about it, he would. Obviously he didn't.

She dumped hot beans into a bright yellow bowl.

"Take these in and sit down," she said. "Billy is just putting on the salt and pepper."

Cain picked up a steaming green bean and popped it into his mouth. The vegetable made a satisfying crunch between his teeth.

"Cool," he said, sounding just like his nephew. "Real potatoes and beans that haven't been cooked to death. I have high hopes for the chicken."

"Chickens," she corrected. "The way Billy eats, I cooked two whole fryers, and bought extras of favorite pieces."

"Breasts?" he asked, deadpan.

"Feet," she retorted. "Nice and chewy."

His face relaxed into a smile. "I'm glad I met you, Shelley Wilde. I would have sworn nothing could put me back in a good mood, but you do it with a few words."

"Chicken feet."

He was still laughing when he walked into the dining room. She was close behind, carrying a platter heaped high with crispy pieces of fried chicken. He seated her formally, ran the backs of his fingers down her sleek hair, and sat across from her.

As they ate, Cain began to pry information out of his nephew with a quiet persistence that reminded Shelley of Nudge stalking beans.

"How's it going in math this summer?" Cain asked.

"Okay."

"Is that A-OK, B-OK—"

"C-minus," Billy said glumly.

"Fractions?"

"And decimals and algebra. Algebra! I'm only in the seventh grade!"

Cain poured gravy over his second helping of mashed potatoes. "What about English?"

"Don't ask." Billy pointed at the drumstick on his plate. "Can I eat with my fingers?"

"I don't know," Cain said, looking up with interest. *"Can* you?"

"Of course I—oh. *May* I eat with my fingers, Shelley?"

"Miss Wilde," Cain corrected.

"Shelley," she said firmly. "And yes, you may. It's not fried chicken if you have to use a knife and fork."

Billy picked up the drumstick and dug in eagerly.

"How much homework do you have to do this weekend?" Cain asked after a few moments.

Billy gave his uncle a wary glance. "You've been talking to Dad."

Cain waited for an answer.

The boy sighed and said in a disgusted tone, "Lots."

"Do you know how to do it?"

"I'll figure it out tomorrow."

"Maybe you'd better figure it out tonight. I won't be here tomorrow."

Shelley looked up sharply. Cain caught the motion out of the corner of his eye, but he kept his attention on his nephew.

"I thought you were going to be here until Dad gets back," Billy said.

"I wanted to. But—" Cain made a cutting gesture with his hand. "I've got to go back to the Yukon for a few days. There was an accident."

"Serious?" Shelley asked, remembering his anger.

"Someone bent a hammer over my site engineer's thick skull."

Billy looked startled, then whooped with excitement. "Did he really, Uncle Cain? Did they fight?"

He slanted his nephew a look that made Billy lower his voice very quickly.

"Yeah," said Cain. "They fought. Like two bloody kids in a school yard sandbox."

"Schoolchildren don't use weapons," she said.

"You haven't been to school lately," Billy muttered.

"Did they arrest the man?" she asked Cain.

"Why bother? It's the Yukon. Besides, it was his wife they were arguing over."

She struggled not to smile, then gave in and laughed.

"Some things are pretty much the same no matter where in the world you are," she said, shaking her head. "My dad used to say he spent more time sorting out people than snakes."

"Amen. Except that I spend more time sorting out fools than rock strata." He looked directly at Shelley. "I'm sorry, mink."

She turned away very quickly, not wanting to show how unhappy she felt about having Cain leave.

"No problem," she said neutrally. "Traveling men . . . travel."

His mouth flattened. He turned to his nephew. "When will your mother be back?"

The boy paused, took a mouthful of potatoes, and muttered, "After breakfast."

Something about his manner made both adults look at him.

"Breakfast tomorrow?" Shelley asked gently. "Or some other breakfast?"

For a moment she thought Billy wasn't going to answer. Then, with elaborate casualness, he picked up another fat drumstick. Just before his teeth sank into the juicy meat, he shrugged.

"Some of her parties last a week. It's okay, though. Lupe does the wash and cooks for me, and Mother always gets home before Dad."

The boy's face changed as he remembered that his father wasn't coming home to his mother anymore.

"Anyway," he said fiercely, tearing into the drumstick, "it all works out."

Cain said something soft and vicious that only Shelley heard. She put her hand over his forearm as though restraining him. The tension in his muscles told her how angry he was.

"I'm sure it does," she said evenly to Billy. "This time it will work out a new way. Cain will bring over your clothes and schoolbooks. You'll stay with me until JoLynn gets back."

Nephew and uncle started to talk at once.

"No arguments," she said.

"But—" Cain began.

"Save your breath. I've spent hours trying to figure a way to trap Billy into being around when Squeeze gets hungry. This is a definite gotcha."

Billy looked hopefully at his uncle.

"If you give Shelley one bit of trouble, I'll peel you like a grape," Cain said. "Got it?"

"Got it," Billy said instantly.

"Speaking of Squeeze and hungry," she said, "I'd better check the aquarium lid."

"Nudge?" Cain guessed.

"In a word. She just ghosted down the stairs toward my room."

Shelley got up and walked quickly down the stairs. She wasn't worried about Squeeze, but she needed an excuse to get away and finish off a few details.

Billy's presents, to be exact.

She pulled the gifts out of her closet and set them on the bed. They looked bright and rather odd. She hadn't remembered until she was home again that she had no wrapping paper. After a fast search, she had found some outdated foil wallpaper samples that worked almost as well.

"No ribbons," she said. "That's what I forgot. What are gifts without at least one ribbon? Let's see. What can I substitute? Yarn, beads, tinfoil flowers . . ."

Inspiration hit.

"Perfect. Unless the critter has the rips."

She went to Squeeze's glass cage. The snake was definitely sluggish rather than racy. It was lying loosely coiled, slightly cool to her touch. Altogether normal for a reptile that wasn't sunning itself on a desert rock.

She lifted Squeeze out and went to the bed. With a few quick motions she arranged the boa's coils around various presents. Then she pulled the blinds, turned off the light, and stood by the closed door in the dark room.

"Cain? Billy?" she called through the door. "Could you come down and help me with Squeeze for a minute?"

Bits of conversation floated down the stairs as the two males speculated on what trouble Squeeze and Nudge could have gotten into in such a short time.

The door opened. Cain's hand felt around for the switch. He found Shelley's fingers.

"What the—?"

"Happy birthday, Billy!" she said, flipping on the light.

The boy's eyes widened in surprise. He looked from Shelley to the bed and then back to her as though he couldn't believe his luck.

"How did you know? Even Mom didn't remem—" His voice cracked.

"Squeeze told me," Shelley said quickly.

Blinking fiercely, Billy went toward the bed. He bent over Squeeze, hiding his face.

"Boy, I'll never trust you with my secrets again, snake. You're such a blabbermouth."

Hesitantly the boy's fingers touched a brightly wrapped package.

"Well, go on, get to it," she said. "You can't expect Squeeze to wrap *and* unwrap your presents for you."

Billy looked up for an instant. His flashing yet almost shy smile made Shelley want to cry.

She watched with an ache in her throat as the boy draped the quiet snake around his neck and picked up the first present. He unwrapped the package while keeping up a running commentary on babbling boas and how in heck did Squeeze manage all the sticky tape.

Cain's hand curled around hers. He lifted it from the light switch to his lips and brushed his lips over her palm.

"You're a special woman, Shelley Wilde."

His fingers tightened and he kissed her hand again, pulling her close, rubbing his cheek against her hair slowly, savoring the unique fragrance and feel of her. Smiling, she relaxed against his warmth, taking pleasure in the feel of him against her back.

"Thank you," he whispered. "Billy hasn't had an easy time of it lately."

"No thanks needed. I haven't had so much fun since I was a kid myself."

Billy whooped as he pulled a book out of the stiff wrapping paper.

"Cool! His newest book. I didn't even know it was out yet. And it's illustrated by one of my favorite artists."

Eagerly he read the first few paragraphs. He turned the page, devoured a few more lines, then remembered where he was. Carefully he set the book aside and went to work unwrapping the next present.

"How did you know what he likes to read?" Cain asked against her ear.

"Snakes are very talkative creatures."

"Chicken feet."

She smiled. "Would you believe a little breaking and entering?"

"Billy's room?"

"Actually, Lupe let me in. After that it was just a matter of time. His room is like he is. Vivid and open."

The boy gave another whoop and waved an art book in their direction.

"Look, Uncle Cain! Now I can show you what Gorpian fighting slugs look like, and Tannax Four weirdmasters, and . . ." He scanned rapidly through the index. "Cherfs! They even have cherfs!"

Shelley felt the silent laughter go through Cain as he pulled her even closer.

"I can hardly wait," he said to his nephew. Then he spoke very softly against her ear. "What in hell is a cherf?"

"Don't ask. Dreadful creatures."

They nearly lost Billy to an art book with exquisitely drawn alien landscapes, but finally the lure of the last, biggest package was too much. He lifted it, rattled the box cautiously, and began unwrapping it slowly. Though he was eager to see what was inside, he was reluctant to open the last present.

Gradually a glittering silver dragon emerged from the mounds of tissue paper. With a sound of awe and disbelief, he lifted the sculpture and turned it reverently in his young hands.

"It's . . . it's way, way beyond cool," he said. "Look at those scales and teeth. And the claws!"

"Careful," she said. "The artist made everything very pointy."

He touched the curving fangs and claws.

"Sharp, too," he said admiringly. "This dragon is

no wimp. Bet he eats knights for breakfast and armies for dinner and kings for dessert."

Squeeze shifted on Billy's body. Human warmth was beginning to make the snake lively. A dark, forked tongue flicked rapidly over the dragon. The snake rested its head on the silver dragon and gave Shelley a long, unblinking look.

"Do you think he approves?" Cain asked her.

"I think it's time for Squeeze to go back in the box. Check it out."

He did, and spotted Nudge stalking closer to the action. He took two steps, scooped the snake from around Billy's shoulders, and stuffed the boa gently back into the aquarium.

Nudge watched the whole thing with normal cat curiosity but no real bloodthirsty intent.

Cain put the heavy lid in place.

Squeeze tasted the glass and watched the cat.

"Think they'd ever be friends?" Billy asked.

"As long as there was a referee," Shelley said dryly, "they'd both survive. They might even enjoy it."

"Let's not put it to the test tonight," Cain said. "I'm too tired to referee a bobcat and a boa constrictor. Let's round up your loot and go back upstairs."

As soon as he and Billy had an armload of presents, Shelley shut the bedroom door behind them. She raced past them up the stairs, shutting off lights as she went.

"What is this, a test of our night vision?" Cain demanded.

' She acted as though she hadn't heard.

"Ouch," Billy said, bumping into his uncle. "Your boots are hard."

"Guys could break a leg in the dark," Cain said loudly.

"So slow down," Shelley yelled from the kitchen.

She pulled Billy's cake from its hiding place in the cupboard. Their voices were getting closer.

"Slower!" she demanded.

Hastily she lit the candles one after another, dancing with impatience as the limp wicks reluctantly caught fire.

Billy and Cain found the dining room table the hard way. Thumps and mutterings came from just beyond the kitchen.

"Close your eyes!" she called.

"What difference would it make?" Cain asked.

"Can I sit down first?" Billy asked.

"I don't know. *Can* you?"

From there the conversation degenerated into the amusing kind of crossfire that was more common between brothers than nephew and uncle.

Each time Shelley laughed at a comment, her hand jerked and the match missed a candle.

"Shelley?" Cain called.

"Patience. I'm in here working on my night vision."

A few moments later, he came into the kitchen with an armload of dirty dishes. When he saw her bent over the birthday cake in the dark kitchen, her eyes alight with reflected fire and her mouth curved in a secret smile, he wanted to dump all the dishes in the trash and carry her away into the night.

But he didn't. He simply put the dishes in the sink, and watched her, smiling as she was smiling, his gray eyes brilliant with the tiny dance of flames.

Finally all the candles were burning at once. She picked up the cake tray and carefully began walking.

Cain waited for her signal to open the door to the dining room.

"Are your eyes closed?" she asked Billy.

"Yes."

"Don't peek."

He didn't dignify that with a reply.

When they walked into the dining room, he was sitting upright, scowling fiercely to demonstrate that his eyes couldn't possibly be closed any tighter.

Once she set the cake in front of him, she began to sing "Happy Birthday." The good-natured, off-key rumble of Cain's voice joined in.

As soon as the last word was sung, Billy's eyes popped open. His expression when he saw the loaf cake was worth every bit of time Shelley had spent on it.

Against chocolate-icing hills and lemon rivers, fantastic animals played, their figures lit by birthday candles. The miniature beasts glittered and ran with flame as though they were actually alive and strolling across their tasty landscape.

For a long time Billy simply sat and stared at the fantasy in front of him. His eyes were wide and bright with unshed tears.

"Make a wish," Shelley said.

He bent over and blew mightily.

Suddenly the dining room was dark.

"Good job," Cain said, flipping on the light. "That wish is a sure thing."

While he dished out ice cream, Shelley wiped icing from the miniature beasts and lined them up by Billy's plate. He watched her almost shyly. When he caught her eye, he smiled.

"Thank you," he said.

"My pleasure." Her hand rested for an instant on Billy's fine blond hair. "I'm trying to remember. Are you too old for a birthday hug?"

Without getting up, Billy threw his arms around her waist and buried his face against her. He was surprisingly strong, nearly squeezing the breath out of her, but she didn't complain. She just hugged him in return and silently asked herself again why a child like Billy had been given a mother like JoLynn.

Later, as Shelley helped the boy carry his presents out to the pickup truck Cain had used to transport the dirt bikes, Billy asked his uncle the very question she had been afraid to put into words.

"How long will you be gone?"

"I don't know. Climb in. You better carry that dragon in your lap."

Billy swung lithely into the truck and held out his arms for the box holding the silver dragon.

"A week?" the boy persisted. "A month?"

"A week, maybe less."

But Cain didn't sound like he believed his own words.

Probably a lot more than a week, Shelley thought bitterly. *And why in God's name should I feel hurt? It's Billy who needs Cain in his life, not me.*

She looked away from Cain and concentrated on tucking a sack full of presents next to Billy's feet. When she finished, she straightened and ruffled his hair gently.

"See you tomorrow."

"Thanks again," he said.

The smile she gave him was genuine. "You're welcome."

She stepped away from the cab, but still didn't look in Cain's direction. Her childhood had taught her to hate good-byes.

And this was definitely good-bye.

The pain she felt frightened her, telling her that she had ignored the harsh lessons of her childhood and marriage. She had given too much of herself to Cain, too quickly. Her physical hunger for him was bad enough. Her mental hunger could destroy her.

She had to end it now, right now. It was time to cut her losses and move on, repeating the rituals of her childhood all over again.

"So long, traveling man. Hope everything works out for you in the Yukon."

Cain heard the finality beneath the polite words.

She turned away without looking back. Quick strides took her away from him, up the dark walkway to her home.

He shut the truck door. Hard.

"Stay put," he told Billy. "I'll be right back."

All Shelley heard was the sound of the truck door slamming. She opened the front door to her home and closed it behind her. Then she stood a few feet inside her home and measured the extent of the damage.

Her hands were shaking. Tears were closing her throat. She wanted to scream at her own stupidity.

I've known Cain a few days and already the thought of weeks and weeks without him takes the color out of the world.

Savagely she reminded herself that nothing important had changed. She still had the life she always wanted. She still had a satisfying career, she still had the home she had dreamed of during all the rootless years of her childhood. She had achieved every goal she had set for herself after her divorce.

I have everything.

Except Cain.

The front door opened. He glided inside with the silence and grace of a cat. The door shut behind him with a definite thump. Long arms wrapped around Shelley, dragging her close with frightening ease.

"You forgot something," he said flatly. "Fight if it will make you feel better, but it won't matter. I'm stronger than you and fighting it hasn't done me a damn bit of good."

He pinned her to the hard length of his body while his mouth broke open hers so that he could find all the softness and heat she was trying to deny him. He devoured her with a force that shocked him. He tried to slow down, to temper the anger and fear that had exploded in him when he had seen her turn her back and walk away as though he were no more than Billy's chauffeur.

Only when he tasted her tears running hotly over his lips did he succeed in controlling himself.

"Shelley," he said urgently, saying her name again and again as he kissed her with ravishing tenderness. "Shelley, don't ever turn your back on me like that again. I need you too much."

"But we've only known each other a few—"

"I know myself," he said, cutting across her words. "I've needed you forever."

He kissed her deeply, gently. She trembled and softened against him. Then she kissed him with a hunger that was more than sexual, as though she could store him up against the lonely times ahead.

"You need me, too," he said, "even though you're having trouble getting used to the idea." His arms tightened, then released her. "I'll come back. And you'll be here for me."

The front door opened and closed softly, leaving Shelley alone with silence and tears, the bittersweet taste of a traveling man on her lips.

Chapter Twelve

⟨⟨⟨ The math workbook looked as frayed as Billy had before Shelley began helping him. Now she was sitting on the floor near him, because she had discovered that he preferred doing homework where Squeeze couldn't snake off and hide.

The boa delighted in curling up inside desk drawers, beneath sofa cushions, and in sunny corners behind furniture. After a few frantic hours of turning the house upside down looking for a rosy boa, she had decreed that the snake stayed in her bedroom, where the hiding places were limited.

At the moment, Billy was sitting cross-legged wearing Squeeze coiled around his narrow waist.

"But if they don't tell me the length or the width of the room," he argued, "how can I—Nudge, back off—know the area?"

Nudge gave the boy a hurt look and stopped pawing at Squeeze, who was slowly uncoiling from the boy's waist.

Warily Shelley kept one eye on the wildlife and one eye on the math.

"You do know the dimensions of the room," she said.

"I do?"

"Think about it. How long is the room? Not in feet or inches, but as though you were describing it to a friend."

He frowned and pushed aside a snaky coil that was covering a diagram in the math book.

"Twice as long as it is wide?" he asked finally.

"Good!"

"Yeah, but they want feet and inches and stuff."

"We're getting there. Now, if—back off, cat."

She snagged Nudge by the scruff. The cat batted with sheathed claws at a firm section of boa slithering by.

"If you call the width X—enough, Nudge!—what would you call the length?" she asked.

"Twice X?"

"Close."

"Oh, two X, like in problem three."

"Right!"

Dawning excitement lit Billy's lean features. "Then the area is X times two X, right?"

"Twice right."

He gave her a quick smile and bent over the workbook.

She held on to Nudge and watched the boy attack the assignment with real enthusiasm. He wrote confidently and rarely erased. Once he had accepted the

idea that X could stand for anything, anytime, anywhere, he was happy to put X to use.

As Shelley had guessed, he had a quick, inquiring
mind, though at first it had been a test of wills to get
him to use his mind for anything other than stubborn-
ness and evasion.

To Billy's surprise, she had proved to be more
stubborn than he was and every bit as quick.

The intercom buzzed.

"That's probably your mother," Shelley said. "Go
ahead and let her in."

Squeeze slithered off in a heap as the boy bounced
to his feet. The snake started coiling across the room
in search of new mountains to conquer.

Billy pressed down the intercom button. "Door's
open, Mother, c'mon in. We'll be up as soon as
Shelley helps me with my last math problem and we
put Squeeze away."

He flipped off the intercom and flopped on the
bedroom floor with the coltish grace that only teenagers have.

Shelley stared at him, surprised that he hadn't run
upstairs to say hello to his mother. After all, he hadn't
seen JoLynn for six days.

"This can wait while you say hi," Shelley said.

"She won't care," Billy said absently.

Lying down, head propped on his hand, he leaned
over the math book. He frowned as he tried to arrange
the various parts of the algebra problem in his mind.

Nudge, who had as fine an appreciation of warmth
as any snake, immediately took up residence along the

boyish midsection that Squeeze had abandoned. That made it awkward for Billy to write, but he didn't complain. He and Nudge had been bunkmates for the past six nights.

Out of the corner of her eye, Shelley saw Squeeze begin to climb her dresser. She reached out, captured the snake's tapering tail, and began gently dragging the adventurous boa back across the carpet.

Squeeze turned and looked over his nonexistent shoulder at her, but made no attempt to escape. The instant she let go, the snake flipped a coil over her wrist and tried to drag her over to the dresser. When that didn't work, the boa decided to try higher up on her arm.

"Forget it, snake," Billy said without looking up. "She's got a lot more X on her side than you do."

Nudge batted at the pencil that was wig-wagging so temptingly across the paper in front of her black nose.

"Cat, you're getting to be a pest," he said, but his tone was more absent than threatening. "Shelley?"

"Hmm?" she asked, peeling Squeeze off her neck before he could settle in.

"They left something out of this one."

She stretched out full-length on the floor to get closer to the math problem. Billy turned the book so that she could read it along with him.

Squeeze and Nudge found themselves nose to nose across an open math book. The snake's tongue flickered like a slender black flame. The cat's whiskers quivered with equal interest.

Shelley swept aside a rosy coil just as it snaked toward Nudge.

"They say that B equals ten," Billy said, "and C equals A, and two A equals B. Then they ask what C equals. How the heck should I know, when I don't know what A equals?"

"How many Bs does it take to equal A?"

Billy frowned and began talking through the problem under his breath. After a minute he looked up. "It only takes half of a B to equal one A."

She waited expectantly.

"Oh, I get it now," he said. "Cool!"

He bent over the book and began writing. With an expert swipe on one hand, he fended off both Nudge and one of Squeeze's coils. Shelley looped the coil around her own upper arm so that the boy could work in peace. Sort of.

"B is ten and A is one-half of B," he said, his voice filled with the excitement of discovery once again. "So one-half of ten, which equals five, which equals A, which equals C. That's simple."

"But not always easy," a voice said from the doorway. "A lot of life is like that."

With a startled sound, Shelley rolled over and looked up. "You're back!"

Even though Cain was tired, dirty, and irritated as hell about the mess he had found waiting for him in his condo, he smiled down at the woman lying at his feet. It would have been impossible not to smile. There was a rosy boa peeking out from her shining, loose hair. A huge coon cat's paw patted her other shoulder in search of the snake's elusive head.

"Hi, Uncle Cain," Billy said, writing quickly. "I'll be with you in a minute."

"No hurry. It's been years since I've been to the circus." He sank to the floor and sat Indian-fashion. "You must be the snake lady."

"Actually, I'm the lion tamer."

Her voice was husky with surprise and something more, something that sent a kick of pleasure through his tired body. She was as glad to see him as he was to see her.

"Lion tamer, huh?" he asked lazily. "Then this must be the lion."

He reached over her shoulder, grasped Nudge firmly by the scruff, and lifted her.

The cat dangled from his large hand with a complete lack of concern. The only movement Nudge made was to twist her head in order to follow Squeeze's movements.

"You've done a hell of a job taming this one," he said.

Shaking his head, he lowered Nudge to the floor well away from both snake and lion tamer. Immediately the cat began closing in on Squeeze.

"Billy?" Cain said.

"Yes, sir?"

"Concentrate on your math for a few moments, okay? I've got an X factor of my own that's been missing for six days."

The boy glanced up in time to see his uncle pull Shelley onto his lap. For an instant Billy looked startled. Then, smiling, he bent over his workbook and concentrated on math.

"Hello, mink," Cain whispered.

The kiss he gave her was very discreet, almost chaste. Yet a tremor rippled through him when their lips touched. For him, six days had felt like six months.

It had been the same for Shelley. She came eagerly to him, nestling against his chest, snuggling in like a cat.

He gave a hidden sigh of relief. He had spent a lot of time wondering if she would be happy to see him or still angry at the way they had parted.

"Hello, stranger," she whispered. "Welcome home."

Her fingers threaded through his sun-streaked hair, stroked his stubble-roughened cheek, and delicately traced his mouth. Then her hand came to rest just above the opening of his khaki shirt, where his warmth called to her.

His pulse accelerated visibly beneath the tanned skin of his throat.

She smiled almost sadly even as she touched his pulse with her fingertips. She had tried to build defenses against Cain while he was gone. Many times she had spun possibilities in her mind around his return. She would be polite, aloof, totally in control.

Safe.

Yet when he had walked in unexpectedly, her defenses had vanished at the exhaustion she saw in the deep lines of his face. All thought of keeping her distance fled. All she wanted to do was ease the strain she saw in him.

She curled closer to him and traced the tired lines on his forehead and either side of his mouth as though she could take his fatigue into herself, freeing him.

Slowly Cain rubbed his unshaven cheek against her hair. Silky strands caught and tugged slightly before falling away.

"I must feel like a cactus," he said, "and look worse."

She glanced up at him with green-and-gold eyes that saw each line, the dark circles beneath his eyes, and the heavy shadow of stubble blurring his jawline.

"You look . . . wonderful."

"Chicken feet," he whispered, kissing her eyelids gently, closing her brilliant eyes. "I look like hell."

"Not to me."

His arms tightened around her. He pulled her even more closely against him and buried his face in the dark silk of her hair.

"Home at last," he said with a sigh that was almost a groan.

"Yes," she whispered.

The sense of homecoming she felt in his arms frightened her. Then she let fear and unhappy memories slide away. She held on to the moment and the man with an intensity that was new to her.

Cain felt her arms slide around his back. The soft woman-warmth of her rested trustingly against his body. He shifted her until she fit against him breath for breath, heartbeat for heartbeat.

Slowly they closed their eyes and rocked each other, saying with touch what they could not say aloud.

"Uncle Cain, I hate to tell you this, but that's not Shelley's arm snaking around your neck."

He opened one eye.

Squeeze's polished black eyes stared back at him unblinkingly.

Cain flicked his tongue in and out like a snake, but more slowly.

Squeeze froze, transfixed by the odd sight. Slowly the snake's narrow body gathered more tightly as the boa readied another coil for Cain's neck.

Shelley laughed soundlessly, amused by the look on Cain's face.

"Need any help?" she asked.

"Can you talk snake?"

She flicked her tongue in and out with a speed that equaled Squeeze's.

Cain's eyes changed to a smoky gray as he watched her quick pink tongue.

"I accept," he whispered, bending down to her.

"Uncle Cain—"

"I know, I know."

One strong hand captured Squeeze's head and the other grasped a muscular coil.

Shelley slid off his lap and out of the way while he peeled the snake from his neck. Man held boa constrictor at eye level.

"Feeding time at the zoo?" he suggested.

"Looks like it," Billy agreed.

"Are you prepared?"

"Yeah. We got a rat today."

"Bon appétit."

He unloaded the snake into his nephew's arms just as the doorbell rang.

"I'll get your homework," Cain said.

"I'll get the door," Shelley said. "Feed that critter before he starts hunting Nudge."

"They're friends!" Billy objected.

"Not when one of them is hungry."

The doorbell rang again. Several times. She flipped on the intercom. "I'll be right there."

Without waiting for an answer, she turned off the intercom and started for the front door. She was grateful for an excuse to vanish. Billy was already opening a small cage. Inside was the boa's lunch—a white rat that had been run ragged in some psychologist's lab project.

When she opened the front door, an impatient JoLynn stood on the other side. Despite the lavender smudges under her eyes, she looked good enough to serve to a king.

Abruptly Shelley became aware of her own tousled hair, faded jeans, and oversize cotton shirt tied in a knot at her waist. All that could be said for her outfit was that it was just right for playing with a snake, a cat, a boy, and an algebra book.

"Lupe said Billy's been staying with you," JoLynn announced.

"Yes."

"Tell him to get ready. I'm running late." Suddenly JoLynn's jade-green eyes widened.

Shelley knew without turning around that Cain had just walked up behind her.

"Well, well, well, just look at the iron man," JoLynn said sarcastically. "Wouldn't your wide-eyed piece of ass let you out of bed long enough to shave?"

Shelley's mouth flattened. All that prevented her from tearing into the other woman was the fact that Billy might come upstairs at any moment.

"What's the matter?" Cain asked carelessly. "Couldn't you get laid even once in six days?"

A flush climbed beneath JoLynn's porcelain skin. "I can have all the men I want and you know it."

"Yeah. And you can't keep a one of them, can you?" His voice was like a whip. Then it changed. His tone became like his eyes, cold and pitiless. "If you run your mouth at Shelley's expense again, you will regret it," he said distinctly. "Any questions?"

The dislike in his voice was so intense that JoLynn took a step backward. She looked from Cain to Shelley and then back again.

For an instant Shelley was certain she saw pain in those incredible jade eyes.

"I'll wait for Billy out here," JoLynn said, her voice stretched to breaking. "Tell him to hurry."

"If you were that eager to see him, you wouldn't have been gone so long, would you?" Cain asked.

"Jealous?" she asked, smiling at him with unmistakable invitation

"Of what?"

"You know."

"I sure as hell do. Too bad it took Dave so long to figure it out that the fucking he got wasn't worth the fucking he got."

Before the last words were out of Cain's mouth, JoLynn was hurrying toward her car. Her high-heeled sandals clicked harshly on the flagstone walkway.

He watched her retreat with eyes the color and warmth of ice. Then he pulled Shelley's shoulders against his chest and gently stroked her arms.

"I'm sorry, mink. She has a poisonous tongue. I don't want you or Billy hurt because I won't crawl into bed with her."

"She . . . really wants you."

Shelley felt his shrug and then his breath stirred against her hair.

"JoLynn wants whatever she can't have. Dave loved her anyway, the kind of love most women would kill for. But not her. She almost killed him instead."

"Sad," she whispered. "So damned sad."

"Don't feel sorry for that one. It will give her a weapon to use against you."

"Why did Dave leave Billy with a woman like that?"

"He couldn't reach me in time. He couldn't take Billy to France, because he's behind in school. The divorce was rough on him. And JoLynn pleaded so nicely to have custody of her son for just a few weeks, please, pretty please, and don't forget to bat your eyelashes at the judge."

"Why would she bother? She certainly hasn't tried to spend time with her son."

"Simple. She wants to keep her hooks in Dave."

"But if she doesn't love her husband, why would she care? I couldn't see the last of my ex-husband fast enough."

"JoLynn isn't you. She wants whatever she can't have—until she gets it. Then she looks for another boy-toy."

Slowly Shelley shook her head, thinking of Billy.

"Now that she no longer has my brother," Cain said, "she wants him, so she's using whatever weapon is at hand."

"Even her own son?"

"Especially him."

"Can't his father do something?"

"Dave doesn't understand what's going on. He was so pleased that JoLynn was finally showing an interest in being a mother. He never was very bright where JoLynn was concerned."

"What if—" Shelley cut off her words abruptly.

The sound of Billy talking to Nudge came clearly through the living room behind them.

Cain gripped her gently, then released her as his nephew walked up.

"Where's Mother?"

"She decided to wait in the car," Cain said, his voice completely neutral.

Billy threw him a very adult, sideways glance but said nothing more on the subject of his mother. He shifted his one-armed grip on his suitcase and school-book and turned to Shelley.

"Squeeze was good and hungry. He won't do much of anything but sleep for a few days now." He looked at her almost shyly. "Uh, thanks for everything. It was fun."

She held out her arms. He let go of his suitcase to give her a hard hug and a brilliant smile.

A horn honked three times.

Shelley handed Billy his suitcase.

"Your mother said she was in a hurry. I'll see you soon. And if you get stuck on homework, call me. Promise?"

"Okay. Thanks again."

"I enjoyed having you."

He searched her eyes for a moment, more adult than child, looking for truth beneath the polite words. Then he nodded his head and grinned.

When the horn called again, he turned and trotted down the walkway to his mother's flaming-red car.

"Billy," Cain called.

"Yes, sir?"

"If your mother—if you need anything, anything at all, call me."

The boy understood what the adult was reluctant to put into words.

"Thanks, but I don't think she's real mad at me. And even if she is, it won't last long."

"With her, nothing does," Cain said.

But he said it too softly for his nephew to hear.

After the car left with an impatient bark of tires against pavement, Cain put his arm around Shelley's shoulders and led the way into the living room.

As the door shut behind them, she suddenly realized that she was alone with him.

Truly alone.

Chapter Thirteen

The look Shelley gave Cain was half wary and entirely unsettled.

He lifted his arm from her shoulders and bent to pick up the two suitcases he had left by the front door.

She eyed the luggage unhappily. *Is this what he meant when he told me that I would be here for him when he came back? Does he assume that he's moving in with me?*

When Cain turned and faced her, he was holding his suitcases in polite expectation of being shown to a room.

She just looked at him.

He saw the wariness in her expression. If he hadn't been so tired and irritable, he would have laughed.

Maybe.

Then again, he might have done just what he was going to do now.

With long strides he headed for the stairway to the lower levels of the house.

"Where are you going?" she called.

"To take a shower."

Her mouth opened. She shut it and hurried after him.

"Right now?" she asked.

"Right here. Right now."

"But—"

"It seems," he said, talking over her, "that some damned fool of a contractor tore up my bathrooms."

"Yes, I told—"

"My plumbing won't be put back together for at least a week. I don't feel like waiting that long for a shower."

Too late, she remembered what he had said about redoing his condo.

All I ask is that you get the contractor to do the work while I'm gone.

"Oh, God." She raced downstairs after Cain. "It's my fault. I'm sorry."

"Why? Are you the contractor?"

He dropped his bags in the spare bedroom. In front of her rather dazed eyes, he proceeded to make himself comfortable. First he yanked off his scarred work boots. Socks followed. Before they hit the floor, he was unbuttoning his khaki shirt. He pulled the shirttails out of his jeans with quick motions of his hands.

After one look at the male pelt curling down his chest, Shelley closed her eyes.

It didn't help. Not only could she still see him in her mind, all she could think about was the moment six days ago when she had licked a drop of water from his body.

Oh, God.

Quickly she opened her eyes, thinking self-control would be easier that way.

It wasn't. He was unbuckling the worn leather belt that held up his jeans. She opened her mouth.

Nothing came out.

"Are you?" he asked.

"Am I, um, what?"

"A damned idiot of a contractor."

His hands never paused as he undressed. The zipper descended with a brisk, efficient sound.

She closed her eyes and tried to gather her scattering thoughts.

"No, I'm not a contractor." *I might just be a damned idiot, though.* "I, uh, can't even hang pictures straight."

"How are you at scrubbing backs?"

"Cain . . ."

It was all she could say.

In the silence that followed, she clearly heard the whisper of his jeans sliding down the length of his legs and the soft thump as he kicked the heavy cloth aside.

"Not so good at backs, huh?" he said with mock sympathy. "No problem. I'm a great believer in on-the-job training."

Her eyes snapped open. "What?"

His hands went to the elastic band of his briefs.

She retreated, slammed the door behind her, and yelled at him through it.

"Cain Remington, what the hell do you think you're doing!"

"Taking a shower. By your cowardly actions, am I to assume that you're not going to scrub my back as an apology for tearing up my house?"

"I, uh, that is . . . Damn! I thought you'd be gone at least two weeks, so I gave the contractor the go-ahead."

"I figured that much out all by myself, two seconds after I tripped over the goddamn toilet they left by the front door."

"You're angry."

"I haven't had a shower for three days and I haven't eaten for eighteen hours."

"Is that a hint?"

The only sound that came through the door was that of water being turned on full force in the shower.

Shelley let out a breath she hadn't known she was holding and pushed away from the door.

Discretion is the better part of valor and all that, she told herself briskly. *An apology and a platter of ham sandwiches might get me off the hook.*

Besides, I can't really blame him. If I came home dead tired and found a wreck instead of a haven, I'd be furious.

She went to the kitchen, made several thick sandwiches and a pitcher of fresh lemonade, and tiptoed back down the stairs. The sound of running water came through the door. Apparently he was enjoying the luxury of a long, steamy shower.

With one hand she opened the door, juggling the tray. Using her hip to open the door farther, she backed into the room.

It was quiet. Too quiet. The shower had been turned off.

"Lunch is on the dresser," she called, warning Cain that he wasn't alone any longer.

The bathroom door opened. Freshly shaved and bathed, he walked into the room wearing a towel around his hips and a mist of water shining in his hair.

Shelley started to retreat again.

He gave her a sidelong glance, rummaged in his suitcase, and faced her with clean jeans in hand.

"I assume if I start to dress, you'll run out on our unfinished conversation again."

"Count on it."

"Mink," he said, as though confirming the endearment he had chosen for her. "Soft and wild and very, very shy. Don't go away, mink."

She watched the bathroom door close behind him. A few moments later, he was back. The jeans he wore were faded and soft, fitting him like a pale blue shadow.

No man should look that good in jeans, she thought distantly. *It just isn't fair*.

The waistband didn't come to his navel. Dense, curling hair made a wedge across his chest and drew a dark line down the center of his body. The line widened just beneath his navel, foreshadowing the thicker hair below. Water drops sparkled everywhere, shifting and gleaming with each breath he took. Like a sculpture by a master, he called to her mind and her senses at the same time.

"Why did you tell the contractor he had two weeks?" Cain asked calmly. "I said I'd be gone a week."

"Yes, but . . ."

Vaguely she waved her hand. Not once did she look away from the water drops sparkling on his chest.

"But?" he prodded.

"I assumed that meant at least two weeks and probably a month."

He waited for her attention to shift back to his face. When it did, he spoke quietly. "Is that what he did?"

She blinked. "Who?"

"Your ex-husband. Did he say he'd be gone a day and stay away a week?"

"Something like that."

Cain started walking toward her.

"I'm really sorry," she said quickly. "I didn't mean to mess up your—"

"When are you going to realize," he interrupted, reaching for her, "that I'm not like your ex-husband?"

She watched his face come down toward hers and realized all over again that he had the most beautiful mouth she had ever seen. Hard and yet sensual, cleanly curved and utterly male.

His mouth hovered just above hers. His eyes watched her. He made no attempt to hide the hunger that had only increased with each hour he spent away from her.

She watched his smoky gray eyes and remembered how wonderful his mouth had felt on her lips, the pulse in her neck, the hard tips of her breasts. She was aching to feel those caresses again.

"What are you thinking?" he asked softly.

"That I'll die if you don't kiss me."

The husky confession drew a thick sound from him. His mouth closed over hers hungrily.

She opened herself to him, inviting him into her soft heat, shivering when his tongue rubbed hotly over hers. Her fingers flexed, sending her nails into his thick hair even as his palms worked down her back to the firm curves of her hips.

When his hands were full of her, his fingers clenched in sensual luxury. She made a startled sound that was also a muffled cry of pleasure.

Slowly he caressed every part of her mouth, lingering over the special softness behind her lips and the sliding delicacy of her tongue. Then he groaned and thrust deeply into her, filling her with a prowling, probing sensuality.

Hungrily she flowed over his hard male surfaces, trying to fit his body as perfectly as his mouth fit hers. His hands kneaded her hips as he held her hard and close. Then he moved slowly against her, proving beyond doubt that he was not in the least like her ex-husband.

Cain wanted her. The proof of his desire caressed her with every sliding movement of his hips.

By the time the kiss ended, Shelley could barely stand. A strange weakness consumed her, turning her bones to honey and her blood to liquid fire. She clung to him, feeling helpless, almost afraid, needing him in a way she didn't understand.

"Cain? I feel . . . dizzy."

He was surprised by the confusion and shadow of fear in her voice. In the next breath he realized that despite her headlong response to him, despite her obvious sensuality and hunger for him, despite having been married, Shelley Wilde didn't know what real passion did to a woman's body.

"It's all right," he whispered.

He shifted her in his arms, soothing her where he had once aroused. Then he laughed softly and rocked her close against his chest.

"It's better than all right," he said. "It's incredible."

Her eyes asked the question she was too shaken to put into words.

"This is the way it should be between a man and a woman," he said simply. "Wildfire, clean and hot and pure. Touching you is like putting a torch to dry chaparral."

"What about you? Is it . . . is it the same when I touch you?"

"Let's find out."

He lifted her fingers from his chest and slid them down his body until they hovered just above the blunt ridge of his hunger.

"Touch me, mink. Watch me burn."

She settled on him so lightly that even her delicate fingertips barely registered the caress.

Cain's aroused flesh was far more sensitive than mere fingertips. The hesitant caress she gave him was pure fire. Every muscle in his body tightened. When she ran delicate fingertips over the length of him again, he closed his eyes and shivered.

She looked at his face, wondering if he was enjoying the gentle intimacy as much as she was. His face was drawn with what could have been pain, making his mouth a hard, sensual line. Standing on tiptoe, she traced the line with the tip of her tongue. At the same moment, her hand moved warmly over him.

Smiling, her own eyes half closed, she watched him burn.

"You're not going to run away from me now, are you?" he asked.

"Run?" She laughed breathlessly. "I can barely stand."

"That's Mother Nature's way of telling you it's time to go to bed."

"Are you weak, too?"

He kissed her lips gently despite the hunger racking him. Slowly he lifted her in his arms and walked toward the bed.

"The man gets a few extra minutes of grace," he said, placing her on the bed and coming down beside her in a controlled rush. "But I'll tell you, each time you kiss me I can feel it all the way to my knees."

"We're going to be too weak to do anything," she said, half laughing, half serious.

His smile went from tender to very male.

"That's not quite the way it works," he said, unbuttoning her blouse.

"It isn't? Are you—sure?" Her breath caught as his fingers traced a line of fire down to her waist.

"Very."

The knotted tails of her blouse gave way to his determined fingers.

"You see," he said, "once you get smart and lie down, you get strong again. Very, very strong."

"I'll take your word for it. I'm still at the weak stage."

She couldn't help shivering with a combination of nerves and desire as he took off her blouse and bra. When his hands came back to her body, her breath stopped in her throat.

Please, God, don't let me flinch when he touches my breasts.

Shelley didn't want painful memories from the past to spoil this moment. She didn't want Cain to be angry or hurt and withdraw from her. She wanted to feel again the extraordinary fire that had swept over her at the beach when his mouth had caressed her so urgently. She wanted to forget everything a humiliating marriage had taught her. She wanted to burn in her lover's arms, consuming him, consuming herself.

Yet when Cain's hands came up to her breasts, she froze.

It was just an instant, but he felt it. His hands stilled and his mouth tightened.

"I'm sorry, don't be angry," she said in a rush. Tears filled her throat, strangling her. "It's not you, it's me. I told you. I'm no good at—"

His mouth stole her fearful words and replaced them with a deep, gentle kiss. Long fingers caressed her breasts, teasing the tips until they were ruby-hard.

Streamers of fire ran down to her thighs. She arched against him, burning for him. She twisted into his touch, increasing the sweet pressure of his fingers.

"Your ex-husband didn't want you to burn," Cain said roughly, "because he knew he couldn't put out the fire. I don't know if I can, either, but I'm sure as hell going to enjoy finding out."

His hands went beneath her back, arching her toward his beautiful, hungry mouth.

"I like it when you burn," he said.

His teeth raked lightly over her nipple. She gasped with pleasure. Then he drew her heavily into his mouth.

The world spun away. She forgot her past experience, the husband she could never fully arouse, the doubts she had about herself as a woman. She forgot everything but the rhythmic pull of Cain's tongue and teeth and lips.

Waves of sensation swept over Shelley, shaking her with their force. Her head fell back and her eyes became unfocused. She gave herself to his lovemaking with an elemental abandon that was more arousing to him than any declaration of passion could have been.

She didn't know how long she was held suspended between his powerful hands and his caressing mouth. She knew only that she had never felt more desirable, more desired.

Then she discovered even that wasn't enough.

She had to have more of him, give more to him, make him burn as she was burning. She threaded her hands into his hair, letting it slide between her fingers. The feeling was deliciously sensual. His hair was damp from the shower and hot with the passion that radiated through both of them.

Her fingernails scored lightly over the bunched muscles of his shoulders. Then her palms rubbed across his burning skin, savoring every bit of him she could reach.

It still wasn't enough. She was consumed by the need to feel his tongue against hers, to taste his heat, absorb it, become part of it. Yet she couldn't tell him what she wanted. She could barely even say his name for the sensual vise gripping her.

As though he knew her need, he lifted his head from her breast and took her mouth without restraint, crushing her back into the bed with the force of his kiss.

She didn't complain about his weight. She gloried in it and in him. Wrapping her arms around him, she pulled him even closer, needing the masculine heaviness of his body as he settled between her legs. He pushed sinuously against her, seeking the waiting softness, silently asking if she wanted him. Instinctively her hips moved against him, telling him that she burned.

"Shelley?"

"Yes. Hurry."

Swiftly he peeled off their remaining clothes, reached into his discarded jeans, and pulled out a small foil packet.

"Next time you can help me with this," he said, ripping apart the foil. "But this time I don't feel like playing. This time I just want to be inside you."

An instant later, his hands were stroking her urgently from her ankles to her forehead and back. He wanted to slow down, to savor her heat and hunger, but control was sliding away from him with each broken breath he took. The raw hunger burning him was like nothing he had ever experienced.

When his fingers found the hot, soft center of her, he groaned at the proof of her arousal. He bent and took her mouth fiercely, ravishing her with thrusts of his tongue as he wanted to ravish her with thrusts of his body.

She came apart beneath the sensual assault, crying out her pleasure, twisting up to him, telling of the fiery need racing through her, shaking her until she could only call his name again and again. Blindly her hands slid down his body until she touched him and knew the full measure of his need.

He made a hoarse sound. In an agony of pleasure, he moved between her soft palms. Then he captured her hands and pulled them back up his body. He bit her palms with hungry sensuality, wanting to devour and cherish her at the same time.

"God, how I want you," he said through clenched teeth.

She couldn't even answer. All she could do was lift up to him in a silent plea.

Long fingers slid down her flushed body and sank into her satin depths, caressing her until fire melted her. Breath hissed through Cain's teeth. He closed his eyes and deepened the caress, savoring the liquid silk of her response. With a shudder he withdrew slowly and lay on his back, not touching her at all.

She turned restlessly toward him, wanting him.

And then she saw his face. His expression was harsh and tightly drawn, as though he was in pain.

"What's wrong?" she whispered.

"I want you—too much."

"I don't understand."

She touched his jawline and felt the shudder that took him with even such a simple caress. At that moment she had no doubt that he wanted her as no man ever had. To be wanted like that made her feel as though she was breathing fire. Heat twisted through the core of her, bringing a wild kind of strength. She had never dreamed such wanting was possible.

But he was retreating from her with every rough breath he took.

"Tell me what's wrong," she said. "I want you."

"I know."

Hungrily, gently, his fingers moved up her inner thighs until he knew once again the satin heat of her.

"I can feel how ready you are for me," he said roughly. "So soft, so hot."

Her hand touched him. "And you're ready for me, aren't you?"

He gave a harsh crack of laughter. "Hell, yes, I'm ready."

"Then why . . . ?"

"It's been so long since you've been with a man, you're as tight as a virgin."

Even as he spoke, he caressed her slowly, deeply. Her breath broke and she melted over him again.

"Cain," she said urgently. "Please."

He fought against the savage need to bury himself in her willing body. "I'm too damn hungry, mink."

"What?"

With a despairing curse, he wrapped her hand around his tightly sheathed flesh.

"You're small," he said curtly. "I'm not. I'm afraid I'll hurt you."

Visibly fighting for control, he withdrew his touch from her body again.

Shelley felt empty, aching. Slowly she kissed his cheek, his neck, the tangled mat of hair on his chest, the dark line leading to his navel.

"You won't hurt me," she said against his skin.

He couldn't speak for the sudden hammering of his blood. The butterfly softness of her lips brushed over him in a caress that tightened every muscle in his body.

Then, hungrily, she tasted the strip of hard flesh that was still naked beneath the condom.

"Shelley—"

"I'm empty, Cain."

He turned swiftly and pinned her to the bed, filling her with a single powerful movement of his body. She cried out at the sudden penetration, but it was a cry of pleasure, not pain. The shivering, melting heat of her body told him just how great that pleasure was.

It was no less for him. He moved inside her again, filling her all over again, dragging sweet cries and liquid fire from her, setting her completely afire, burning her, burning with her. Snug within her body, he rocked against her, feeling a pleasure so great that he could only groan.

At each movement of his hips she cried out and her nails licked like flames over him. Abruptly her body tensed. Her eyes opened with surprise as pleasure exploded into a consuming ecstasy.

Cain saw the instant of her surprise. Then he felt the liquid heat and satin pulses rippling deep within her. He set his teeth and willed himself not to move. He wanted it to last forever, to stay joined with her endlessly, savoring the hot, wild instant when she first knew ecstasy.

Another tiny convulsion swept over her. Her heat rippled around him again, tugging at him. He fought against his own need but it was too late, control slipping away, ecstasy claiming him as completely as it had claimed her. With a low cry he arched into her until they couldn't be any closer. Then he gave himself to her and to the deep completion he had found only in her.

For a timeless moment they burned together, giving each other a shimmering pleasure that neither had ever known before.

Chapter Fourteen

Slowly, slowly, Shelley came back to awareness of the late-afternoon sun slanting through the bedroom. The light turned Cain's body into a golden sculpture so perfect she couldn't help tasting him to see if he was real.

Cradled in his arms, she smoothed her lips over the resilient muscles of his shoulder and chest. Smiling lazily, she savored the memories that licked over her like another kind of sunlight. She decided it was fitting that the man next to her was bathed in radiance, a god cast in gold, for no mere mortal could have shown her that paradise was a place of ecstatic fire.

His stomach growled beneath her cheek. If he was a god, he was a hungry one.

She laughed softly and nibbled on his flat belly.

"Could I interest you in some ham sandwiches and fresh lemonade?" she asked.

"Who do I have to kill?"

"No one. I slaughtered the lemons myself while you were in the shower."

She slid a bit farther down his body, closing her teeth on the skin over his stomach, savoring the taste of him. He ran his hard thumb down the length of her backbone to the generous crease below her waist.

"Mink," he said huskily. "Soft and wild."

His body tightened in sensual reflex as her mouth drifted even lower, where he was now fully naked.

"But no longer shy," he said on a swiftly indrawn breath.

She turned her head quickly, looking up at him. He was right. She felt no shyness with him, simply a *rightness* that was like homecoming, a feeling of being wholly alive.

The sudden movement of her head sent her hair drifting over him, covering him like a loincloth made of silk. His breath caught in a husky groan as the cool, soft strands rubbed over him and slid caressingly between his thighs. Heat and heaviness shot into his veins, making him stir beneath the silky veil of her hair.

"Should I be shy?" she asked, resting her cheek on his abdomen. "Is that what you want?"

"What I want would shock you."

"Tell me," she said quickly. "I mean it. You gave me so much. Let me give you everything you want."

He laughed gently. His fingertips caressed the dark arch of her eyebrow, the hollow beneath her cheekbone, the soft curve of her lips.

"Cain?"

"You gave me everything I wanted and then taught me how to want more."

"More?"

"Then you gave me that, too. Right now, you could skin me with a dull knife and I'd thank you every inch of the way."

He saw the puzzlement in her hazel eyes, the frown drawing together her eyebrows.

"What do you mean?" she asked.

"You really don't understand, do you?"

There was no mockery in his voice, only wonder that someone so naturally sensual could be so innocent.

"But that shouldn't surprise me," he said. "You haven't slept with enough men to know the difference between sexual release and the kind of mutual pleasure we just had."

He traced the line of her mouth again, loving its softness and promise of heat.

"I didn't believe that kind of pleasure existed," he said simply. "Until you."

Her tongue touched his fingertip briefly, then vanished. The caress was like the moment when she had licked a water drop from his chest, a touch that was violently arousing simply because it was spontaneous.

He eased his fingers around to the back of her head, kneading her scalp. His breath hesitated when she slid her cheek from his abdomen to the musky, thick hair just below. The movement sent her own much-softer hair sliding over him again. His body hardened even more, magnifying the beat of his heart with each second.

"What about you?" he asked.

She made a humming, purring sound that almost tickled against his body. Almost, but not quite. The difference was pure fire.

"Are you sure I didn't hurt you?" he asked.

The soft breath of her laughter spread over his ultrasensitive skin.

"I almost fainted, but you didn't hurt me. I didn't know a man and woman . . ."

Her voice trailed off as she discovered the intriguing changes taking place in him again. Her tongue flicked out.

His breath came in hard.

"I've just discovered the problem with that kind of pleasure," he said. "It satisfies me all the way to my soul."

Delight swept through Shelley. She loved knowing that she could both arouse and satisfy Cain, a man of laughter and intelligence and strength, a man whose male sensuality and hunger spoke to her own elemental feminine core.

"Is that a problem?" she asked, tasting him again.

"Knowing how good it's going to be makes me want to bury myself in you all over again, and then again and again."

"Yes." She dragged her hair slowly over him, tasting him, loving him. "Again and again. I want to . . ."

She froze as she heard her own thoughts. *I want to possess Cain. I want to keep him locked within my body so that no other woman could ever take him from me.*

He saw the darkness expanding in her eyes and wondered what was wrong.

"Mink?"

She looked at him strangely, as though she were suddenly afraid of him.

"What is it? Did I hurt you after all?" he asked. "We don't have to make love again now, if that's worrying you. Just being like this with you is more pleasure than I ever expected to have from a woman."

Slowly she shook her head.

"Your hair," he said. His voice broke. "Do that again. It's like a cool kind of fire wrapping around me."

Another wave of possessiveness swept through Shelley. She couldn't bear to think of him going from bed to bed like her ex-husband, making sweet, sensual demands on other women. And answering their demands in turn.

"Shelley?"

Cain's voice was as gentle as the fingers stroking her cheek. She took a ragged breath and forced herself to relax.

"You didn't hurt me."

"Are you sure? When you felt me getting hard again, you looked frightened."

"It's not that. I just realized—" Her voice broke.

The newness of her feelings overwhelmed her, shaking her. She couldn't think clearly enough to be tactful or to duck his questions. All she could think of was the truth she had just discovered.

"I don't want you to be with other women," she said starkly. "It was bad enough with my husband. With you, it would . . ."

She stopped talking, closed her eyes, and concentrated on trying to control her emotions.

"Shelley."

After a moment she looked at him. His eyes were a silver blaze of desire.

"You weren't listening very well a moment ago, were you?" he asked quietly. "I've never known this kind of pleasure with another woman. I never will. It's you, mink, not me."

"But I'm not like this with other men."

"Then I guess we're stuck with each other."

His smile was both gentle and fierce, like his eyes, like his fingers caressing the nape of her neck. He pulled her up his body and kissed her until she forgot her fear of losing him. Her arms went around his neck as she met and matched his hungry kiss.

Finally, tenderly, they released each other, oddly soothed by the knowledge of how easily each could arouse the other. She buried her face against his neck, breathing in the warm male scent of him. After a moment she began to laugh softly.

"Your stomach is growling again."

"There are two parts of a man's body that he doesn't have a hell of a lot of control over. His stomach is the other one."

"I've got just the thing."

"You certainly do."

His hand smoothed down her body until her breath caught and her lips parted in surprise. She hadn't realized she was still so sensitive.

"How about sharing it with me?" he whispered.

Laughing, she nipped his shoulder and slid out of bed. The sandwiches were where she had left them, on the dresser. She picked up the tray and started across the room. When she looked at the bed, her steps slowed.

Cain was watching her as though he had never seen a woman before that moment. His glance went from her tumbled hair to her toenails, then back to the feminine curves between.

Heat shimmered through her in a tingling wave. Suddenly she was very aware of herself.

Completely aware.

Her mouth went dry. She felt as if she were looking at her own body through his eyes, seeing for the first time the ripe invitation of her nipples, the beckoning curve of waist and hips, the dark hair gleaming at the apex of her thighs, the hot inner softness that so perfectly matched his body.

"Shy again?" he asked huskily.

"I—not really. I've just never seen myself through a man's eyes before."

"Then you finally know how sexy you are."

"To you," she whispered. "Yes."

She started toward the bed once more, feeling strangely light, as though a weight had been taken from her. She had always believed in herself as a person, but this was the first time she had been confident of herself as a woman.

When she bent over to set the tray on a bedside table, he caressed her lazily. Long fingers stroked her legs and the smooth skin of her inner thighs. Slowly, inevitably, his hand moved higher, until finally his fingertips rubbed over the soft, sultry flesh he longed to taste. Smiling, he watched her shiver at his slow penetration. His thumb sought and found the sensitive knot that was still flushed and sleek with passion.

A burst of heat and golden weakness shot through her, making her sway slightly. She started to say something, but the words were lost in a gasp as his thumb moved again, sending lightning through her.

He felt the sensual tensing of her body as vividly as she did.

"Cain? I—"

Words died as she melted over his hand.

"I love feeling your response," he said.

"We just—your lunch—"

She gave up and braced herself against the bedside table while he caressed her with a slow sensuality that consumed her.

"Don't worry, mink. I'm not going to make a meal out of you."

He leaned over and nibbled on her thigh.

"Dessert, now," he said thickly, "is an entirely different matter. Would you be my dessert, Shelley Wilde?"

When she answered, her voice was throaty, unrecognizable. Eyes half closed, she was looking at Cain's sun-streaked hair feathering across her thigh.

"I've never been dessert," she said. "What's it like?"

"I don't know. I've never wanted to make dessert of a woman. It seems we're destined for a long list of mutual firsts."

His mustache smoothed against her skin. His tongue flicked out, almost tasting her. Then he turned his head away from her too-tempting warmth and bit her thigh with measured force. When he felt her shudder and sway against him, he cursed quietly and released her.

"Wildfire," he said in a low voice.

He looked from the fine trembling of his hands to the sudden, heavy urgency of his body. He knew that even if he took Shelley now, he would want her again and again. There was no end to his need of her, and no beginning. He had always needed her.

He always would.

"My God," he said, disbelief and passion roughening his voice. "Do you know how much I want you?"

Shelley sank down onto the floor and slumped against the bed. She took a long, ragged breath and fought for control of the female body that kept astonishing her with its reckless passion.

"I can see the headlines now," she said. " 'Man and Woman Starve to Death in Bed.' "

He lay back and laughed despite his insistent sexual hunger for her.

She took another long breath and began to laugh

with him, releasing them from the tension that had wrapped hot, silken coils around her.

And him.

The certainty of her ability to arouse him was like wine heating her blood. It was all she could do not to test the boundaries of her newfound sensual powers. The only reason she didn't was the memory of how exhausted he had looked before he showered. Obviously he had gone short on sleep as well as on food and baths while he was in the Yukon.

When Cain's hand appeared over the edge of the bed, blindly seeking her, she grabbed a sandwich and plopped it down against his palm.

"Here," she said. "I refuse to be a three-day wonder for the *Enquirer*."

"Sounds like fun to me."

"Eat."

"Are you telling me I'm going to need my strength?"

"Yes!"

Hand and sandwich disappeared. Sounds of quiet munching drifted down to her. She rested her forehead against her knees and tried to think of anything but his utterly male body stretched out naked on the rumpled sheets.

She sensed a movement above her head and looked up in time to see another sandwich disappear off the tray. Her own stomach entered a loud complaint.

The hand reappeared, waving food under her nose. The sandwich was already half eaten.

"You called?" he asked.

She grabbed his hand and sank her teeth into the sandwich, just missing his fingers.

"Come up and eat with me, mink."

"Can I trust you?"

"I doubt it. Want to find out?"

Shelley rose to her knees and peered over the edge of the mattress.

All six feet three inches of Cain was sprawled at ease against the lemon-yellow sheets. He was propped up on his elbow, quickly reducing the sandwich to a memory. The color of his body hair ranged from streaks of spun gold where the sun had touched him to very dark where it hadn't.

Yet it was what lay beneath the symmetry of flesh and bone that appealed so strongly to her. The depth of her attraction to him increased with every bit of laughter he shared with her, his generous sensuality, his kindness to Billy, even his icy anger at JoLynn's cruelty. There was an essential goodness in Cain, a clean inner strength. It was more compelling to her senses than any arrangement of male skin and bone and muscle would ever be.

As she watched him, emotions condensed within her, filling spaces she had never known were empty, filling her until she thought she would overflow with tears.

"It isn't fair," she said.

"I offered to share."

"Not the sandwich."

"Then what?"

"You. Men aren't supposed to be beautiful."

He tossed the last bite of sandwich back on the tray and turned to look at her. The color of his eyes went from blue-gray to silver as he read the simple truth in her expression.

To Shelley, he was beautiful.

The uneven smile he gave her made her want to laugh and cry at the same time.

How could I give so much of myself to him so quickly?

There was no answer except the truth she already knew: she had given Cain much more than her body. Too much.

She kissed the callused fingertip that was touching her as though she were a dream come true.

"I'm not beautiful, mink. Hell, as you pointed out when we first met, I'm not even handsome."

"I was wrong."

Smiling, he stroked her cheek and shook his head.

To keep from reaching for him, she crossed her arms on the mattress and rested her chin on them. She looked him over with the same attention she brought to judging a piece of art.

"Someone like Brian or JoLynn might have more surface prettiness," she said. "But you can't see *into* them. They're . . . muddy."

"Like your ex?"

"And yours. But you aren't muddy. You're clean and strong all the way to your soul. That's what beauty really is. The rest is just distraction."

"Then you're the most beautiful woman ever born."

He lifted her onto the bed and cradled her against

his body. There was no hungry passion in his embrace. He simply held her, needing to feel her warmth, the stir of her breath against his neck, the feminine strength of her arms holding him in return.

His hands moved over her without sensual demand. The feel of her reassured him that she was real rather than a dream born out of his own loneliness, a loneliness that had been part of him for so long that he didn't even think about it until it was gone.

He wasn't lonely any longer.

The realization went through him like a shock wave, changing everything in its wake.

Shelley made an odd sound and pushed slightly away.

"It's okay," he said. "I wasn't about to ravish you again."

"How disappointing."

His chest moved in silent laughter.

"Not that I blame you," she added. "Look what I did."

Very gently she touched his chest. Beneath the cushion of hair was a bruise.

"Not likely, mink. You'd have to take a hammer to me to leave a dent like that."

"Then what was it?"

"Like I said, a hammer."

"You're joking."

"I wish."

The thought of anything hurting him went into her like a knife. "What happened?"

"A slight difference of opinion."

"Over what?"

"The usual. Whiskey and a town bike."

"A bicycle?"

"No. A woman. The kind anyone can ride."

Shelley winced. "Did you see a doctor?"

"No point."

"Why?"

He stroked her hair, trying to soothe the tension he felt vibrating through her. When that didn't work, he pulled her head toward his mouth and kissed her lips.

"It's no big deal," he said.

"Then why won't you talk about it?"

"Because human stupidity pisses me off."

"You must spend most of your time in an advanced state of pissed-offness."

He laughed and lay back again.

She curled along his side and waited.

"You know the geologist and the engineer I was having trouble with?" he asked finally.

"The ones who were fighting over the, uh, town bike?"

"Yeah. I got up there just in time to break up a nasty little brawl."

"That's when someone used a hammer on you?"

"My own damn fault," he said, yawning. "I was more worried about the guy with the pistol. Drunks are really unpredictable."

Her mouth went dry.

"When I went after the gun, Joe and the woman

jumped me. I got the gun away from Ken and blocked most of the hammer blow. Then I knocked some sense into the two men.''

A ragged, indrawn breath was Shelley's first comment.

''Does this happen often?'' she asked faintly.

''No. When it does, it's usually between miners, not engineers, and I just let them have at it, so long as they're pretty evenly matched. But Ken was a miner before he was anything else. Two drinks, one flashy piece of ass, and he goes ballistic.''

''Aren't there any police?''

''Were there many cops in the Sahara?'' Cain asked wryly.

She closed her eyes, remembering. There had been times when she and her mother retreated into their tent. That was when her mother took a well-oiled pistol out of a false compartment in a suitcase. Then mother and daughter waited quietly behind canvas walls.

In time, Shelley learned to shoot and care for the pistol herself. Even before then, she was squinting through the slit where the tent flaps didn't meet. More than once she had watched her father talk to angry men with a shotgun in the crook of his arm.

''No police until after the fact, and usually not even then,'' she said. ''Dad had to take care of things himself.''

''It's the same in a mining camp. It's up to the camp boss to keep order.''

"Are you the camp boss?"

"No, Ken is. Unfortunately, the town bike in question—"

"Lulu?"

"Yeah. Joe's wife. She was the one with the hammer."

"Oh, Lord."

"If she'd been a man, I'd have broken her arm." He shrugged. "As it was, I told Lulu if she ever came at me again, I'd take her down like any man."

"What about Ken?"

"He'll be looking for a new job as soon as his arm heals."

"His arm?"

"I broke it. I don't like guns, especially when they're pointed at me."

"I . . . see. And the husband?"

"Joe took Lulu back to their cabin. I don't know what happened after that."

"I doubt if a good time was had by all."

"I hope not," Cain said bluntly. "I didn't see Lulu the rest of the time I was there, which was fine with me. I was too busy trying to get things running again to worry about some troublemaking slut."

The contempt in Cain's voice chilled her. It was the same cold disdain that came when he mentioned his ex-wife or JoLynn.

Town bike.

Even Shelley had felt the sharp edge of his tongue when they first met.

Spinster. A woman who can't hold a man.

"You don't like women very well, do you?" Shelley asked quietly.

And she had just discovered that she was very much a woman.

Chapter Fifteen

The silence stretched for so long that Shelley decided Cain simply was going to ignore the question. Then he sighed, raked a hand through his shaggy hair, and began talking.

"Too many women are on power trips," he said. "They want every man they see. But they don't really want men. They just want men to want *them*."

The tension in his body was plain to her. His muscles were as hard as the line of his mouth. He turned and looked at her.

"I haven't liked women for a long time," he said evenly. "Then I saw a woman standing in a shaft of sunlight with a snake draped over her arm. She was handling it so gently . . ."

He traced the line of her eyebrows with his thumbs.

"And she handled a lonely boy just as gently," he said, his voice slow and deep. "She had no reason to be gentle, nothing to gain. She was simply a loving kind of woman."

"A spinster who couldn't hold a man?"

253

His laughter and warm lips brushed over her forehead.

"There I was, all intrigued by you," he said, "and you couldn't hold your nose high enough when you looked at me. Yeah, I was pissed off."

"It never occurred to me that you saw past Jo-Lynn's, uh . . ."

"Tits?"

"Let's not forget her ass."

"I did a long time ago. It's called growing up."

Shelley's smile faded when she saw the intensity in Cain's eyes.

"That's why you intrigued me," he said. "You were real all the way to the bone. No games, no lies. You had the kind of honesty I'd given up hoping to find in a woman."

She turned and kissed his palm. Then she bit it.

He laughed and caressed her lips with his thumb.

"When I saw you lighting candles on Billy's cake, I knew I had to find out what it was like to have an honest, loving kind of woman in my bed."

"So what was it like?" she asked, her voice light. But there was no laughter in her eyes as she watched him.

"You taught me that some dreams come true," he said simply.

"Some dreams are nightmares."

"Not this one. I've finally found a woman who is strong and tender, smart and honest, civilized and wild."

His warm breath mingled with hers in a kiss. When

it ended, she tilted back her head and looked directly in his eyes.

"Cain, I'm not wild. I'm a homebody."

"Look out that wall of glass and tell me you aren't wild."

She looked across his chest to the tall windows that gave the guest bedroom a spectacular view of the steep hills. Even as she rejected the truth of what he said, she had to admit the land called to her at a level deeper than words, deeper than thought, deeper than denial.

Soon twilight would come, and with it the moist sigh of an ocean breeze reversing the hot Santa Ana winds. The sea air would bring life to the empty land. Evening would be a chaparral-scented coolness sliding down hot ravines. Deer would begin to glide out of cover, picking their way through the brush on delicate feet. Raccoons would sneak up to drink from her pool, followed by opossums. Sometimes there would be the amusing black-and-silver elegance of a skunk strolling by.

And always there were jackrabbits freezing at the first sound, alert for the coyotes that moved like tan shadows through the concealing brush.

This was Shelley's favorite time of day, when the sun was easing its fierce grip on the land. Everything glowed with a rich, mystic light that whispered to her to go out to the untamed hills and explore them, to walk in places where man rarely went.

Cain watched her looking at the land and knew that he was right. Whether she admitted it aloud or not, she was too honest to hide her reactions. She loved the wild places where animals were more common than man and the wind was more common than any life.

"So I like a good view," she said. "So what? Everyone does."

"What makes a good view is a matter of opinion."

"Meaning?"

"Meaning the windows in this house are oriented toward the land rather than the city lights."

She shrugged. "I can see lights at night."

"You can, yes. But it's the view of the land you truly enjoy."

"Lots of people like a view that isn't cluttered up by houses. That's why oceanfront property is so expensive. Does that mean that everyone who lives along the beach wants to live in a wilderness?"

The challenging note in her voice made him pause, but not for long. What he was trying to point out about her basic nature was too important to shove under the rug.

Even though she plainly wanted to.

"JoLynn covered up her windows because she's too silly and shallow to respond to something as wild as the sea," Cain said quietly. "You chose walls of glass facing away from the city because you need to see something untamed in the midst of all the concrete and macadam."

She tossed her head impatiently.

He didn't take the hint.

"There is wildness in you," he said. "You can't hide it. Why even bother to try?"

She stiffened beneath his caressing hand, withdrawing from him without moving away.

Yet he sensed the change in her as surely as he would have sensed a change in his own heartbeat. He watched her with clear, unflinching eyes.

"Why do you deny that you're not a complete homebody?" he asked.

"Because it isn't true."

"Give me a better explanation."

She shifted restlessly. "I love the hills for their tawny colors and the way light transforms them. They're as superb as any piece of art created by man."

"You love them because they *weren't* created by man. The hills are wild."

She turned and watched him with wary hazel eyes.

"You're wrong. I'm a homebody." She smiled, trying to soften the hard edge of her voice. "People come in all different types and sizes. Like you. A big, rangy traveling man."

And the most beautiful person I've ever known.

Her sad smile made Cain's breath catch. Her eyes were brilliant with what could easily turn into tears. His gut instinct told him she was saying good-bye all over again.

"You can't dismiss what we have so easily," he said.

"Who said it was easy?"

Before he could answer, she covered his mouth with her hand.

"No, please," she said. "We can't change what we

are. But we can share ourselves, can't we? For as long as it lasts?''

"It will last forever. I love you." His fingertip touched her lips delicately. "And that's another first. I've never told a woman I loved her."

The words swept through Shelley, destroying and creating at the same time, changing her whether she willed it or not. Tears trembled in her eyelashes. She didn't know whether to laugh or cry or scream or just plain run from the certainty in Cain's silver eyes.

Homebody and traveling man joined forever.

It will never work.

Losing him will hurt like nothing else in my life ever has.

"Cain . . ."

Her voice was small, anguished. Frightened.

He kissed her very gently.

"Don't cry. As soon as you know why you're afraid of your own wildness, you'll know that you love me as much as I love you."

She shook her head and fought not to lash out at life's whimsical cruelty, matching JoLynn with Billy and a homebody with a traveling man.

Cain sat up and looked down at the slender, dark-haired woman who was as stubborn as she was sensual.

"I'm tempted to make love to you right now," he said. "I could make you come apart in my arms. You would cry your pleasure and your love for me to the skies."

She looked at the burning assurance in his eyes. Hunger raced through her. So did fear.

"But that would only scare you more," he said, turning away. "So show me your hills, homebody. I've never hiked through a piece of art."

For a moment Shelley simply lay on the bed, watching Cain as he got up and started putting on the clothes he had shed with such impatience earlier. Then she got up herself, trying to equal his calm.

She couldn't. She was clumsy getting dressed. Her hands were shaking and her thoughts were a jumble.

"We should take a canteen," he said. "Do you have one in that big bedroom closet of yours?"

The casual question shocked her. It was as though he had never looked at her with luminous, unflinching gray eyes and spoken of love. She swallowed hard, yanked on her jeans, and turned to face him.

He wasn't even looking in her direction.

"Yes, I have a canteen."

She was pleased that her voice was almost as matter-of-fact as his.

"Knapsack?" he asked.

"Yes."

"Hiking shoes?"

"Not in your size."

"I have my own. What about you?"

"Right next to the canteen."

He smiled lazily at nothing in particular, as though he had just won a bet with himself.

"Know a place where we can picnic in your hills?" he asked.

Slowly she nodded again and watched his smile soften the lean lines of his face. Emotion rippled through her. His smile was so beautiful to her that she simply wanted to stand and stare at him.

"Let's go," he said. "I'll make some more sandwiches while you gather the gear."

With a feeling of unreality, she watched him walk out of the room.

He doesn't believe what I told him. Or is it just that he doesn't really care?

Alone in the room, Shelley stared out the window at the mysterious, alluring hills. Slowly she shook her head.

He cares. Not enough to change his roaming ways, of course. On the other hand, he's never had a real home, so he doesn't know what he's missing.

Yet I know he feels something more than just desire for me. He might say he loves me in order to get me in bed, but there wouldn't be much point in lying about his feelings now. Why bother? He got what he wanted.

So did I.

Sensual memories shimmered through her, making her catch her breath. She was honest enough with herself to know that Cain could have her again and again, for as long as he stayed.

Not just for the sex, although God knows it's good. But because I . . . care for him. Too much.

Homebody and traveling man.

God, what a mess.

Biting her lip, she stood motionless, trying to bring order to the chaos of her emotions.

She couldn't. Every scent in the room, every velvet shadow in the rumpled sheets, every crumb on the sandwich tray—everything reminded her of his generous lovemaking.

Enough running in circles, she told herself briskly. *I'll do what I always do when life closes in and I can't think.*

And what she did was hike in the hills. That was why every item of gear that Cain had mentioned was neatly stacked in a corner of her closet, waiting to be used. At least once a week she slipped away into the hills with her knapsack and a cold dinner. She loved to sit out there in the stillness with twilight sliding into night, watching while shadowy bits of life ghosted through the chaparral in search of food, prey, or sanctuary.

Eagerly Shelley finished dressing, gathered the hiking gear in her arms, and went up the stairs, taking them two at a time.

Cain looked up from making sandwiches and smiled at her as she came into the kitchen with an easy, cross-country kind of stride. As he had guessed, she was at home wearing hiking boots.

"I poured the last of the lemonade into the canteen," he said. "If you want to take something else, I have an empty canteen in the truck."

"Lemonade is fine with me. It's cool at night. We won't be gone long enough to really need water."

"That's the way I figured it. Did you pack a flashlight?"

She hesitated. Somehow there was more statement than question in his words.

"I always have one in the knapsack," she said.

"Knife? Matches? Compass?"

"And a first-aid kit and a survival blanket that can either reflect or absorb heat," she said dryly. "Did I miss anything, O mighty trail master?"

"Nope."

He gave her a sidelong glance, then returned to making sandwiches, neatly stacking slices of ham on the bread.

"Drop the other shoe," Shelley said.

He smiled slightly. "Quick, aren't you?"

"Mink usually are. So what are you trying not to say?"

"For a homebody, you sure know a lot about surviving in rough places."

"I learned the hard way. That," she said distinctly, "was before I had a home."

All he said was, "Got something to wrap these sandwiches in?"

"Third drawer from the right."

While he rummaged, she went to the refrigerator.

"I've got some fried chicken left from last night," she said.

"Billy must have been off his feed."

"No. I got smart. I cooked enough for five normal appetites. That way there was enough left for him to take a piece or three in his lunch bag."

Cain snickered.

"Go ahead, laugh," she said. "But I never really

understood the expression 'hollow leg' until I saw
Billy eat. While he was here, I made a quadruple
batch of chocolate chip cookies. Twice.''

When she looked up from packing chicken in the
knapsack, Cain was watching her with a gentle smile
that made her heart turn over.

"A loving kind of woman," he said softly.

"It comes with being a nice, tame homebody."

But her voice wasn't nearly as contrary as her
words. It was impossible for her to argue with Cain
when he smiled at her like that.

"Next time I'll come back before my nephew eats
the last cookie."

Shelley's eyelids flinched at his calm acceptance of
the fact that he would be going away again.

And coming back.

"I hid some cookies in the red coffee tin on the top
shelf of the cupboard over the refrigerator," she said,
reaching for a kitchen chair. "I thought you might not
have outgrown your taste for them."

"Does that mean you have?"

"Are you kidding? Those cookies have three of the
basic food groups—sugar, grease, and chocolate."

He lifted the chair from her hands and put it back
under the table.

"Remember?" he said. "You have a man in your
home now."

He leaned past her and opened the cupboard above
the refrigerator. Sourly she noted that he didn't even
have to stand on his tiptoes.

"This the one?" he asked.

But even before he spoke, he had pried open the lid. The scent of chocolate curled against his nostrils.

"This is the one," he said, breathing in deeply, filling his lungs. "Damn, but that smell brings back memories."

"Good ones?"

"The best. Seth loved chocolate chip cookies. After Mom married him, the cookie jar was always full. Laughter and love and the smell of chocolate."

The gentle, remembering kind of smile on his face slid through the defenses Shelley was trying to re-build. She felt like putting her arms around him and holding him, telling him with her touch that she was glad to share his memories and his smile, glad just to be with him.

She didn't realize that she had followed her impulse until she felt the warmth of his chest beneath her cheek. His arms wrapped around her, returning her hug.

"I'm glad you have some good memories of child-hood along with the bad," she whispered.

Cain kissed her hair and breathed in deeply again, but this time it was her scent he was savoring.

Gentle, generous, sexy, he thought, kissing her hair again. *And scared.*

I better remember that, or my gut tells me I'll find myself out on my ear, wondering how I let the best thing I've ever found slip through my fingers.

After the painful lesson of his first marriage, he had learned to trust his instincts, rather than fight them. He didn't know just why Shelley was frightened of loving him, but he had no doubt that she was. Reluctantly he released her.

"It's your knapsack," he said, handing her the wrapped sandwiches. "You know the best way to pack it."

Without seeming to, he watched her work. She put the hard things on the bottom, the soft things on top, and the uneven things away from the side that would rest against her back. Then she shook the knapsack gently to see how everything would travel. She fished out a sandwich that was determined to hide beneath the heavy tin of cookies and packed it in a different place.

Every move she made was casual and skilled. Each motion revealed how many times she had loaded up this knapsack and headed for her tawny hills.

Tame homebody? he thought sardonically. *Yeah. And I'm Tinkerbell.*

No matter how much she protests her high state of civilization, she spends a lot of time out in those wild hills.

He started to tease her again about the difference between her words and her actions, but stopped himself just in time. The wariness had only begun to fade from her green-and-golden eyes. He would be a fool to call it back, sending her into hiding again.

Cain was a lot of things. A fool wasn't one of them. Not since his first, disastrous marriage.

"I'll take that," he said, reaching for the knapsack.

"I'm used to it. Anyway, it's too small for you."

"Let me take a look at the straps."

He lifted the knapsack out of her hands and lengthened the straps so they would fit over his much wider back and shoulders. Then he put on the knapsack, straightened out the straps, and shrugged his shoulders to settle the weight in the center of his back. He moved with the ease of a man accustomed to carrying a much bigger, heavier pack.

"Fits fine," he said. "Lead the way."

She didn't bother to argue. She simply walked out into the bronze-and-scarlet evening.

As soon as they left the landscaped walkways of the pool and garden, heat welled up from the ground as though they were walking on an oven. Cain had been in enough deserts to know that the chaparral's thick growth was deceptive. The soil beneath the brush was dry and stony.

"A road to nowhere," he said.

Shelley looked at the twenty-foot-wide plowed strip of ground that ran all around her property.

"Fuel break," she said. "The hills and mountains around Los Angeles are covered with them. Fire roads, too. People use them when the fire season is closed."

"They make good bike trails."

"Enjoy them while you can. It's been dry lately. The fire season could open at any time. Then the hills will be closed to bikes and hikers."

"But not to you."

"I don't smoke, I don't target-shoot, and I don't build fires. Nobody even knows I'm out there."

A footpath led across the fuel break. Shelley

followed the dusty trail without looking. She knew every inch of it, because she had made it throughout the years of hiking from her house into the hills.

"Does it work?" he asked.

"The fuel break?"

"Yeah."

"So far, so good. Some of the houses have been here ten years."

Cain looked from the brush that covered the steep hillsides to the strands of expensive houses that had been built on the highest ridgeline of each range of hills.

"Fire burns uphill," he said.

"Not lately. The brush around here hasn't burned for almost a hundred years."

Frowning, he looked from her house to the wild land. The chaparral was more a low forest than tall brush. Twenty feet high, thick, tangled, desert-dry; in fire season the chaparral was a tawny threat surrounding her home.

"I'm surprised you didn't choose a nice green valley," he said. "Safer that way."

"Uglier, too. The view stinks as much as the air. Up here you can breathe. At least, most of the time."

"Don't like being closed in, huh?"

She didn't answer.

Mourning doves burst out of the chaparral just beyond the fuel break. Graceful, darting, leaving a wake of liquid cries, the rosy gray birds flew off into a distant, twilight ravine that was too steep for man to disturb them.

The informal footpath ended in a wall of chaparral two stories high. Shelley eased sideways into the thick, often prickly growth.

"Watch your eyes," she said. "There's no real trail, just a way I've found to get in and out of the ravine."

Cain waited until he was far enough behind that the branches she pushed aside wouldn't snap back across his face. Then he followed her into the chaparral, automatically adjusting his stride to keep the knapsack from snagging on every brittle branch along the way.

Despite the rough ground and the lack of any real trail, Shelley made very little noise. Completely at ease, she moved with the smooth economy of effort that was learned only through long experience in the wild.

Smiling, watching her, Cain silently enjoyed her gift of becoming part of the land. She passed through it with little more disturbance than the flight of a bird.

Tame, is she? A homebody?

Like hell she is, he thought with cool satisfaction. *She's hiking down a steep hillside, moving as gracefully as a dove through chaparral that hasn't been touched since white man came to California.*

And she's enjoying every step because the land is wild, untouched.

But he kept his insights to himself. He didn't want to argue with her just now.

Give her time. She isn't stupid. She'll see the truth.

The ground at the bottom of the ravine was covered

with rocks that had been rounded and smoothed by water. The stones told him that despite the seasonal drought, when hard rain came, the gullies filled with enough water to push boulders around.

There was no water now. There was only a slight easing of heat. Sunlight barely penetrated the chaparral. The treelike bushes surrounding Cain were at least three times his height, often more. Twilight pooled thickly in the shadows. The air was hot, pungent with the odors of resins and herbs.

Shelley turned back toward him. She spoke softly, letting her voice blend with the twilight. "In the winter, if you sit very still, you can watch the animals coming to drink at this seep."

He looked where she was pointing. Dried moss carpeted an area not much bigger than the knapsack. The seep had no moisture now. It looked more like a small, rumpled brown throw rug than a water hole.

"This used to run year-round," she said. "The winter before last was terribly dry. This one was worse. The seep stopped flowing."

"What happened to the animals?"

"They come to my pool to drink. Even the rattlesnakes."

"And you let them."

"They were here long before I was."

She crossed the ravine and began to climb quickly up the far side. Several hundred feet up the hill, where bedrock shelved to make a small clearing in the chaparral, she stopped and looked at him expectantly.

Without a word he took off the knapsack and spread the survival blanket. She watched, catching her breath from the last, steep scramble. Then she realized that his breathing wasn't the least bit disturbed.

"You must do a lot of hiking," she said.

He heard the wistfulness in her voice and almost mentioned it. He stopped himself just in time.

"A fair amount," he said. "Satellite photos are good for narrowing the choices, but nothing beats walking the land."

"Or scrambling."

"Yeah. Mother Nature tucks the most useful minerals in the damnedest places."

"You love them, though. The wild places."

He glanced up from setting out the picnic. He expected to see disapproval in her eyes even though there had been none in her voice. He saw only her acceptance of him.

Traveling man.

We can't change what we are. But we can share ourselves, can't we? For as long as it lasts.

"Yes, I love wild places," he said evenly. "Just as you love the bit of wildness you allow yourself."

She looked at his eyes. They were the color of twilight now, watching her with a certainty she couldn't deny and couldn't share.

"Look around you," he said, gesturing to the chaparral. "In some ways, this is as wild as any place I've ever been."

"That's ridiculous. Los Angeles is all around us."

"Is it? Since the beginning of time, how many

people do you think have stood here, right here? A thousand? A hundred? Ten?'' Softly: ''Two, Shelley. You. Me.''

''That's not the same as being wild.''

She took the knapsack and began putting out food. As far as she was concerned, the topic was closed.

''How is it different?'' he asked.

It was a reasonable question.

She didn't have a reasonable answer.

''I don't know,'' she said tightly. ''I just know that it is. I can have this and a home, too. But don't worry. I don't expect a traveling man to understand that.''

He hesitated, knowing he shouldn't push her. Yet he couldn't pretend that she was anything but dead wrong.

''Home isn't a place,'' he said. ''It's an emotion. Like love. Don't hide behind the elegant walls of what you call a home. Let yourself love me. That's the only home either one of us needs.''

Her head snapped up. ''Home isn't—''

He kissed her swiftly, stopping the words. When he lifted his head, he smoothed his thumb over her lips.

''No more, not yet,'' he said. ''Listen to me, love. Please. Then I won't speak of it again, I promise you.''

Breath held, he waited for her decision, watching her face with hungry eyes. Just when he thought he had lost her, she nodded her head. He touched her lips with his thumb, wanting to kiss her, knowing he shouldn't. Not yet.

Maybe not ever again.

"I want to laugh with you, argue with you, make love with you until there's only one of us, not two," Cain said quietly. "I want to marry you and spend my life with you."

Tears magnified the hazel darkness of Shelley's eyes.

"We belong to one another in a way that has nothing to do with when we met or how long we've known each other," he said. "I've always known you, always loved you. It just took me years to find you. Too many years. Don't waste any more of our lives. Be with me, marry me, *love me*."

Shelley's tears ran hotly over the fingers that were caressing her lips.

"You don't have to give me an answer yet," he said gently, relentlessly. "In fact, I won't let you. Right now you think that loving a traveling man will destroy all your dreams, all that you have, even destroy *you*."

She took a broken breath and went pale at hearing her worst fears spoken aloud.

"So that's it," he said. "That's why you're afraid of me and the wildness in yourself. Don't be, mink. You won't lose your home. You'll find it. We'll make a real home together, in each other's arms."

He kissed the hot tears gleaming on her eyelashes, her cheeks.

"Cain—"

"Let's just be with each other for a while," he said quickly. "You'll gild my home and when you're done, we'll talk again."

"But—"

"Say yes, my love," he whispered.

She didn't know whether he was asking for her agreement not to argue now or for her promise to love him in the future. She knew only that she couldn't say no to the man whose lips were gleaming with her tears, the man who held her so gently, the man who knew her so terrifyingly well.

But she couldn't say yes, either.

Why not? she asked herself with eerie calm. *You have nothing to lose that isn't already gone, do you?*

Do you?

"Shelley?"

Slowly she nodded her head.

Chapter Sixteen

A full moon was just rising above the hills, softening their stark outlines with a pale orange glow. Stirred by a breeze, the chaparral rustled just beyond Cain and Shelley's picnic place. All that remained of dinner was a chicken wing she was gnawing on and the taste of lemonade on his mustache.

"What happened when you took in the ore samples?" she asked.

"Guess."

"Politics as usual."

"Bingo."

She worried a morsel off the bone, licked her lips, and sighed. "What was the usual kind of politics down there?"

"Corrupt. A few weeks after I left, I learned that the Minister of Development's brother-in-law had studied geology and was certain that there were no iron deposits anywhere around. And tin or manganese? Impossible."

"The official really believed his brother-in-law rather than the ore samples you brought?"

"He really did. So there I sat, with a sackful of ore that could have launched a decent, home-grown metal industry, and listened to an idiot tell me there was no useful ore in his country."

"What did you do?"

Cain shrugged. "I went to the military tribunal that was running the country between elections. I dumped the ore on a colonel's desk, told him that the Minister of Development was a horse's ass, and left."

She laughed and shook her head at the same time. "I'll bet they ran you out of town."

"I didn't give them the chance. I caught the next plane north."

"And that was the end of it."

"Not quite. Three days later, the colonel called me in L.A. Seems that the Minister of Development's brother-in-law—who happened to be the Minister of Trade—was getting a percentage on all steel imports into the country."

"The brother-in-law didn't want a local steel industry, is that it?"

"Yeah. Local steel would have cut into his profits, so the trade minister did his best to sink my recommendations."

"But didn't you say the country had a huge trade deficit and needed to cut back on imports?"

"The country's needs came in a bad second to the Minister of Trade's greed," he said flatly.

"It's not always like that. Some governments care about the people."

"Not if the people in question are poor or not blood relatives of the ruling class. When the needs of poor people and the greed of rulers collide, there's a wild scramble at the money trough. Guess who wins—the needy or the greedy?"

Even the softly descending night couldn't hide the weariness and disgust in Cain's expression.

"Sometimes the good guys win," Shelley said after a moment.

"Not very damned often. I can't tell you how many times I've found resources that might have taken the *under* out of underdeveloped country, and had my discovery ignored or bungled because a handful of highly placed people didn't want any changes."

"It seems that they'd figure out that if the country gets richer, the people in control get richer."

"Don't hold your breath. Once the tiger of change comes to a country, no one can predict who's going to ride and who's going to get eaten. The rulers know that better than anyone. They kill the possibility of change wherever they find it."

"Not a happy picture."

"The world isn't a happy place," he said sardonically. "Ninety percent of the population live somewhere between the Stone Age and the Dark Ages. And the children . . ."

He shrugged and made a defeated gesture with one hand.

"I know," she said, taking his hand. "It used to

tear at me, seeing the children smile despite their fevers and running sores. Simple aspirin was a miracle drug. Penicillin was the hand of God touching them.''

Long, callused fingers interlaced with hers. He held on to her like a thirsty man holding on to the hope of water. After a time he started talking again.

She listened intently, hungry to know more about him. His silences told her that he rarely spoke with anyone about what he had seen.

''There were times when I'd strike ore in a really beautiful place,'' he said slowly. ''After the first rush of discovery wore off, I'd be tempted to keep the find to myself.''

''Tired of fighting with corrupt governments?''

''Partly. And partly, I just didn't want to ruin the place. Mining isn't a pretty process.''

''Neither is starvation.''

''Yeah. That's the hell of it. Even if I file an accurate report, there's no guarantee that the kids will be better off. But if I don't file a report, there's no chance at all for most of the kids. Their lives will be short and brutal.''

''What an awful choice to make, the beauty of the land or the laughter of a child.''

His fingers tightened in hers.

''Usually there isn't a real choice,'' he said. ''You go with the kids. But sometimes the country is reasonably wealthy or already has enough of whatever mineral I find.''

''Then what do you do?''

''I keep my mouth shut, refund whatever I've been paid, and walk away.''

''Do you do that often?''

''Not nearly as often as I'd like to. Someday I'll show you the places I haven't talked to anyone about. They're as beautiful now as the day God made them.''

She looked at his face. It was all but concealed from her in the gathering darkness.

''Tell me about your favorite place,'' she said.

''It's tucked up in the Andes, way up, a thousand miles from anywhere. Too high for jungle, not high enough for year-round ice. The mountains are green and black, steep and wild, and the sky is blue all the way to the center of the universe.''

''I know that kind of blue,'' Shelley said. ''I haven't seen it for a long, long time. The air is absolutely pure, like being suspended in fine, fragile crystal. One sound, one careless movement, and it will shatter around you.''

He smoothed his mustache over her fingers. ''Yes, it's exactly like that.''

''How did you find your special place in the Andes?''

''I was following a river up to its source. The water was clean and cold and so pure it was almost invisible. There was no trail, no sign that any man had ever walked where I was walking.''

''What about the natives?'' she asked.

''Not even them. The land was too steep and rocky to farm. The people in the last village I went through told me there was no way up this mountain, no pass to the other side, and that those who dared disturb the sleeping mountain gods never returned.''

Shelley leaned closer, looking at the pale gleam of Cain's eyes, the darkness of his eyelashes, his lips softly curved in a remembering smile. She didn't have to ask him why he was smiling. She knew.

There was a quality to the truly wild places of the earth that was unique. They joined humanity's forgotten past to its mysterious future. Untamed places humbled and elevated civilized people, teaching them that some things must be taken as they are, untouched, their wildness both a reassurance and a challenge to the restless human soul.

"I was looking for one kind of metal and found another," Cain said.

"Gold?"

He nodded. "It was a placer pocket no bigger than my knapsack. The gold nuggets in that hole were so pure I could draw designs on them with my fingernail."

Her eyes widened. "My God."

"Yeah. I worked downstream from that point, using a plate from my mess kit to pan for gold."

"And?"

"Barely any traces."

"But where did it go?"

"Where it came from is the megamillion-dollar question," he said dryly. "You want the mother lode, not a litter of baby nuggets."

She laughed and leaned forward, listening, watching.

"The pocket of nuggets lay just below a point where a network of tributary streams joined the main river," he said.

"Where did the streams come from?"

"They drained several peaks. The gold could have washed down from any one of them. The nuggets were rounded smooth, so they had come some distance in the water before they were trapped in the placer pocket."

"What did you do?"

Her voice was husky. She was caught between his words and the rough silk of his mustache stroking her fingers.

"If I brought back the handful of nuggets I'd found," he said, "thousands of men would rush in and tear up that place with hydraulic jets."

Without knowing it, she bit her lip and shook her head at the decision he had faced.

"If I could have pinpointed the source of gold," he said finally, "I'd have burned candles for the children at the village church and walked down out of the mountains to file my report."

"But you didn't."

"No. I kept my mouth shut. The mother lode could have been anywhere within five thousand square miles."

"Talk about a needle in a haystack. Even a solid gold one . . ."

He nodded. "Then there was the fact that this particular government was already making several billion dollars a year in the cocaine trade and spending every dime of it on wine, women, and weapons.''

"Déjà vu all over again.''

"Over and over and over. I didn't see how a handful of gold would make much difference to the dirt-poor natives. But losing their mountain gods would destroy them.''

He kissed her hand and added softly, "It was the most beautiful place I'd ever seen. I needed to know that the mountain was still there, still whole, even if I never had a chance to see it again.''

"Landscapes of the soul,'' she said, remembering his words. She kissed the backs of his fingers gently. "Thank you.''

"For not filing the report?''

"For being the kind of man you are.''

He lifted her, settling her between his legs so that her back rested against his chest.

"I wish I'd had you to talk to before now,'' he said, kissing her temple. "No matter where I was, I always felt like a stranger in a strange land. Totally alone. I'd come out of the mountains or the desert and go to the conference tables and try to make men understand what I'd seen.''

"Did they?''

"Not a word of it. The people who knew the wild didn't know the city, and the people who knew the city were afraid of the wild. The only common ground we had was developing resources so that the next generation had a chance at penicillin instead of disease.''

"My parents talked a lot about that. They had a hard time making people listen, in or out of the country."

"They should have tried waving cash," Cain said. "Revolutionaries and tyrants, bureaucrats and brigands, they all come to a point when you talk money. Cold cash is the universal language, not the needs of children."

The bitterness in his voice reminded Shelley of some of her own memories.

"I wish I'd been there for you to talk to," she said.

"I could have used a—" Quickly he bit back the word *wife* and said, "A real friend."

"I used to dream of having someone like that," she admitted. "None of the kids I met knew how I felt. Nobody else had lived in the wild and the city and everywhere between."

He pulled her closer, saying without words that he understood the kind of loneliness she was describing.

"When I'd talk about a desert spring," she said, "city people wouldn't understand the miracle of water. When I'd talk about the astronauts, desert people wouldn't be able to comprehend men on the moon."

Cain smiled slightly and smoothed his cheek over Shelley's hair.

"It seemed like every time I made some progress in understanding," she said, "Dad would wrap up whatever project he was working on and we would leave. That's when I began to hunger for a home of my own."

"Was it a specific geography you wanted, or simply a place where people understood you?"

"That's what home is, a place where people understand you."

"And L.A. is your home."

"Yes." Her voice was soft, certain.

"Who understands you in L.A.?"

He felt her stiffen and knew the answer—nobody in Los Angeles understood Shelley.

Yet she insisted it was her home.

"Look out just beyond that line of houses," he said, pointing. "The moon is the color of pale gold, like the flecks of light in your eyes."

She shivered when his lips nuzzled beneath her hair to find the sensitive curve of her ear. But it was more than his touch that made her tremble. Each word he had spoken was a pebble dropped into the calm pool of her determination, words setting off ripples that went clear to her soul, threatening her security, her happiness, her very idea of home.

He doesn't understand, she thought wearily. *How could he? He never went through the hell I did for the sake of wild places.*

Maybe if he understood, we could stay together.

A shaft of pure longing went through her, a homesickness for something she had never known. A sharing of tears and laughter, hopes and fears, triumphs and failure.

A sharing of life.

"When I was seven," she said, "we were staying in

a tent somewhere in the Negev. There was a moon like this one. Fever moon.''

Her hands gripped his forearms. Her voice was thin, strained. Tension vibrated through her. She had never spoken about her terrible fears and equally wrenching hopes.

''We'd only been in that camp two days,'' she said. ''We must have picked up the sickness in the city. Dad was out in the field with most of the workers, doing the initial survey. The guide was the only one who spoke English. He was with Dad. Mom and I stayed in camp. She got sick first.''

Cain's eyelids flinched. His arms closed reassuringly around Shelley.

Her hands moved restlessly over his forearms as though she was trying to convince herself that she wasn't seven anymore, wasn't alone, wasn't a terrified child watching her mother slide into delirium.

''She was hot when I touched her, as hot as the desert sand. Hotter. Then she started talking and laughing and crying. It scared me. She was talking to grandparents I knew were dead. I didn't know what to do.''

''You were only seven. No one expected you to do anything.''

If Shelley heard, she didn't respond to the soothing words. Her fingers closed around his wrists with punishing force.

''Mom started calling for Dad. I ran out into the night. The moon was like tonight, the color of brass.''

Cain looked at the brass-colored moon above the hills and held her even closer.

"There were two men out tending the pack animals," she said. "No one spoke English. No matter how much I cried and pleaded, they didn't understand that my mother needed help."

He wanted to kiss her, to stop the torrent of painful words. But he didn't. He simply held her and ached for the frightened child she had been.

"Finally I dragged one of the men toward the tent. He refused to come inside. Then he heard Mom laugh and babble and scream. He turned and ran away."

Cain murmured softly against Shelley's hair, rocking her very slowly, holding her. After a minute she took a ragged breath and kept on talking, wanting him to understand just how deep her need for a home went.

"Years later, I realized that the man had shown great courage even to walk as far as the door of our tent."

"He was Muslim?"

"A very devout one. In his culture the price of being alone in a tent with another man's woman was death. I didn't know that. All I knew was that I was terrified and he ran. Mom didn't recognize me. I was afraid to leave her, so I sat next to her, holding her hand and crying until the fever took me, too."

Shelley's fingers loosened their grip on his forearms. She leaned back heavily against his chest and pulled his warmth around her like a cape.

"Dad came back sometime before dawn. The man

hadn't just run away. He got on a camel and tracked Dad by moonlight. They nearly ran the animals to death getting back to us.''

With a long sigh, she rubbed her cheek against Cain's arm and finished the story.

''We all survived. But after I woke up, I made a vow. When I was an adult, I would never, ever go to a place where if I called for help, my only answer would be an alien jumble of syllables. I would find a place where people understood me, *and I would never leave*.''

Cain was afraid to speak, afraid to push Shelley any more on the subject of understanding and security and home.

''How did your mother feel about it?'' he asked finally.

She shrugged. ''After that she just made sure there was a native woman in camp if we had Muslim workers.''

''An English speaker?''

''Mom didn't care. Just so there was someone who could make our needs understood to the men in an emergency.''

''A practical woman, your mother,'' he said approvingly.

Shelley hesitated, turning his words over in her mind.

''I never thought of it that way,'' she said slowly. ''If I'd been Mom, I'd have climbed on the first camel and left.''

''Without your father?''

Sighing deeply, she acknowledged defeat.

"No. Mom loved Dad more than anything else on earth. She must have. God knows she put up with enough."

"I'll bet she loved the desert, too."

"You're right. The worst arguments she and Dad ever had came when she wanted to go exploring. Sometimes she and I would sneak away and ride out into the desert just to listen to the silence."

Cain's breath wedged at the thought of a woman and a child roaming alone through the vast, trackless deserts of the world.

"That was a damn fool thing to do," he said flatly. "No wonder your dad raised hell."

She laughed and shook her head.

"You sound just like Dad. Mom was no fool. She could track and ride like an Arab, and she taught me to do the same. I was safer in the desert with her than I was in a city taxi."

He thought it over and nodded. "I'm going to enjoy your parents. Where are they now?"

"Some godforsaken strip of coastal South America where it never rains for years at a time."

"The Atacama Desert."

"You've been there?"

"Once. Briefly. Next to the moon, it's the driest piece of real estate within reach of man."

"Or snake," she said. Then she whispered, "That's another first."

"What is?"

"I've never talked about the fever moon before. Not

even with Mom. But I've dreamed of it. I still do. The helplessness terrifies me.''

''Why? You have a home now, a place where people understand you. The dream shouldn't be able to touch you.''

Though Cain's voice was matter-of-fact, the words were like stones dropped into Shelley's calm certainty, sending questioning ripples through her.

Frightening ripples.

For a heart-stopping second, she was seven again, alone in the middle of a desert, holding the hand of a mother who didn't recognize her.

He felt the sudden stiffness of her body and cursed his too-quick tongue. The fact that his questions were reasonable only meant that she would fight them—and him—all the more strongly.

Before she could deny or argue or retreat, he tilted her face up to his and changed the subject in the oldest way of all.

''Have I mentioned that you taste even better than chocolate chip cookies?'' he asked as he bent down to her mouth.

She accepted his kiss with a relief that quickly became passion. The ripples that went through her now had nothing to do with uncertainty or fear. They came from the excitement of his tongue teasing hers. Turning slightly within his embrace, she let her head slide into the crook of his arm, giving herself to him, hiding nothing of her response.

To Cain, her sensual honesty was the most potent aphrodisiac imaginable. He kissed her with an honesty that was equally potent. The embrace deepened and lengthened until they were breathing raggedly, straining to be closer and then closer still, wanting nothing between them but the mingled heat of their bodies.

His hand moved from her face to her throat, caressing her skin, traveling slowly down her body. He hesitated, then stopped short of her breast.

She made a small sound and put her hand over his, urging him to touch her.

"It's all right," she said. "I won't freeze on you again."

Between the words she kissed his lips, his chin, the pulse beating in his throat.

"Truly," she whispered. "I know now that you won't make fun of my body. Touch me, Cain. I want you to touch me."

"I want that, too."

His voice was rough with the difficulty of restraining himself, yet his hand was very gentle on her breast. He teased the hidden, aching nipple.

"I want to do more than touch you, mink. I want to tear off your clothes and feel you all hot and—"

Abruptly he stopped talking. His hand trembled slightly as he removed it from her breast.

"I think," he began carefully.

"Good, one of us should," she said quickly. "It's your turn."

He laughed and ached to bury himself in her, warming himself body and soul.

"We'd better get out of here," he said. "I think we'll set fire to this dry brush."

"Maybe I'd better do the thinking. Spontaneous combustion is a myth."

"Want to bet?"

His hands shifted and he lifted her, arching her breasts toward his mouth. Her thin cotton blouse and delicate bra weren't much of a barrier. He felt the instant, hard rise of her nipple against his tongue.

"You win," she said. "Spontaneous . . ."

The word became a moan that was also his name. The sultry heat of his mouth, the exciting edges of his teeth, and the insistent rubbing of his tongue sent streamers of fire from her breasts to her thighs. She dug her fingers into his thick hair and twisted against him, wanting him until she could barely breathe.

Slowly common sense returned to Cain. Groaning, he tore his mouth from her breast.

"I don't want to bruise your soft body on this granite," he said. "But, God, I want you!"

With a hungry sound he kissed the wildly beating pulse in her throat. She tilted her head to the side, giving him as much of her skin as he wanted to take.

And he wanted it all.

"Which one of us is doing the thinking?" he asked.

Her only answer was fingernails biting sweetly into his scalp, asking him to bend down to her once more.

"I was afraid of that," he said.

With a swift movement he lifted her from her nest between his legs.

In the moonlight Shelley's face was half gold, half wild, and her blouse clung to the breast he had kissed, outlining the hungry ruby peak.

He couldn't stop himself from bending over her untouched breast. His tongue flicked out, his teeth nibbled, and then he held her close and hard against his mouth. He didn't let her go until the nipple was erect and the cotton clung wetly, outlining her arousal.

Finally he raised his head and admired her breasts through the nearly transparent cloth.

She watched his hungry silver eyes. "Is it your turn to think?"

"Yeah."

"So what are you thinking?"

"I'm a great believer in symmetry."

"Symmetry, huh? I've never heard it called that before. My turn now."

Smiling with anticipation, she reached for the buttons on his shirt.

He caught her hands, biting them not quite gently from her palms to her fingertips. Then he stood up, pulling her to her feet as he did.

"Enough teasing, mink. I'm going to have a hell of a time walking as it is."

"I wasn't teasing."

"I know. That's what's driving me crazy. Come on. I've got an idea."

"Symmetry?"

"Yeah. Cool water and a hot mink."

"Sounds like there's something missing."

"Don't worry, I'll come up with it."

Laughing, she took a step, winced, and rubbed her hip. Sitting on the rock had stiffened her muscles.

"Now that I'm thinking again," she said, "as a

chair or a bed, granite leaves something to be desired.''

''Comfort?''

''Everything,'' she retorted.

Despite the rapid beating of her heart and breaths that wanted to break into fragments, Shelley started picking up picnic items and stuffing them into the knapsack. Every movement spoke of her impatience to be off the rocky hillside and in Cain's arms again.

Too late, she realized that the flashlight was at the bottom of the sack. She fished for the light, muttering tribal curses that made him laugh out loud.

''Hand it over to the thinker,'' he said.

''The stinker?''

''Mink hunter, actually.''

''Doesn't rhyme.''

''Minker does.''

She tossed the knapsack in the direction of his laughter. He caught a strap and rummaged inside until he felt the cold metal cylinder of the flashlight. He pulled it out.

''I'd claim a kiss as my finder's fee,'' he said in a deep voice, ''but I don't trust myself.''

Her lips parted even as she closed her eyes and tried not to see his hungry, beautiful mouth.

''That makes two of us who can't be trusted,'' he said, wrapping one of her hands around the flashlight. ''Here. Turn something on besides me.''

''Promises, promises.''

''It's a fact. Want me to prove it? But I'm warning you, you'll be on the bottom.''

For a moment she was tempted. It showed clearly in the line of her body swaying toward him.

Then she turned around and began walking briskly toward her home.

the...

Chapter Seventeen

Shelley hardly needed the flashlight to find her way back home. The moon had shed its bronze veil. Now it was a flat, silver-white circle pouring light over the land.

A surprising amount of moonlight filtered through the chaparral. Only at the bottom of the ravine was it completely dark, as though night had run down the hillside and pooled thickly, gathering strength to overcome the moon.

The sound of the waterfall curled down the dry ravine toward them, whispering of coolness. Along with moonlight and the murmur of water, the scent of flowers sifted through the chaparral.

Cain watched the night with every sense alert, heightened. He loved the wild places of the earth. The place Shelley had chosen for her home was one of them.

But she doesn't see that, he thought. *It's all around her, a part of her, and she denies it.*

He hoped she wouldn't hurry to finish gilding his

house. He didn't know how long it would take her to realize that they were good for each other.

If she ever admitted it.

She will, he vowed. *She has to. She can't be so wild in my arms and still think of herself as tame.*

Trying to talk to her just makes it worse. But there are other ways to get past her fear. She forgets all about tame and civilized when we make love.

Anticipation spread through him, speeding his heartbeat.

As they approached the edge of Shelley's yard, the waterfall breathed moisture into the dry air. The pool rippled with silver invitations and silky promises.

"Hallelujah," he said. "If only all hikes ended like this."

With that he sank down on one of the long cushions that lined one edge of the pool. Laces raced through steel-rimmed holes as he untied his boots with flying fingers.

Before she had taken off more than her hiking shoes, he was shucking off his jeans and underwear. From the corner of his eye, he saw that she was unzipping her jeans. He began unbuttoning his own shirt. As soon as he was halfway done, he smiled wickedly. She was just stepping out of her jeans.

"Last one in does dishes for a week," he said.

Shelley took two steps and hit the pool in a long, running dive. When she surfaced, she flipped hair out of her eyes and grinned up at him.

"Thanks," she said cheerfully. "I hate doing dishes."

"Wait a minute. You're still wearing your blouse, among other things."

"All you said was 'last one in.' You didn't mention what I should or shouldn't be wearing."

He threw back his head and laughed, conceding the game to her.

Her smile widened in triumph. Blinking water from her eyes, she watched while he pulled off his shirt and tossed it aside. Moonlight ran down his body like a ghostly caress. He was naked, utterly male, and completely at ease with it.

Cain had always been attractive to her. Now he was compelling. Without warning, desire shot through her, hot satin petals unfolding deep inside her body like a flower blooming in darkness.

She didn't know how long she treaded water and simply looked at him. Finally she realized that he was sitting cross-legged on a cushion at the edge of the pool.

He was watching her. And he was smiling.

"How's the water?" he asked.

"Water?"

She tried to focus on words. All she could think about was the moment when he would slide into her, filling her.

"Water," he agreed. "You know, the stuff you're trying to walk on."

"Oh, that."

"Yeah."

"Water," she said, looking at him.

"This water, to be precise." He grinned. "Forget it. I'll find out for myself."

Though he was smiling at her, his arousal was vivid in the moonlight as he leaned forward far enough to dip his hand into the pool. The water and the air differed only in texture, not temperature, and the scent of flowers curled around him like a caress.

"Like you," he said. "Warm. Silky. Perfect."

Anticipation gathered heavily in him. Despite that, he didn't move to get into the water. He needed to know that she, too, found a sensual Eden waiting to be explored in the pool, the night, the lover who wanted her in so many ways.

"Beautiful night," he said, "beautiful water, beautiful woman."

She treaded water with easy grace.

"Why do I get the feeling that you're not paying any attention to me?" he asked.

"You couldn't be more wrong," she said huskily.

For a few moments longer she memorized everything about the man sitting by the pool, as naked and potent as the night itself.

"Cain . . ."

"What is it, love?"

The endearment set off another wave of warmth in her, another petal unfolding deep inside her.

"Don't you want to swim?" she asked wistfully.

"Do you?"

"Come in and find out."

He straightened his legs and slid from the warm air

into the equally warm pool, barely disturbing the surface of the water. Without warning, he pushed off from the side and knifed underwater toward her.

When his fingers wrapped around her ankles, she took a quick breath, expecting to receive a dunking for staring at him so openly. Instead, his strong hands kneaded up her calves to her knees, then to her thighs, then to the wisp of nylon circling her hips. His fingers burrowed beneath the thin fabric of her panties and swept them down the length of her legs.

He surfaced a few inches away from Shelley, dangling her bikini underwear from his finger. He tossed the scrap of cloth onto the flagstones.

"You're way overdressed for the occasion," he said.

"I was in a hurry. Something about dishes, I think."

"That was several minutes ago. You're still mostly dressed."

"Have you ever tried to undress while treading water?"

"Nope. I've got both feet on the ground."

"Lucky you," she retorted. "I'm in over my head."

"No problem. I'm big enough for both of us. Hang on."

He walked to where she was treading water. She braced herself on his shoulders.

"Better?" he asked.

"Much."

"Can you breathe okay?"

"Sure."

"I must be doing something wrong."

He reached beneath the water and pulled her close. Her breath caught when she felt his hard, blunt flesh pressing between her thighs. The thought of holding him inside her body again made her shiver in pure anticipation.

"Enough swimming," she said huskily. "Let's go to bed."

"I like waterbeds."

"I don't have one."

"That's what you think."

His mouth closed over hers and his hard tongue searched her mouth intimately. His hands spread beneath her hips, caressing and supporting her at the same time. He bit her neck lightly, repeatedly, hungrily, until she arched into the caresses, demanding something less teasing.

"I'd unbutton your blouse," he said, "but my hands are full right now."

Slowly he flexed his fingers, curling them into the luxurious curve of her hips. Then he shifted her until her legs were wrapped around his waist.

Her breath hesitated, broke, came out in a rush. Though he could have taken her, he didn't. But he wanted to. She could feel his arousal brushing against her own soft, hungry flesh.

"You're still wearing too much," he said. "Undress for me."

His voice was like his hands, low and urgent, caressing her. Then he saw the surprise on her face at his request. He smiled slowly.

"Another first?" he asked.

She nodded.

He sipped at her mouth with tiny kisses. His hands smoothed over the backs of her thighs and hips. There was both reassurance and arousal in his touch.

"It's all right," he whispered. "Let me see how beautiful you are wearing just moonlight."

A combination of sensual excitement and shyness made Shelley's hands tremble. Clumsily she found the first button on her blouse. She pulled at the smooth mother-of-pearl. It slid away from her fingertips. She captured and lost it again. Finally she managed to hang on to the slippery button long enough to worry it through the hole. The second button was even more difficult, for it was not only wet, it was completely underwater.

"I'm no good at this," she said unhappily.

"Does this help?"

He walked a few steps backward, bringing both of them closer to the shallow end of the pool. As he moved, her body lifted a few more inches out of the water.

Frowning, she struggled with the button. He watched her gleaming, smooth fingers. When he couldn't resist any longer, he bent and kissed her hands. It still wasn't enough. He captured each finger in turn, learning every surface with his tongue.

The feel of Cain's warm, slightly rough tongue sliding between her fingers dissolved Shelley. She dragged at breath but still couldn't get enough. Light-headed, she fought to free the button with one hand while he caressed and nibbled on the other.

His teeth closed on the pad of flesh at the base of her thumb. Desire shot through her.

"If you keep that up," she said in a shaky voice, "I'll be hours getting these damned buttons undone."

"There's no hurry. We have all night. Literally. The whole night."

His voice was deep and certain. He lifted his head and looked at her eyes. Slowly his hands explored the sleek, flexed muscles of her thighs. Fingertips traced first her hips, then the cleft between. From there he slid down to incredible softness, and lingered.

She gasped as he skimmed the sensitive folds of flesh. She tried to say something, but could only say his name. Her eyes were black with desire, gleaming in the moonlight. Though she seemed to shiver, cold was the last thing on her mind. She was burning.

His breath quickened with each rippling response of her body to his touch.

"Undress for me," he whispered.

Long fingers circled her, plucked delicately, and retreated. His eyes watched her, praising her, promising her pleasures she couldn't imagine.

She forgot to be embarrassed or shy. Her fingers grabbed buttons and pushed them through button-holes.

He watched her progress with frank hunger. His eyes were half closed, as sensual as his mouth. Waiting.

She didn't know what he was waiting for. She didn't even care. She just wanted to give it to him, whatever it was, and take from him what she needed more with every quickened beat of her heart.

Finally the last button was undone. The tails of the blouse floated out behind her hips. He kissed her collarbone and the hollow of her throat, the sleek curves of her neck and shoulders. As he caressed her, he eased farther backward into the shallow end of the pool.

With every slow step he took, less of her was concealed by the warm pool. He kissed each new inch of skin that was revealed. He didn't stop walking until the surface of the water lapped at her sensitive nipples, teasing them into dark, tight peaks.

His teeth closed over the lacy edge of her bra once, twice. Then he released her.

"Almost there," he said. "Just one more bit of clothing left."

Cain lifted his head and looked into her eyes, waiting, silently asking that she finish undressing herself for him.

Old fears turned in her, old taunts, old mockeries of her as a woman. The bra was her last bit of covering, of armor, of safety.

And he was asking her to take it off.

Not with words, which she could have countered. He was asking her in silence, knowing exactly what he was doing. He wanted her to give herself to him in a way that she had given herself to no man, to trust him not to ridicule her.

Stop being such a coward, Shelley told herself. *Cain won't belittle me. He saw all of me this afternoon and didn't complain about fried eggs and other small blessings.*

Yet she could no more stop herself from hesitating now than she could have prevented herself from freezing the first time he tried to touch her breast. Like fear, pain and humiliation were great teachers. Lessons learned from them bypassed the mind and went directly to the reflexes.

Clumsy again, her fingers moved to the clasp that lay between her breasts. Finally she managed to take hold of the small fastening and undo it. Wet lace clung to her breasts as though the clasp had never been released.

He looked into her eyes, waiting.

And then Shelley knew that she would have to remove the lace with her own hands, unmistakably offering herself to him.

Cain saw the instant of understanding in her eyes, felt it in the sudden, subtle tension of her body.

"I love you," he said softly, waiting.

With fingers that shook, she peeled away the lace. A moment later, she bared herself to him in an intimacy that went beyond simple nakedness.

Strong hands shifted, lifting her until her breasts were free of the pool's liquid embrace. Water ran silver down her body and back into the pool. A few drops remained behind, forming a fragile web of diamonds on each breast. Her nipples gleamed like miniature jeweled crowns.

He tried to speak, to tell her how much her trust meant to him and how beautiful she was, but he had no words that touched the depth of his emotion. With aching slowness he lifted her higher.

As the warm support of the water vanished, she braced herself against the muscles of his upper arms. Breath held, she watched while his mouth came closer to her. His lips parted. The tip of his tongue licked diamond drops from each dark crown.

She felt unspeakably beautiful as she watched him caress her. The velvet of his tongue touched her sensitive nipples; the pale flash of his teeth caught and held her for more darting, probing caresses. Then he drew her into the heat of his mouth until she closed her eyes and made tiny rippling sounds of pleasure.

Finally he lifted his head, but instead of lowering her back into the pool, he brought his mouth once more to her breasts. He tasted them with gently savage nips that made her arch against him, wanting more, needing more, demanding it.

He watched her through half-closed eyes, savoring the sight of her abandoned to him in the moonlight, radiant with the wildness he could draw out of her depths.

She laced her fingers into his hair and tugged, drawing his mouth to her breast again.

"Love me," she whispered.

He took her into his mouth and caressed her until both of them knew it wasn't enough. When neither of them could wait any longer, he took her to the side of the pool and set her on one of the cushions.

Her blouse clung wetly to her arms and back. Her legs dangled on either side of him, sheathed in warm water from her toes to her knees. She watched him with wondering eyes. Her hands rubbed slowly along his arms and shoulders. It was obvious that she enjoyed the feel of his water-slicked skin stretched over muscles drawn taut with desire.

"Soft enough?" he asked. "I want you to be comfortable."

She nodded, unable to speak.

"Good," he said. "I've waited long enough for dessert."

He turned his head to kiss her vulnerable inner thighs. Her breath caught and her body jerked. With a thick sound of anticipation, he gently sank his teeth into her smooth flesh. His mustache stroked against her skin as his hands parted her legs with lazy, caressing motions.

"Cain," she whispered. "You're right. We've waited long enough. Come up here with me."

She speared her fingers through his hair, tugging on his head, wanting to feel his mouth on hers, wanting him to climb out of the pool and lie with her on the cushion.

Instead, he slipped her legs over his shoulders. She made a startled sound and opened her mouth to ask a question. Her thoughts splintered into pure sensation as she felt his mouth caress her with an intimacy she had never imagined.

A firestorm of sensations raced through her, turning her blood to molten gold. She could say nothing, do nothing, not even breathe. Her body was wholly his.

The flower hidden within her bloomed in a hot satin rush. She moved helplessly against him, aware of nothing but his hungry mouth. Each movement of his lips and tongue and teeth told her that she was exquisite, perfect, a gift from mountain gods who understood what this man wanted in a woman.

Shivering, crying, she twisted between his hands, burning for him, burning him in turn. She didn't know the exact instant when he came out of the water and buried himself within her. She only knew that when the night came apart around her again and again, he was there to cling to, he was there to drink the cries from her lips; that he filled her to overflowing.

Then he crushed her to his own body. Ecstasy ripped through him, tearing him apart with a pleasure so intense it was like pain.

Gradually Shelley became aware of the moonlight and night around her. Cain's breath was warm against her cheek and the weight of him was unbelievably sweet on her body.

She ran her hands over his shoulders and back and hips in long, slow sweeps, wordlessly enjoying his warmth and resilience. She could hardly believe that he was real, that she was real, that a man and a woman could give each other such extraordinary pleasure.

His lips brushed over her closed eyes, her cheeks, her softly smiling mouth.

"What are you thinking?" he asked.

"This is a dream." She traced his flawless mouth with the warm tip of her tongue. "You're a dream. Don't wake me. I'll die if I wake up."

"I've already died."

He kissed her with a tenderness that made her throat ache with emotion. Then he moved as though to separate their bodies. She tightened reflexively, holding him within her.

"Don't go," she said huskily. "It feels so right to have you like this."

He whispered her name and his love against her lips. Then he gently began to leave her.

"I'm crushing you," he said when she moved again to keep him inside her. "You can barely breathe."

"I don't care."

"I do. I have so many things I want to share with you tonight, tomorrow, all the nights and days in the world."

He kissed her, then nibbled at the ticklish spot he had discovered behind her ear. He laughed softly when she squirmed against him.

"I can't do much with you if I mash you flat, now, can I?" he asked reasonably.

He nipped her stomach lightly, then circled her navel with his tongue.

"What did you have in mind doing with me?" she asked with a lazy smile.

He stood and pulled her up with him.

"Water sports, among other things," he said.

"Water sports?"

His agreement was muffled against her neck. He licked up the perspiration drying on her skin.

"Like swimming and water polo?" she asked.

"Like showers and baths and Jacuzzis and pools and lakes and rivers and oceans."

She looked at him and thought about a whole world of possibilities. It was a dazzling prospect.

"Didn't you know?" he whispered. "Mink are incredible in the water. Nothing else on earth like them."

"You're thinking of otters."

"No, I'm thinking of one very special mink."

Cain's eyes gleamed down at Shelley. He peeled off the wet blouse and bra that still clung to her.

"Come with me, mink. It's time you learned the fine art of back-scrubbing."

"And then what?"

He lifted her across his chest.

"Then I'll dry your hair and your soft, lovely body. I'll carry you to bed. And then I'll kiss every bit of you."

"When do I get to kiss every bit of you?"

His whole body tightened as he read the sensual curiosity and anticipation in her eyes. He bit her full lower lip with exquisite care.

"Any time, love. Any time at all."

Chapter Eighteen

⌒⌒ "Did you say that there aren't enough minerals for a full-scale mining operation?" Shelley asked, holding the phone tightly to her ear.

"Not in these conditions," Cain answered. "The Yukon is hell on equipment."

She strained to hear his voice. It sounded rough and thin, as though the words were being dragged through dry cereal. The rasping, echoing quality reminded her of every minute of the ten days he had been gone.

"But the Canadian government hasn't given up," he said. "They want me to expand the survey."

Her heart sank. "Now?"

"Next summer, when the snow melts and the sun never sets. Only a fool looks for ore in the dark under snowdrifts as big as a house."

Shelley waited for a burst of static to pass.

"That must be something to see," she said.

"The snow?"

"All that daylight. Hour after hour after hour, day after day after day."

"I'll be glad to see the sun, period. It looks . . ."

There was a crackle and a hiss. Then the connection cleared enough that she would pick up every word.

". . . winter. This storm came early and is staying late. We haven't had a window worth mentioning for days."

"Will you be able to fly out?"

"We've been trying. It's looking better, but I can't say when I'll get to L.A."

The hollowness that settled in Shelley's stomach at the thought of not seeing Cain tonight surprised her. She had been counting on it more than she knew.

"I'll wait for you at the airport," she said.

"It could be dawn before we get this bird back to L.A."

"I don't mind."

"I do. I don't want you sleeping in a chair at the airport because the weather closed in again up here."

"But—"

"I'll just go straight to my place and crash. I haven't slept much in the last ten days."

Neither had she, but she didn't want to say it aloud. He would ask what was wrong. Nothing was, except that she missed him until she couldn't sleep.

"I . . . hope you get out," she said.

"Are you all right?"

"Fine."

Neither of them believed it.

"Damn this weather!" he said savagely. "I love you. I should be with you right now. I miss talking to you, holding you, hearing you laugh."

She smiled even though he was thousands of miles away and couldn't see.

"I was looking forward to curling up with you," she said. "I wanted to tell you about the tangle Nudge and Squeeze and Billy got into and my new client who collects stationery from every high-class bordello in the world, and the sound of wind in the chaparral under the moon, and . . . lots of things." She laughed oddly. "I sound like an idiot."

"You sound like you've missed me."

She swallowed. "I have."

"My silver lining in an otherwise damned black cloud."

"You sound so tired," she said. "Will you be able to sleep on the plane?"

"Depends."

"On the weather?"

"On who wins the toss. Miller sprained his hand, so I'm backup pilot."

Static didn't conceal the sound of Shelley's sharp breath or the protest she made.

"Don't worry, mink. If I'm not up to flying, I'll ground myself. I didn't live this long by being a fool."

"Be careful," she said urgently. "I—I—miss you. So much."

"I love you."

The connection broke.

She looked at the dead phone and swallowed hard, fighting a wave of loneliness.

Why do I feel like crying? He'll be home soon. If not tonight, then tomorrow.

He'll come home to me.

Blindly she hung up. Feeling adrift, she paced through The Gilded Lily, her home away from home. Usually the shop reached out and folded her into a hundred small tasks and fifteen matters too urgent to be ignored.

Usually, but not today.

There was work all around her, but she didn't see it. She walked right past a stack of new catalogs that had just come in, their glossy pages brilliant with the lure of the rare and the original. File folders of new clients and works-in-progress lay scattered across her desk, needing the kind of attention only she could give.

She looked away from them. Her restless glance fell on a new shipment from Shanghai. Bits of packing material and dust still clung to porcelain and jade bowls. The elegant pieces begged to be cleaned, appreciated, and displayed.

When Shelley had placed the order six weeks ago, she had been impatient to have the bowls arrive, to feel their luminous curves and cool weight against her palms. Yet when the items had actually arrived this morning, it had been a struggle for her to work up enough interest to open the box, check that the contents agreed with the shipping manifest, that the manifest agreed with her original order, and that nothing was damaged.

Some other day I'll appreciate them.

Some other day I'll get excited about Mr. Masterson's unique ocean cottage and Ms. Luther's delight in shadow and texture.

Some other day, but not today.
Today all I want is Cain.

Absently she ran her hands over the soothing, sensual lines of the sculpture called "I Love You, Too." She tried to list all the things that she had to do, but could think only of the man who wasn't there.

What it would be like to canoe down rivers and across lakes that had no name, to chip rock samples from river cliffs that had never known the touch of man, to smell the fragrance of cedar and see the mysterious aurora whisper across the face of an unknown sky?

Will he find another landscape of the soul in the Yukon? Will he bring it back to me with words, share it in the peace of his voice and the clear depths of his eyes?

Does he miss me one-tenth as much as I miss him? Will he stay with me this time, or will he go as he so often has gone in the last six weeks? A day here and two days there. A week. An eternity of loneliness.

Traveling man.

After a time Shelley loosened her grip on the sculpture's smooth body.

He'll come back. He said he would.

In the past six weeks she had learned that Cain Remington was an honorable man. A man who kept his promises.

He hadn't pressed her to marry him, to say that she loved him, despite the fact that she was certain he wanted to. Instead, he had simply, thoroughly, showed her that she could trust and enjoy him.

They went to auctions together, sat together on the couch, and looked through catalog after catalog. They laughed at some of the bizarre things people bought and put in their houses. They discussed what might or might not fit into his home.

Yet whenever it came to the point of actually deciding on something to go into Cain's penthouse, he changed the subject or distracted her with a touch or a smile or another story out of his past, another landscape of his soul.

She hadn't pressed him for cooperation on remaking his home. She was as aware of his deadline for her answer as he was.

And she was afraid.

You'll gild my home and then we'll talk again.

For the first time in her life, Shelley didn't want to complete a job.

When the streams of workmen and plaster dust descended on his condo, Cain had packed his suitcases and appeared on her doorstep. She had let him in with a smile and a hug. She loved the idea of having Cain living in her home.

Without a word she had bypassed the guest room and led him to her own bed. There, beneath the silver radiance pouring through the skylight, they discovered many paths to fulfillment. There they fell asleep with their bodies intertwined. There they awoke in a warm tangle of soft kisses and softer words.

The contractor was finished with Cain's penthouse now. For weeks it had been ready for her to add her special touches. Painted and tiled, carpeted and polished, the basic lily waited to be gilded.

Shelley had moved heaven and earth, performed minor miracles and threatened loss of business, paid special handling fees and outright bribes; and the furniture Cain wanted had been delivered last week.

Each piece was unique, made to her exact specifications of size and color, fabric and wood. Forest green and tawny brown, sand and teak, rare accents of teal blue like the hidden flash of a wilderness lake; shades and tones of individual colors overlapped from room to room, giving the effect of walking through a civilized but not domesticated landscape.

I should have finished the penthouse weeks ago.

But each time she had tried to pin down exactly what her very special client wanted in the way of gilding, he had phone calls to make or Billy was coming over or Cain was too tired to look at catalogs or he was too hungry or sleepy or big or small or not there at all.

Shelley knew why he was ducking the small decisions.

She was ducking the big one.

In all the ecstasy, in all the peace, in all the laughter and easy silence, she had said nothing about marrying him, living with him, loving him. She had simply taken the joy as it came and tried not to let his absence rip holes in her life.

Yet it did.

"Shelley?" Brian asked.

Startled, she looked around. "Yes?"

"What's going on?"

"Nothing. Why?"

"I've been calling you from the back room, but you didn't answer. I thought you'd gone home."

The combination of irritation and concern in his voice told her she had been stroking "I Love You, Too" for a long time, lost in her own thoughts, her own fears. Abruptly she stepped away from the sculpture's silent, seductive promise.

"Sorry," she said briskly. "I was thinking about one of the jobs I'm working on."

"Remington's house?"

She hesitated, knowing that Brian resented Cain. "Yes."

"Any problems?"

"No, not at all. Why?"

His shrewd blue eyes narrowed. "It's unusual for you to take so long on a project."

"Cain is an unusual man."

"Shelley Wilde, Queen of Understatement." Brian's tone was mocking, but his smile was almost sympathetic.

"What does that mean?"

"Any man who can have you walking around in a daze is a hell of a lot more than 'unusual.' He's a candidate for a full page in the *Guinness Book of World Records*. If Remington gave a postdoctoral seminar on how to screw a woman senseless, I'd be the first to sign up."

"It wouldn't work," she said tightly.

"Not to worry." He held up his hands in mock

surrender. "I gave up on seducing you a long time ago. I'll stick to women who appreciate handsome, civilized blonds who are dynamite in bed. Did Mrs. Kaolin's jade come in with that last shipment?"

"Speaking of women who appreciate handsome, et cetera," Shelley said sardonically.

"You should try it."

She gave him a long, level look, seeing him as a man for the first time in years. His smile reminded her of a newly fallen angel—white, shining, and already more than a bit corrupt. He was measuring her with eyes that had known a thousand women and would know a thousand more.

"I thought you gave up," she said.

"Maybe I changed my mind."

"I didn't."

"Something sure as hell changed. You're different, babe. I get the feeling you've learned a lot about screwing since Remington got in your pants."

"Start looking for another business partner."

Brian looked surprised. "Hey, all I meant was—"

"—since I'm Cain's lover, I must be available to every other man who comes along," she finished coolly. "I understand how a man like you would think that. For you, women are toilet paper. The color and texture might change from roll to roll, but otherwise it's business as usual."

"None of my women have complained."

"Toilet paper isn't noted for its wit. The white jade belongs to Mrs. Kaolin."

"And you belong to Cain Remington. No problem. Message received. What about the woodcuts for Mr. Ming?"

"They haven't arrived yet," she said through her teeth.

"I'll check on them. Take the rest of the day off, partner. You look like you need it."

Whistling, Brian headed toward his office.

She looked around the room as though she was a stranger who had wandered in off the street. She felt odd, dislocated, almost dizzy. Her familiar world was slowly, relentlessly tilting on its end and she was sliding into the unknown.

How had Cain put it? *Stranger in a strange land.*

The sculpture beckoned irresistibly. She took a deep breath and hung on to the wood with both hands. The cool, smooth curves calmed her.

After a time Shelley knew what she had to do.

"If Billy phones," she called to Brian, "tell him Cain's flight was delayed by a storm. We'll pick Billy up tomorrow after school."

Brian stuck his head out of his office. "Thanks for reminding me. That's why I was looking for you."

"Billy?"

"Yeah. He called about fifteen minutes ago. His dad arrived today. Something about getting married here rather than in France, and he'd pick up Squeeze as soon as he could. Does that make sense?"

She smiled, hearing Billy's delight in the garbled message.

"It makes perfect sense. He's going to have a family. A real family."

Once again she looked around the room, feeling like an outsider. She took a deep breath and tried to shake off the uprooted feeling.

"Do you need the small van today?" she asked, her voice strained.

"No." Brian took a step toward her. "All kidding aside, Shelley, are you all right?"

"I'm fine. I'll bring the van back tomorrow."

"Anything I can do?"

She looked at the sculpture. "Yes. Carry this out to the van for me."

"Where are you going?"

"I have a renegade lily to gild."

"Remington, huh? About time."

But that was the only comment Brian made while he carried "I Love You, Too" out to The Gilded Lily's delivery van.

Shelley secured the sculpture in one of the van's many padded compartments. Then she got in and drove home, trying not to think about what would come after she finished Cain's penthouse.

What will I do? I can't live with a traveling man and I'm afraid I can't live without him.

She had only one hope. She clung to it more tightly than she did the steering wheel.

Once Cain sees how wonderful I've made his home, how warm and inviting and just plain perfect it is for him, he'll see that he doesn't have to roam. Everything he needs is here.

Holding onto the wheel until her hands ached, she said the same words over and over to herself, desperately wanting to believe they were true.

Desperately afraid they weren't.

Two distant smudges against the mountains caught her attention.

Smog? she thought, distracted.

A quick look convinced her that the dark streaks didn't come from smog. The autumn day was hot, brilliant, swept clean by the powerful, seasonal Santa Ana winds. The air was oven-dry and crackling with static electricity.

Fire, she decided. *At least two.*

With the critical eye of someone who has weathered many fire seasons, Shelley measured the distant smoke plumes. One was nearly white, which meant that firemen were already at work pouring water on flames, turning midnight smoke to a pearl gray. The second plume was still dark and untouched, a dry, black thunderhead boiling toward the mountains.

She kept an eye on the dark column after she got on the freeway. By the time she turned off onto surface streets again, the smoke was showing billows of white and gray, thinning before her eyes. Someone had reached the fire.

Sirens blared and honked behind her. She pulled over to the curb as a fire truck raced by. Two more trucks followed quickly. A fourth truck lagged.

She waited patiently for the heavy truck to catch up to the others. As the owner of a hillside home surrounded by chaparral, she had nothing but approval for the city, county, and state firefighters who kept the lid on southern California's easily burned wild lands.

Ninety-nine percent of the time, the firemen managed to do the impossible, holding the fires down to a handful of acres. The remaining one percent was a preview of hell. Flames one hundred feet high, smoke that blackened the day, incandescent embers that rode the back of the hot wind and spread burning seeds of destruction.

That was when the Sierra Deuces came, heavy-bellied planes flown by certified madmen. The aircraft swooped down through a blinding chaos of smoke, flying low enough for the pilots to see the shape of the land and the fire that was consuming it. Then, when they were over the worst of the flames and the updraft from the fire raged around them, shaking everything, the planes opened their bellies and dropped maroon veils of fire retardant.

On the flanks of the fire below the planes, hundreds of men fought with shovels, brushhooks, bulldozers, and curses to stem the flaming tide. Eventually the firefighters won and the skies were swept clean again by the very wind that had fed the flames.

Silently Shelley prayed that this wouldn't be the fire that got away, burning the land down to bedrock, leaving nothing behind but black scars.

It looks like they're getting a handle on it, she told herself, staring through the hot windshield. *They'll hold it down to a few hundred acres. Unless the wind shifts . . .*

A fifth fire truck blasted down the boulevard. No

more equipment followed. Gradually cars pulled back into the traffic lanes, resuming whatever business had brought them out into the hot day in the first place.

Shelley took her place in the shifting steel river of cars. Traffic thinned to nothing as she turned off on the narrow, two-lane road that snaked through the hills toward her home. No smoke stained the sky here. There was nothing but pouring sunlight, dry chaparral whispering, and shadows rippling and changing, made and remade by the restless desert wind.

As soon as she parked the van and walked up to the front door with the key in her hand, Nudge appeared out of the shrubbery. She yeowed softly, rubbing her supple body against the back of Shelley's knees with unusual vigor.

"Take it easy. You're going to knock me off my feet."

But even as she spoke, she bent down and rubbed the cat's broad head. Nudge leaned into the touch. When she stroked down the muscular feline back, Nudge purred and arched against the stroking hand.

"Cain's right. Just like a woman." Then her breath caught. "Or a man."

Memories of his response to her touch poured through her—his body tightening until every inch of him was hard, gleaming with heat, and then his deep groan when she explored him with her curious, hungry mouth.

The door key dropped to the flagstones with a small, ringing sound.

"Shelley," she muttered to herself, "if you keep

thinking about Cain like that, you're going to drop something that's a lot more valuable—and breakable—than a house key.''

The interior of the house was cool but not cold. Her air-conditioning was the kind that came from open windows and a built-in system of air recirculation.

She descended the stairs to her bedroom in a controlled rush, stripping off clothes as she went, organizing what had to be done in her mind. First on the list was some comfortable clothes. Then came the packing boxes in the garage.

''The gilding is going to begin, Cain Remington, with or without your help. I just hope I choose the things you want.'' She took a deep breath. ''No, I *know* I'll choose what you want. We like a lot of the same things.''

With a feeling of cheerfulness that bordered on insanity, she changed clothes, bounded up the stairs, and began gathering boxes from the garage. She piled them in the upper-level living room, along with huge plastic bags full of packing material.

''All right. Now it begins.''

She went to a large storage closet that was concealed behind red cedar identical to the rich paneling she had chosen for Cain's home. Inside the closet was everything she had collected for use in her own home. With each season, she changed some of the living room displays, refreshing her eye and keeping her appreciation of the art sharp and new.

Since the day she had agreed to gild the penthouse, she had begun gathering things from her own home, selecting the art that had pleased him. One such piece was the framed Landsat photo of the Sahara that had been in her shop; an identical photo had hung downstairs in her home. Now it was in the closet, waiting to be taken to a new home.

A Japanese screen painted with a flying crane and a spray of bamboo came from her living room. The piece was one of her favorites; it raised simplicity from a virtue to an art of unsurpassed serenity. Cain had looked at it for a long time. When he had finally turned away from it, he had seemed refreshed.

"Definitely the screen," she said under her breath. "And the geese, symbol of the north and freedom."

The geese were modern decoys done by a master carver from Maine. Part of her winter art, the birds were graceful, elegant, both lifelike and an abstraction of life. The tension between what was real and what wasn't gave the birds enormous power.

Working quickly, she pulled out a tawny piece of eighteenth-century Peking glass and set it next to the geese. Her next choice was a Korean Kiri chest for Cain's bedroom, then two seventeenth-century Chinese fur storage chests.

"Yes, I'll need those," she said, scanning the closet shelves, "and that, and this, and . . ."

The shelves rapidly emptied. Soon a flawless, deadly samurai sword lay next to the Peking glass. It was followed by an intricately carved Aztec weapon called an atlatl.

"Now . . . yes, the rugs. And the mask. And

the . . ." She laughed and shook her head. "Why don't I just admit it and empty the closet?"

Navajo rugs, whalebone masks, cedar carvings of bear and salmon and killer whales. A brass telescope that was more than a hundred years old. A four-hundred-year-old copy of a Tang Chinese horse that was so alive she was tempted to tether it to a lamp so it wouldn't prance away.

When the closet shelves were bare, she went to a special cupboard that held framed oils and watercolors. Among the oils were California landscapes done by turn-of-the-century American Impressionists. The paintings' sensual colors and textures beckoned like a refreshing breeze.

There was also a series of waterbirds and birds of prey done by a Native American artist trained in France. The combination of a hunter's appreciation for the life-and-death reality of the birds, plus an abstract artist's eye for fluid lines, summed up the birds in a few strokes and muted colors.

Then she added a wild card, a Charles Maurin pastel of a dancer. Surrounded by her rippling, floating costume, the woman was like a butterfly with endless, filmy wings, an innocent temptress poised amid shifting colors.

Even after the closet was empty, Shelley still wasn't satisfied. She went to the various display cases in her living room, removing the pieces that had most appealed to Cain. The fact that they were also her favorites didn't stop her.

He had been drawn to them. They would be his.

Carefully she removed the Balinese dancer, the ivory chessmen, and the Eskimo woman. Other, smaller things followed. Soon the display cases were as bare as the closet.

"No big deal," she said to Nudge, who was warily circling the items laid out on the floor. "I can fill in with stuff from the shop."

If I need to.

But that was something she wouldn't say aloud, even to herself.

Gently she lifted out the last item in the display case. It was the bemused opal jaguar with a ruby butterfly resting on its golden claw.

"I'd love to hang St. George and the dragon over Cain's bed," she said to the cat, "but Billy has it for now."

Nudge ignored her mistress in favor of investigating the jaguar.

"The universe of stars! Of course. It will be perfect."

She raced downstairs to her office, where the dragon had once hung. It had been replaced by the art she had found while shopping for Billy's birthday.

For a few moments she stood in front of the luminous universe of the painting, watching the swirling stars and enigmatic faces, worlds without end, mysterious landscapes unknown to man. The painting haunted her. It hinted at something about time and space and the tiny, stubborn condensations of energy known as life.

Cain had been drawn to the painting as surely as he had been captured by the jaguar and the butterfly. After he had looked at it for a long, quiet time, he had turned to her.

What do you see there, Shelley?

I don't know. I only know that once I saw it, I had to have it.

He had smiled suddenly, a take-no-prisoners kind of smile, but he hadn't said another word.

"What did you see, Cain?" she whispered in the empty room. "What is there in this ageless, limitless sky that made you smile at me like a man who had just been given everything he ever wanted?"

There was no answer. There wouldn't be until he came back home.

To her.

Chapter Nineteen

⌒⌒⌒ It was midnight before Shelley finished gilding the penthouse. Soaring and at peace, excited and serene, content and on the edge of tears, she walked alone through the rooms. Everywhere she looked, she saw the proof of what she felt for Cain. In every color and texture, in every unique piece of furniture, in every carefully chosen piece of art.

There's nothing more I can do. His home is as perfect as I can make it.

Come home, love. Come and stay with me.

Torn between hope and fear, tears running down her face, she stood in the middle of the home she had created. She didn't hear the front door open and close, didn't hear Cain's sudden intake of breath when he saw her.

Then his arms closed around her and she hung on to him until she ached. The rasp of his beard stubble across her cheek felt more wonderful to her than a silky caress, and the heavy male smell of wool and sweat was sweeter to her than the fragrance of flowers blooming beneath the moon.

"I m-made a home for you," she whispered.

"I know. When I hold you in my arms, I'm home."

His voice was as uneven as hers. For a time they simply held each other. Then, slowly, her arms loosened and she smiled up at him.

"Come with me. I want to show you your home."

"I'm looking at it."

But he wasn't. He was looking at her.

A shaft of disappointment went through Shelley. She wanted to share with him the home she had created, to give him the gift she had thought so long and so deeply about.

Doesn't he care about his home even a little bit? she wondered in despair.

Just as she opened her mouth to protest his lack of interest, she looked at Cain—really looked at him. His face was streaked with dirt, his eyes were puffy and ringed by darkness, and his skin was drawn. Even his lips were pale, almost bloodless. Instantly she forgot about the gilded home and her disappointment.

"Oh, love," she whispered. "What did you do to yourself?"

He smiled crookedly. "I worked triple shifts."

"Why?"

"To get back to you."

"I—you didn't have to."

"I wanted to. My only regret is that I'm too tired to do much about anything right now. I flew the first leg of the trip and then stayed awake on the second to make sure Miller didn't need a hand.''

Gently Cain kissed her lips and ran his fingers lightly over her face, her shoulders, her arms, as though trying to convince himself he wasn't dreaming. She stood on tiptoe and returned the undemanding kiss.

"You're home," she said. "That's all that matters. Come on. I'm going to scrub your back and tuck you into bed.''

"Sleep with me. And that's all it will be. Sleep. I'm beat.''

"I like sleeping with you.''

"Even when that's all we're going to do?''

"Of course. Being with you is . . . good.''

His laced his hand through hers and followed her down the hall. Paintings called silently to him, a handful of fluid lines evoking birds in flight, birds courting, birds raising their young, a bird of prey soaring in a transparent sky.

"The falcon," he said, slowing.

Her face lit with a smile. "Do you like it?''

"I love it," he said, smothering a yawn. "But it keeps blurring.''

"That's because you're asleep on your feet.''

When she urged him along, he followed her, only to be distracted again by an inviting room opening off the hall.

"Those colors," he said, yawning. "They remind me of a northern forest. And isn't that a Haida carving on the wall?''

"Yes." She tugged on his hand. "Come on. I'll give you a full tour in the morning."

Adrenaline went through Cain like cold lightning, focusing him in spite of his exhaustion.

"You're finished?" he said sharply.

"Yes. You can see it all tomorrow. Now it's more important for you to sleep."

"Shelley? Love?"

She smiled up at him and saw his hunger to know her answer. She also saw the sheer tiredness beneath his need. He had worked around the clock to get back to her.

"It's not gilded until you have the tour," she said. "That will be tomorrow. You're too tired for anything now except sleeping."

For a few moments he fought the truth of her words. Then he gave in to the exhaustion rising in him like a black tide.

"Damn it," he said roughly.

"It's all right. You're home. All the rest can wait. Truly."

He looked at her, trying to read her answer in her eyes. He saw concern and caring and a need to take care of him.

It's all right. You're home.

And he was, for Shelley was there.

Sighing, Cain kissed her fingertips and allowed her to lead him down the hall. She took him straight through the master bedroom, not giving him time to look around. There was no point in stopping to look around. He wouldn't have been able to appreciate anything. His eyes were heavy-lidded, nearly closed. He was a breath away from being asleep on his feet.

While she started filling the huge bathtub, he fell asleep in a dressing room chair. He awoke long enough to help her get his clothes off and slide into the hot, swirling water. She pressed a button and air bubbles thundered through the water.

"God, that feels good," he said. "I'm sore all over."

"Don't fall asleep until I get in."

He smiled slightly. "Don't worry. I won't drown."

Quickly she undressed and got into the water, shampoo in hand. She washed his hair first, laughing when he went under the surface to rinse and blew a mighty stream of bubbles. Then she bathed him with shampoo for bath soap and her hands for a washrag.

And she smiled at him, enjoying being with him, touching him with no thought of being touched in return.

Her pleasure in him was like sunrise for Cain. He watched her face while she washed days of work away from his body. He cupped her breasts in his hands, caressing her simply because she was beautiful to him and he enjoyed that beauty.

She bent, kissed his hands, then resumed washing him, savoring the solid reality of his flesh sliding beneath her fingers. Eyes closed, he sighed and gave himself to the dreamy, undemanding pleasure of her touch.

"Wake up," she said finally.

"Mmmmm?"

"Time to go to bed."

Yawning hugely, he pulled himself out of the hot water. He cursed under his breath when his back and chest muscles reminded him of mossy rocks and a hard dunking in an icy stream.

"Are you all right?" Shelley asked, seeing him hesitate.

"Just stiff. I took a header in a creek."

Her hands and eyes went over him, but found no injury. She dried him with a towel bigger than she was and not nearly so soft. He yawned repeatedly, apologizing; then he yawned again and she laughed softly.

"Face down, sleepyhead."

She aimed him toward the waiting bed and gave him a slight push. Then she wrapped herself in another towel and went to the side of the bed. Sleepily he put an arm around her hips and tugged her close.

"Not yet," she said. "Go to sleep while I rub the stiffness out of your back."

"What about you?"

"I'll be right beside you when you wake up."

With a deep sigh Cain relaxed. Shelley took off her towel, warmed fragrant oil in her hands, and knelt next to him on the bed. When her hands began to knead his body, he groaned contentedly. Smiling, she leaned into her work, massaging from his hips to his shoulders and down to his hands. She kissed the fingertips, the palm of each hand, and smiled when his fingers curled into his palms as though to hold the warmth she had given him.

She worked over him in silence, enjoying just

having him near. She went to his feet and massaged upward gently, firmly, until the long muscles of his body were finally supple again.

"Are you asleep?" she whispered.

His answer was lost in the mattress.

"Roll over, lazy man. The other side of you has muscles, too."

"It's stiff, too."

He rolled over.

Her breath caught. "I thought you were too tired."

"I am."

"You could have fooled me."

Laughing, she slid out of his grasp and resumed the massage. She went from his feet to his calves and then on to the muscular resilience of his thighs.

He groaned when her fingers feathered through the wedge of hair on his abdomen, teasing him by not touching him in the way he needed to be touched.

"Mink?"

"You're too tired. See?"

With a lithe movement she evaded his searching hands.

"Close your eyes," she said gently. "You'll be asleep in no time."

"Shel—"

The rest of her name was lost in a thick sound as she bent over him, her breasts brushing against his aroused flesh as she massaged him from his hips to the pulse beating heavily in his neck. She kissed his neck, savoring the race of his heart.

"Close your eyes," she said. "No, don't move. You don't have to do anything at all."

Her lips rubbed over the curly brown hair hiding the muscles of his chest. His breath came in hard and deep.

"Let me take care of you," she whispered. "Let me show you how glad I am to have you home."

He looked at her for the space of several heartbeats. Then he sighed and closed his eyes, giving himself to her. Gently her mouth moved over one dark nipple and then the other, until both tightened into tiny, hard buttons.

Long fingers searched through Shelley's hair, caressing her scalp even as her teeth closed on a sensitive male nub. She tugged and sucked gently, enjoying the shiver of response that went through his strong body. Her hands searched over his chest, moving slowly, sensitizing every bit of his skin. Her breasts brushed against him repeatedly, intimately, caresses that made fire shimmer through her as certainly as it did through him.

Softly, inevitably, she slid down his body until her cheek was against his hard abdomen and her hair was a dark, silky fire burning between his legs. She moved her head languidly against him, watching pleasure course through the man she loved. With a shiver of desire, she kissed his hot skin, caressing him, cherishing him with lips and tongue and teeth.

Cain groaned thickly and moved against her with a slow sensuality that belied the urgency he felt. When he could take no more, he called her name in a low voice, telling her what her loving touch was doing to him, how much he wanted her, the need to be sheathed in her liquid fire.

His words were as soft and hot and intimate as her tongue against his naked flesh, words caressing her until the satin flower hidden within her body bloomed and she moaned, needing him. With dreamlike slowness she settled over him, wanting to cherish and remember each instant of their joining. Smiling, eyes half closed, she took him wholly into herself, completing both of them.

She bent to kiss him, and the kiss was as hot and as slow and as deep as their joining. She glided over him in rhythms of love and loving. The long, sliding caress of her body made him moan thickly. She moved again and then again, slowly, deeply, using every bit of their mutual hunger, making tongues of fire lick through their bodies.

Tension gathered in him, sensual heat and need growing, taking his body, giving it to her. At the last instant he fought to control himself, holding back, waiting for her.

She knew. She moved slowly, holding him tight and deep. Then she bent down and whispered against his lips.

"I love you, Cain."

The words stripped him of control. With a thick sound, he gave himself entirely to her soft, sliding heat.

She felt ecstasy explode through him in exquisite

pulses. For a timeless instant she savored his release, but his pleasure undid her as surely as her statement of love had unraveled him. Moaning, moving slowly, she gave herself to ecstasy, to him, coming apart around him in a shower of satin fire.

His arms held her for long, quiet minutes, supporting her as she lay limply on his chest. When their bodies were again their own, he held her against him. With one long arm he dragged a quilt over both of them. Sleep pulled at him, but he fought against it.

"Tell me again," he said.

"I love you."

He gave a long, shuddering sigh. "Thank God. I was . . . afraid you wouldn't . . . let . . ."

Cain's voice faded into sleep.

Smiling, she kissed his chin and burrowed into his warmth. Soon she was as deeply asleep as he was.

Shelley awoke to the feel of Cain's hands stroking her body, and his mouth pulling lovingly on her breast, taking her from sleep into sensuality. With a soft sound she shifted closer to him, the hidden flower blooming, her body ready for him in the hot, endless instant of waking.

When his long fingers caressed her and discovered her readiness, he settled between her legs. Hands cradling her face, he moved slowly, pressing against her, touching her intimately without taking her. Eyes still closed, she sought him blindly, aching for him until she cried out.

"Was I dreaming?" he asked.

His teeth closed on her nipple with exquisite restraint, making her arch wildly beneath him. The sultry moisture of her response made his body tighten violently; but even more than her satin heat, he wanted her trust, her love, her life.

"Tell me I wasn't dreaming."

His name was torn from her as fire took her. She felt him slide against her, into her, and then came a slow withdrawal that made her want to scream in protest.

"Do you love me?" he asked.

Her eyes opened, dark and hungry. "Yes."

Still he waited, poised at the point of taking her, his eyes the hot gray of summer rain. He felt her shift slightly beneath him, felt her legs part even more, felt her thighs move slowly over his, asking for him.

"Tell me," he said, his voice rough with passion and restraint. "I have to hear it. I have to know that I wasn't dreaming."

"I love you, Cain."

Emotion transformed his face. She felt the ripple that went through his powerful body like a shock wave. He entered her in a single movement, watching her as she whispered his name and her love again and again, words and movements matching, overlapping, until there were no more words, just cries of ecstasy and completion.

When both of them could breathe again, he nuzzled her hair, her ear, the pulse still racing in her neck.

"I love you, Shelley. I've waited all my life for you."

She smiled, turned to catch his lips with her own, and murmured her love against his beautiful mouth.

"We'll be married as soon as we can," he said, sipping at her lips, her tongue, the soft lobe of her ear. "Three days, right? Isn't that what California requires?"

Before she could answer, he took her mouth in a deep kiss. It was a long time before he lifted his head.

"Would you mind honeymooning in Chile?" he asked.

She caught his lower lip between her teeth and gently savaged it.

"Santiago?" she asked.

"For a few days. Then the Atacama."

"That's where my parents are. Are we going there to see them?"

"It's a big desert, but we'll find them."

"I'd enjoy that, but . . ."

"What?"

"It isn't necessary. We can wait for a few weeks. They'll be in L.A. for Thanksgiving."

"But we won't. Like I said, the Atacama is a big desert. It will take months to do even a cursory mineral survey."

Coolness washed over Shelley. She felt as though her skin was too small, drawing her flesh against cold bones.

"What do you mean?" she asked carefully.

"Basic Resources won a survey bid for the Atacama."

"Oh."

He smoothed his lips over one mink-brown eyebrow, then traced the eyebrow again with the tip of his tongue.

"It's one of the few places in the world I haven't really explored," he said. "I was going to send someone else. Now I won't have to. You love me and you love the desert. Together, we'll listen to the silence, drink wine at sunset, and make love in the cool hours before dawn when the stars are so close they're like a wave breaking over us."

Her body was stiff. She couldn't move, couldn't breathe for the pain slicing through her.

I just made a home for him and all he can think about is leaving it.

"What is it?" he asked. "What's wrong?"

Before she could gather herself enough to answer, he smiled and shifted onto his side, pulling her over with him.

"I'm crushing you again. Sorry," he said, kissing her gently. "You're such a wild thing when we make love. I keep forgetting that you aren't nearly as strong as I am."

Numbly she tried to think, to speak, to understand what had gone so terribly wrong.

His big hand tucked her head against his shoulder.

"By the time we're tired of the Atacama," he said, "the Yukon will be opening again. It's a special place. Few trails and fewer roads, a forest like the sea, green and endless. There are lakes and rivers with no names because no man has been there long enough to—''

''What about home?'' she interrupted, her voice bleak.

Surprised, he drew back until he could see her tightly drawn face. ''When you're in my arms, that's home for me.''

''What about my home?'' she asked.

''We'll be in L.A. a lot of the time. If you want, I'll sell this place and we'll live in yours.''

''This place?''

Abruptly she sat up, throwing off his arms.

''This *place*,'' she said harshly, ''is the home I made for you! But you don't care about that, do you? You can't even be bothered to look at it!''

Pure rage echoed through her words, a rage as great as her passion had been.

Cain saw it. And he was afraid he understood its source.

''Mink?''

''How stupid can one woman be?'' she asked the ceiling. ''I made a home for a traveling man! I fell in love with a man who doesn't want one goddamned thing but whatever is over the curve of the earth!''

''I want you, Shelley. I love you.''

She simply shook her head.

''But you don't love me, do you?'' he asked. ''Not really.''

''That's not true! I love—''

''No,'' he interrupted fiercely. ''You love the idea of home, not me!''

Her eyes opened. They were wide and dry and furious.

His eyes were just as angry. More.

"When will you figure out that we were born to love each other, Shelley Wilde? Or is it just that I was born to love you?"

His eyes closed. Suddenly he looked older than he was, as hard as the lands he had lived in. When he opened his eyes, they were the color of winter.

"You don't trust me enough to admit that you're hungry for new horizons," he said. "Why? What have I done?"

"You don't understand," she said.

He waited, hoping he had missed something, that he was wrong.

"You simply don't understand . . ." she said in an agonized whisper.

It was all she could say. It was the only truth she knew.

"Oh, but I do understand," he said.

With savage restraint he shot out of bed and began yanking on his clothes, talking all the while, words as sharp as knives.

"I'm the one with frightening insight, remember?" he asked. "Well, this is my insight. You don't even love me enough to give up your precious *home* part of the time and travel with me. You don't love me one damn bit."

The pain and bitterness in Cain's voice broke over Shelley, stunning her. He was as hurt and outraged as she was.

"I do love you!" she said.

"Like hell you do. The only thing you love is the idea of a home. You haven't gotten over your childhood. You still don't know the difference between the appearance of a home and the reality."

Fully dressed, he stood in the center of the master bedroom, truly seeing it for the first time—the chests and rugs, the photo of earth-rise over the curve of the moon, the Sahara tiger-striped by sun and wind, the ancient brass telescope, and the swirling universe of stars.

"Nice," he said simply, meaning it. "Very, very nice. And when I leave, it will be as empty as your words of love."

Shelley's breath caught.

"But you don't know that, do you?" he continued. "You don't even admit that there's a whole world out there and the only home that matters is love. Well, I know what's out there, and I'm damned if I'll hide in here with you, playing house and waiting for you to grow up."

He opened the bedroom door, stopped, and looked back at her with eyes as bleak as his words.

"Send the bill to Basic Resources, *homebody*. This traveling man is hitting the road."

Chapter Twenty

As Shelley stood in The Gilded Lily and looked at Billy's father, all she could think about was how grateful she was that Dave Cummings and Cain Remington were stepbrothers, not blood brothers. Dave had dark blond hair, brown eyes, and a quick smile.

If he had resembled Cain in any way, she didn't know if she could have hidden her emotions. In the three weeks since Cain had walked out of his home and her life, she had learned that there was something much worse than crying out in the night and hearing an answer in a babble of foreign language.

Crying out and hearing only silence was tearing at her soul.

"Thank you again for taking care of my son," Dave said.

She smiled wanly. "It was my pleasure to have him around. You have a fine son."

Without really meaning to, she held her arms out to Billy. He didn't need her now that his father was back, but she had missed the boy's laughter and his quick, curious mind.

Billy wrapped his arms around her in a hard hug, smiling with pleasure, silently telling her that he was as glad to see her again as she was to see him. Then he stepped back and looked at her with a child's stunning honesty.

"You been sick, Shelley?"

Dave looked from Billy to the dark-haired woman with the haunted hazel eyes.

"Don't be rude, son."

"I'm not." He looked at her more closely. "You should get to the beach more. You're pale."

"Billy," Dave said warningly, reaching for him.

"It's all right." She touched the boy's cheek. "I've had a lot of work to catch up on."

"Well, now that Uncle Cain is back, you can . . ."

She didn't hear the rest. If she had been pale before, she was white now.

Cain is back.

He hasn't called me.

All the endless hours of loneliness and he still doesn't understand me, still doesn't believe that I love him. Or maybe he has decided that he doesn't love me after all.

Homebody. Child. Playing house.

Dave stepped forward and braced Shelley with his hand.

"Miss Wilde? Are you all right?"

She took a deep breath and tried to smile. "I'm fine. Just tired. I worked late last night."

And the night before, and the night before that—all
the empty nights stretching back to the instant when
Cain had walked out on her, leaving her cursing and
crying in the shell of the home she had made for him.

*Traveling man, loving only the curve of the earth. All
those landscapes of the soul calling to him. A whole
world out there.*

Am I hiding in here?

She tried to push the thought away, but couldn't. It
haunted her as surely as Cain's absence.

Is he right? Am I caught in my childhood?

Distantly she realized that Dave's hand was on her
arm, still bracing her. With an effort she forced herself
to breathe evenly, returning color to her pale cheeks.

"How's Squeeze doing?" she asked in a strained
voice.

"Great," Billy said. "Thanks for giving me that
huge aquarium."

"He looks better in it than the fish ever did. Give
him a squeeze for me. And if keeping him is a
problem for you, bring him back."

He grinned. "No problem. Genevieve kinda likes
him."

Dave ruffled his son's hair affectionately. "That's
because you taught her how to talk snake."

Billy's tongue moved in and out quickly, imitating a
snake. He frowned, not happy with his speed.

"No one does it as good as you do," he said to
Shelley.

Her smiled slipped. Cain had laughed when she had
"talked snake" to him, but the laughter had quickly

changed to passion when her tongue flicked teasingly over him.

"You're still coming to the wedding, aren't you?" Billy asked.

She hesitated. She had accepted the invitation only because she had believed that Cain would be in the Atacama.

But he wasn't.

He was here.

"Please," the boy said. "You promised."

"Billy," David said quietly. "Back off. Miss Wilde is a very busy woman."

"But she promised."

Shelley looked at Dave. There was sympathy in his brown eyes. She wondered what Cain had told his stepbrother.

"Say good-bye, son. I'll be out in a few minutes."

The boy saw his father's determination, sighed, and said, "Bye, Shelley. Thanks again."

"Don't forget to visit," she said.

"I won't."

Just before Billy shut the front door of the shop behind him, he called over his shoulder.

"See you at the wedding, Shelley!"

The door shut fast.

Dave shook his head. "I'm sorry, Shelley—Miss Wilde."

"Shelley," she corrected. "There's nothing to apologize for. You have a son anyone would envy."

Dave looked around the shop before he turned to her with troubled brown eyes.

"You did Cain's penthouse, didn't you?"

She nodded because she couldn't speak.

"I thought so. I've never seen a place that reflected a man's personality so deeply. And a woman's."

"Thank you," she whispered.

"There was more to it than just skill. There was love."

Her eyelids flinched with a pain she couldn't conceal.

"Why did you leave my brother?"

For an instant Shelley thought that she would refuse to answer. But the lure was too great.

Maybe Dave knows something I don't. Maybe he can help me understand why I'm alone.

"Is that what Cain told you? That I left him?"

"No. He hasn't mentioned you at all. It was Billy who told me about you."

Her dark eyelashes closed in a futile effort to conceal her pain.

"Why, Shelley?"

"Ask Cain," she said, her voice low.

Dave laughed curtly. "I'd like to live to see my wedding day."

"What does that mean?"

"Cain and I have been in some hard places around the world. He taught me how to measure men, the signs to look for, the subtle animal signals of violence."

"Insight," she whispered.

"Yes. He has enough for three men."

She wished she could disagree. Deep in her soul she knew she couldn't.

"Cain is a storm looking for a place to break," Dave said simply. "God help the person who triggers him. So I'm asking you. What happened?"

"He walked out on me."

"What?"

"You heard me."

"I heard. I just can't believe it."

"Believe it. I do."

"Shelley, my brother loves you."

"Not enough to stay here with me."

"All the time? Won't your work let you go with him some of the time?"

She didn't answer. Like Cain, she was the owner of her business. She could travel as much or as little as she chose.

And she chose to stay in L.A.

A whole world out there.

Am I hiding in here?

The door to The Gilded Lily burst open and Billy ran back in.

"Shelley, there's a fire near your hills! I heard it on the car radio!"

She bolted out of the shop and stood in the street, straining to see. Wind gusted fiercely, forcing her to squint against the dry rush of air.

But there was no need for clear vision. It was all too easy to see the dense plume of smoke billowing from the direction of her hills. The driving force of the

Santa Ana wind had leveled off the top of the smoky column, flattening it into a long dark flag rippling toward the sea.

Even as she watched, the column boiled up blackly, fiercely, shoving against the harsh wind.

Wildfire, untouched by man.

"Is it—" Dave began.

"Yes."

Without another word Shelley ran back into The Gilded Lily, grabbed her purse, and sprinted to her car.

Dave and Billy were right behind her.

"Anything we can do?" Dave asked.

"No. If the fire is bad enough, they'll have road-blocks out. Only residents will be let through, and maybe not even us. But thanks."

She drove out of the parking lot fast enough to make the tires whine. Within minutes she was on the freeway. The view was better from there. She could see that the fire was at least two ranges of hills east and slightly north of where she lived. Her home wasn't in the direct path of the fire.

Yet.

Small comfort, but I'll take it, she thought grimly.

It was nine-thirty on a hot, dry Saturday morning. The Santa Ana winds would rake the land for the next ten hours, dying back only after sundown. Until then, the wind would blow between forty-five and fifty-five miles an hour, with gusts up to eighty-five. Burning embers would ride the wild gusts of wind, spreading fire from the mountains to the sea.

The closer Shelley got to her home, the more sirens she heard. Fire engines were pouring in from all over the county, but there were only a few roads into the steep, brush-covered hills.

Traffic thickened, slowed, and stopped to allow the screaming parade of sirens to pass. People got out and gathered along the roadside, shielding their eyes from the sun and pointing toward the wall of smoke raging against the brassy sky.

A pale dusting of ash sifted down.

Shelley kept driving whenever she could. Fifteen fire trucks raced past her before she reached the turnoff to her own narrow road. The first thing she saw was a squad car parked sideways across both lanes, blocking them. She stopped abruptly and rolled down her window.

A deputy sheriff leaned down to talk to her. His legs were braced against the stiff wind. He was forced to hold his uniform cap in place with one hand.

"Sorry, ma'am. Unless you live up there, you'll have to turn around. This is a dead-end road. Too many sightseers blocking it and we won't be able to move equipment or evacuate the residents if the fire spreads."

"I live here."

She held out her driver's license. The deputy read the address on it, compared her pale face with the picture, and gave her back the license.

"All right, ma'am, but listen for a squad car just in case."

"In case of what?"

"Evacuation. We're recommending it, but we're not requiring it yet."

Her heart turned over. "Here? We're not in the path of the fire."

"Not at this point. We're evacuating the homes to the northeast. Bulldozers are making a fuel break between you and the fire, and the planes will be coming any time now. Your area should be safe unless the wind shifts."

She let out a long breath. "Thank God."

"But just the same, you listen real good for an evacuation order, hear? Until then, shut off the gas and electricity and load your car with whatever you want to take. Better to be safe than sorry."

Shelley nodded, even though she didn't believe it would happen.

A forced evacuation? Impossible, she told herself. *There's a little ash and smoke in the air when the wind shifts, but the fire isn't that close.*

I'm not going to cut and run just to make some government types feel good.

But she kept her thoughts about evacuation to herself. She didn't want to be forced to stay on this side of the barricade. If just one random ember landed on her cedar-shake roof before she was there to put out the spark, she would lose her home.

And her home was all she had left.

A hard gust of wind rocked Shelley's car and nearly tore off the deputy's hat. She waited impatiently while he got in his squad car, backed it out of the way, and waved her through.

There weren't any fire trucks on the narrow, winding road leading to her home. Fire equipment was concentrated in the next development over, to the northeast. There, fire threatened houses with each hot blast of wind.

Driving up the hill to her house, she saw only private cars heading down to safety. The vehicles were stuffed to overflowing with clothes and paintings, computers and potted plants and pets, whatever each person thought was too valuable to risk losing.

She knew from past experience that some of her neighbors had already made several frantic trips, unloading possessions at a friend's home on the flatlands, beyond the reach of flames. Her neighbors would make the same trip in reverse at sunset, or sooner, when the fire was under control.

It had happened that way in the past. It would be the same now.

False alarm, she thought. *Like the last two times. A precaution, that's all. They aren't really evacuating anyone here.*

Not here. It can't happen here.

She kept repeating the words all the way to her driveway. She leaped out of the car and tripped the main breaker in the electrical box. Then she grabbed a wrench and ran to the front sidewalk. There, set in concrete, were emergency shutoffs for gas and water.

The water valve she ignored. The gas valve she shut off hard and tight.

Nudge appeared at her side. The cat's movements were odd, stiff, edgy. Every primitive instinct was at full alert. Sensitive nostrils twitched, reading danger in the hot, sooty wind. She yeowed once, harshly, and patted Shelley's leg with claws only partially sheathed.

"I know, Nudge. It smells like hell. Literally."

Racing through the house, she shut windows and doors before she threw off her work clothes and pulled on jeans. She hesitated, then hauled out Nudge's car carrier.

The cat saw the cage and tried to bolt.

"No you don't!" she said, grabbing the cat's scruff.

Quickly, firmly, she stuffed an unhappy, spitting Nudge into the cage and carried it out to the car.

"I don't want you to panic and run off into the hills if the wind shifts and you smell a lot of smoke," she explained. "You'd singe every hair on that pretty coat."

The cat squalled in loud protest when Shelley moved away.

"Sorry, Nudge. I've got a long list and a short clock. Take a nap."

Moving quickly, running through the list in her mind, she hauled a ladder out of the garage and leaned it against the overhanging eaves.

"Hope the water pressure holds," she said. "If everyone taps into it at once . . ."

With a silent prayer she turned the hose on full force. There was still water pressure. Not as much as usual, but enough to make the rainbird sprinkler work.

She dragged the hose up the ladder. The sprinkler

attached to the hose chattered wildly and scattered water all around as she scrambled up onto the dry shake shingles. She hooked the sprinkler stand over a roof vent, adjusted the head for a circular pattern and stood back, ignoring the cold stream of water lashing across her with each sweep of the rainbird.

From the rooftop Shelley could see up the street to her left, where the cul-de-sac made a graceful loop. Beyond the curving, single row of houses, flames raged two ridgelines to the northeast. The fire looked like a red-fringed, black blanket being shaken savagely over the tawny hills.

The sound of a large propeller plane throbbed through the air. She squinted, caught a flash of metal, and spotted a Sierra Deuce dropping out of the blue-gray sky. After circling the fiery ridgeline a few thousand feet above the flames, the aircraft slanted down. With a final silver flash, it vanished into the smoke.

Unconsciously holding her breath, she watched until the plane finally emerged again. Somewhere, hidden within the smoke, thousands of gallons of fire retardant were raining down, slowing for an instant the hungry march of flames.

The wind veered suddenly, blowing directly toward her house rather than at a diagonal that would steer the fire past her to the waiting sea. Shelley's heart slammed as the black blanket leaped toward her. The air smelled of smoke. Ashes drifted down into the steep canyon just across the street from her.

No! she thought fiercely. *The wind will shift again. It has to!*

Across the street and beyond the green terraces of the hilltop homes, bulldozers labored on the ridge and in the canyon below. Like huge metal shamans drawing god signs in the dirt, the machines gouged lines of raw earth across the paths fire might take.

The wind shifted again, nearly returning to its original direction. The smoke retreated slightly.

Watching, Shelley prayed that the fiery blanket hadn't shaken off any of its red-hot fringe in her area. If it had, the burning embers would leapfrog fuel breaks and fire lines. Tiny, hidden flames would lick deep within the sun-bleached chaparral; then fire would pool and run together until it leaped fully grown onto the back of the raging wind and rode to new ridges, new hillsides, new houses.

Her home.

It can't be. It just can't.

A cold dash of water across Shelley's back reminded her that there was still much to be done. Her house had three levels of roof to protect. She had put a sprinkler on only one.

Cautiously she walked across the slanting roof back to the ladder and climbed down. She went to the garage, pulled out another lightweight ladder, and hauled it through the redwood gate and down the steep flagstone steps to the second rooftop level of her home. Propping up the ladder, she turned on another hose and sprinkler and dragged it up on the middle roof.

As soon as she positioned the sprinkler to cover as much as possible of the cedar shingles, she hurried down the ladder again and went back to the garage.

By the time she had a sprinkler going on the lowest roof overlooking the pool, she was drenched. Yet as soon as she moved away from the sprinklers, the hot wind dried her with frightening speed.

With a heavily beating heart, she hurried to the built-in sprinklers in the yard and turned them all on. The water pressure was low. Many of her neighbors had left sprinklers running when they fled.

Wind gusted, whipping Shelley's hair across her face, stinging her eyes. A fine mist from the pool's waterfall swirled around her. She turned her face to the dampness. It washed over her like a cool sigh.

"I wish I could breathe that damp air across every bit of my hills," she said. "If only I had a magic wand . . ."

Then she thought of the powerful pump that sucked water out of the pool and returned it in the form of a waterfall.

"Not quite a magic wand, but better than nothing."

She ran down the last steps to the pool pump and filtration system, which was hidden among rocks and greenery. Fumbling in her eagerness, she turned the pump on full. Instantly the waterfall tripled in size, becoming a roaring torrent that pounded down over a third of the pool and flung curtains of mist into the air.

"Every little bit helps," she said, the words both hope and prayer.

Biting her lip, she turned and looked to the southwest, toward the chaparral where she and Cain had walked. The sky was nearly clear in that direction. No more than the thinnest veil of smoke had filtered over there from the fire behind her. Flowers bloomed in splashes of color. Their fragrance filled the sunny day.

It was hard to believe a fire was burning anywhere.

Yet when Shelley turned around, smoke reached toward her home like a hand with black fingers and glowing red nails.

The wind shifted in a single, long moan that swept her hair straight back from her face. Holding her breath, she waited for the wind to shift back.

And waited.

And waited.

Ashes drifted down over her, ashes as big as her palm, ashes still burning at their edges. They cooled before they touched the earth. Behind her, the waterfall pounded with a thunder to equal the wind, sound drowning everything.

Yet nothing could hide the fact that the wind had changed direction. It was blowing very hard now, blowing straight from the fire to her home.

Shelley ran back up on each roof level and moved the sprinklers so that a new section of the tinder-dry cedar shingles would be wet down. Ash fell, streaking her arms. Some of the ash was still warm.

Some of it was hot enough to burn.

"No," she said roughly. "Damn it, no!"

Only a third of each roof had been touched by the sprinklers. It would be at least half an hour before all the roof surface had been watered down even lightly.

Yet as she watched, heat and sun drew steamy evaporation from the damp shingles, drying them, making them vulnerable to fire once more.

A squad car drove slowly up the street. A calm, oddly distorted voice blared out of a speaker. The first part of the message was lost to the wind.

Shelley didn't need to hear the words. She knew the officer was telling people to get in their cars and go down the hill.

"No," she said through her teeth. "It's not that close!"

The squad car passed by the front of the house. Words floated up to the roof.

". . . wind keeps blowing out of the east, the fire lines could be breached," a calm voice said. "There is no reason to panic. There is plenty of time to evacuate. Just get in your cars and drive slowly and carefully down the hill."

Water and ashes running down her face, Shelley stood on the lowest roof and listened to the evacuation order. Slowly she looked around.

The roof was only partially wet.

I can't leave yet. The roof is still dry. Besides. The fire is still at least one ridge over. The wind will shift again before there's any real danger. Santa Ana winds always shift.

The squad car turned at the cul-de-sac and went down the street again, sending the evacuation orders echoing between the smoky, windswept houses. Cars started up and began following the officer down the hill, away from the fire.

No fire trucks came screaming up the narrow road. Despite the evacuation orders, other areas were in more immediate danger from the fire.

"I'm not leaving yet," Shelley said. "This is my home! If I leave now and an ember lands on the roof, no one will be here to put it out."

She glanced around anxiously. To the southwest, over the ravine behind her house, the sky had dimmed from blue to gray. Overhead, the air was darkened by smoke, getting darker with each minute. Ashes rained down. With them came tiny glowing embers.

"After I soak the whole roof, I'll leave. But not before."

Part of Shelley thought the decision was quite rational.

Part of her was terrified.

The wind was blowing directly from the east, and it was blowing hard enough to make her stagger.

Grimly, she climbed to the next level of the roof. The shingles were slippery where water had fallen and crackling dry where the sprinkler couldn't reach. She dragged the sprinkler to another place. Cool, bright water streamed over the roof.

The wind veered slightly, backing toward the north again.

"Thank God," she said. "I'll have time. I probably won't even have to leave at all."

For the next twenty minutes the wind blew less fiercely. She went from roof level to roof level, trying to cover as much of the shingles as possible. When a section of roof was barely damp, she dragged the sprinklers over to wet down another part.

She no longer heard the Sierra Deuces as they made their heart-stopping passes over the flames. She no longer noticed the palm-sized ashes floating down, partially cooled by a descent from thousands of feet. She heard and saw only the job before her, a dry roof and three hoses to drag.

Forty minutes later, Shelley stood on the middle roof level, looking southwest. Sky that had been pure and blue was now the color of slate.

With her heart in her throat, she climbed up to the roof that looked out on the street, where the fire was burning down from the north and east. Each time she had climbed from roof to roof, she had promised herself that it would be the last time and then she would go down the hill.

I'm not being foolish. There's still plenty of time for me to leave.

Even if flames had already jumped the fire line and settled onto the next ridge over from her house, fire burned very slowly going downhill. And if that wasn't enough, there was a fresh fuel break cut through the canyon bottom.

I can move the sprinklers just once more. There's enough time to soak the roof and save my home.

Even as she told herself it would be all right, she glanced at her watch. A sick feeling washed over her. The wind had been blowing from the east for the past twenty minutes. The fire was coming straight at her.

Coughing as smoke raked her throat, she climbed to the peak of the roof. When she reached for the sprinkler, she looked over the peak for the first time in thirty minutes.

A feeling like death went through her.

The hellish glow of the fire was everywhere. Flames were twenty feet high, thirty feet, even higher; flames twisting and dancing over the land in terrible beauty.

A vast, eerie crackling sound filled the air, as though the day itself was burning.

Motionless, barely breathing, Shelley listened to the voice of wildfire raging through chaparral toward the necklace of hilltop homes where she stood.

Wind gusted fiercely.

Wildfire answered with an explosion of flame. Fire consumed the air, the sky, the chaparral, everything but the rocky land itself.

Even before the first embers rained down, scorching her, Shelley knew that she had been a fool to stay. The fire hadn't slowed meekly on the downhill side of the ridge and died along the fuel break. Flames had leaped the whole canyon, wildfire riding the searing wind, chaparral exploding in a firestorm that neither sprinklers nor prayers could turn aside.

Spot fires burned on both sides of the winding road leading down the hill to safety. In some places the small fires met and blended in a preview of the flaming hell to come. Numbly, held in the thrall of the advancing firestorm, she watched tongues of fire lick across the road, cutting her off from escape to the flatlands below.

A high scream rose up from the road, a sound like canvas endlessly ripping. Something flashed darkly, a shadow racing between flames several miles below, a black motorcycle accelerating through tight corners, its rider crouched half off the seat as he leaned into the curves, keeping the bike upright by using his own body as a counterweight.

Abruptly Shelley's numbness shattered into real terror. Not for herself. For the man racing wildfire to be with her.

"Cain! Go back!"

The cry tore at her throat, but the voice of the fire was much louder.

"No! Go back, Cain! *Go back while you still can!*"

The wind tore away her cry. Fire leaped the road behind Cain, in front of him, all around him, caging him in flames.

He vanished within the fire.

Time slowed, crawled, stopped. The only thing still moving was the savage leap of advancing fire.

Shelley screamed, a long sound of anguish that was torn from her soul.

Chapter Twenty-one

Shelley stood rigid, as frozen as time itself, her scream lost in the awful voice of wind-driven fire.

Suddenly a black motorcycle burst out of the flames, its engine revving in a single sustained shriek of maximum power. Cain was crouched over the handlebars, holding the motorcycle to the road with skill and brute power.

Adrenaline swept through her, freeing her. She scrambled off the roof and down the ladder. Embers fell all around, burning her. She didn't feel it.

Down the street a cedar roof blossomed into flame with a terrible soft sigh. Tiny fires burned on her neighbor's roof. Glowing ashes drifted down in a searing rain that shriveled plants as she watched.

She ran to the driveway, yanked open the car door, and pulled a trembling Nudge out of her cage. The cat tried to climb inside Shelley's shirt.

"Easy, sweetheart. Easy," she murmured soothingly. "You're too big for me to handle if you go ballistic. I know you don't like water, but we're going swimming anyway.''

The motorcycle engine's high-pitched cry came closer, dimming the voice of fire. Abruptly the sound changed, tires rather than engine shrieking.

Cain sent the bike into a long, controlled skid that ended in front of her house. He hit the ground running. Behind him, the bike continued on its side across the pavement in a shower of sparks.

Fifty feet away, a neighbor's roof sighed and gave itself to the fire.

"The pool!" she shouted.

Cain couldn't hear her. His helmet was on, black visor down, the plastic pitted and tarnished by fire. He grabbed Nudge's scruff in one hand and Shelley's arm in the other and ran through the front yard.

Suddenly the air was hot, steamy with the sprinklers' artificial rain. Yet the back of Shelley's blouse was dry. She heard the wildfire racing up behind her, felt it reaching for her.

Cain kicked the redwood gate wide open. Side by side, they raced down the flagstone steps through air that was a mixture of steam and smoke and ashes too thick and too hot to breathe.

He didn't wait until the steep path descended to the level of the pool. He literally threw Shelley into the pool from the steps at the head of the waterfall. An instant later, he followed in a long leap, taking the squalling cat with him.

A thunder of water closed around them, absorbing the first, deadly burst of the firestorm as it broke over

Shelley's home. Beneath the water, she opened her eyes on a world gone the color of flames. Instinctively she stayed underwater and headed for the flagstone grotto behind the waterfall. Cain swam alongside, moving powerfully despite his boots, helmet, leather jacket, and a fistful of frantically struggling cat.

Cautiously, remembering the fierce heat that she had felt in the instant before water covered her, Shelley surfaced behind the waterfall. The water was a seething, translucent, sooty orange wall shielding her from the rest of the world. The air was hot, bitter, steamy—but breathable.

The firestorm had passed over.

Cain heaved the dripping cat up onto the stone lip of the pool. Ears and fur plastered to her body, Nudge hunkered down and snarled like the outraged cat she was. She lashed out with unsheathed claws, but he had already snatched back his leather-gloved hand.

Bracing himself on the side of the pool with one arm, he fumbled with his helmet fastening. When the buckle opened, he swept off the helmet. Then he grabbed Shelley and pulled her close. She clung to him, unable to speak, her arms locked around his neck.

"I don't know whether to kiss you or strangle you," he said, his voice raw. "If you ever do something that stupid again, I'll kill you myself!"

Before she could answer, his mouth closed over her lips. She didn't fight. It was what she wanted more than anything else on earth.

He was alive, and so was she.

It was more than she had ever hoped for after she saw his motorcycle engulfed in fire.

When he finally lifted his head, she tried to speak. All she could do was cough harshly. Smoke had penetrated even the waterfall's protective wall.

His hand fastened on her collar, ripping apart her blouse in a single motion. He used the soaking strip he had torn off to cover her mouth and nose.

While she tied the cloth behind her head, he struggled out of his gloves and leather jacket. The jacket showed both the dull scars of fire and the thin, pale scars left by Nudge's raking claws.

When Cain began coughing, she yanked off another piece of her blouse and tied it over his face. As she finished, a brilliant flare of orange lit the ash-gray water. The roof was collapsing, sending fire raining down.

Suddenly reality crashed around Shelley.

Everything I've worked for since I was nineteen is gone.

She had given up everything for her home, including the man she loved. She had lost her home anyway, and had nearly killed Cain and herself in the process. With a low moan she closed her eyes, not wanting to see even the molten reflection of her dying home.

Cain gathered Shelley in his arms and held her while her childhood dream of security burned to ash around her.

Finally the last fiery colors ran down the waterfall

into the pool and did not return. He waited a while longer, holding her, feeling the shudders that ran through her body with each breath she took.

When his eyes no longer smarted from smoke, he pulled the soaking cloths away from his face and hers. Gently he kissed her forehead, took her arms from his neck, and put her hands on the lip of the pool.

"Can you hang on?" he asked, his voice rough from smoke.

She nodded.

He took a breath, eased through the waterfall, and looked around.

The waterfall drowned what he said. It was just as well. The words were as ugly as the smoking debris.

Nothing was left of Shelley's home but random, ruined walls and a scorched cement foundation. The rest was no more than ashes riding on the back of a wild desert wind.

Grimly, Cain dove back beneath the waterfall.

"It's safe now," he said as soon as he surfaced. "There's nothing left to burn."

She bit her lip and nodded. She had expected nothing else.

Even so, it was a shock to come out from behind the waterfall and find a landscape gone black, nothing left but ashes and wind.

So much beauty engulfed and then burned to soot and memories.

The black vision blurred beneath her helpless tears. He touched her cheek with fingers that trembled.

"I'll build it for you again," he said. "Every stone,

every flower, every wooden beam and piece of tile. Everything. You'll have your home again if it's the last thing I ever do. I promise you. You will have your home again.''

Sobs racking her body, she turned to him. "Hold— me. Just—hold me.''

Cain lay on his side in the penthouse, watching Shelley sleep. She was pale but for the traceries of red where burning debris had touched her. When he had washed the soot from her fair skin, each scarlet mark he discovered had been like a knife scoring his own body, telling him how close he had come to losing the only woman he had ever loved.

His fingers tightened in her silky hair as he bent to brush his lips over her cheek.

I'm sorry, love. I never should have left you. Will you be able to forgive me?

Not wanting to wake her, he didn't say the words aloud. He knew she was exhausted by adrenaline and grief. She was vulnerable now.

Too vulnerable.

She'll turn to me because she has nothing left. I don't want it to happen that way. It's not good for either of us.

Yet he knew he couldn't leave her again.

Shelley stirred. Still asleep, she curled more closely to him, snuggling against his warmth.

He drew her closer and he breathed deeply of her sweetness. He didn't know what would happen when she woke up. He only knew that it would be better than waking up alone.

Her eyelashes trembled, then opened.

The first thing he saw was her joy at seeing him. Then came shadows as memory returned. His hand smoothed gently over her hair, comforting her as he would a child.

"I'll make another home for you," he said quietly. "It will be all right, Shelley. You'll have your home again."

"Do you still love me?" she whispered, watching him with eyes that were older, darker, even more beautiful than he remembered.

"Not even hell's own wildfire could destroy my love for you."

"Then I'm home," she said simply. "Wherever I am, when I'm with you I'm home."

His arms tightened. He looked at her as though he wanted to see through to her soul.

"Are you sure?" he asked. "I want to marry you, but not like this. Not because you've lost everything else. That would be unfair to both of us."

Suddenly Cain closed his eyes. If he looked at her, he would take whatever she offered despite the knowledge that they would both regret it later.

"When you have your home again," he said, "then we'll talk about us."

"I'll never have my home again. Its most important ingredient is gone."

He opened his eyes and saw her certainty. Defeat tasted like ashes in his mouth.

"The art," he said roughly. "Why didn't you try to

save it? Some of it would have survived a dunking in the pool.''

She shook her head. Silky tendrils of hair licked across his bare shoulder.

"The art wasn't what made my house a home. Love made it a home. My love. But when you left, you took my love with you."

His eyelashes lowered, veiling his eyes. A muscle moved along his jaw. "Then why didn't you come with me?"

"I didn't understand then. Now I do."

"What do you understand now?"

"Us. You gave me one kind of fire and it burned through all the barriers I had built up against trusting someone else with my life. When you left, I thought that our fire had destroyed me."

Tears came as she remembered her pain and her loneliness.

"Shelley . . ." he whispered. "I never meant to hurt you."

"I didn't mean to hurt you, either. And I did, didn't I?"

"Like nothing I've ever felt before in my life."

Her eyelashes trembled as she tried to blink back tears. She couldn't, so she just let them go.

"It took another kind of wildfire to burn through reality and show me what is enduring and what isn't," she said, her voice husky. "Love is like the naked land. It's real. It's enduring. The structures we build on it might burn or crumble or disappoint us. But love survives like the land beneath the ashes. We can build again.''

She took his hands and kissed them, loving each callus and scar, each lean and graceful finger.

"I lost a lot of things when my house burned," she whispered. "Beautiful things, irreplaceable things. But still *things*. When I saw you coming up the road and the fire burning everywhere—"

Her voice broke and her arms closed around him with a grip that even he would have had trouble breaking.

"When I saw that fire explode over your motorcycle, over you, I would have given everything I've ever had or hoped to have just to know that you were alive. Everything. My art. My home. My life."

With a hoarse sound, Cain buried his face in her hair and held her as though he wanted to take her into his soul. It was a long time before either one of them could speak.

"That's how I felt when Dave called and told me there was a fire near your house," he said finally, his voice thick with emotion.

"How did you find me?"

"I went looking. You weren't at the evacuation center, you weren't at The Gilded Lily, and the bastard at the roadblock wouldn't let me by."

What Cain had gone through showed in every harsh line on his face and in the gun-metal eyes narrowed against remembered pain.

"I knew you were up there protecting your home,

and everywhere I looked there was fire. I . . . went crazy. I had to know you were alive.''

"But how did you get past the police?"

He smoothed his cheek against her hair and let out a ragged breath.

"I took a trail Billy and I had discovered. Then I cut back to the road as soon as I was past the squad car."

"You shouldn't have. If you had been killed . . .''

She didn't finish. She couldn't. She simply held him until she stopped trembling.

"When I found you had come back for the wedding and hadn't even called me,'' she said, "I didn't know anything could hurt that much."

"I didn't come back for Dave's wedding. I came back for the woman I loved. I just didn't know how to go about getting her when she didn't want me."

"But she does,'' Shelley said, smiling through her tears. "I love you. I'll go with you wherever you want, whenever you want. Just let me be with you."

"We don't have to go anywhere. We're home."

"But all those landscapes of the soul calling to you . . . what of them?''

He kissed her forehead, her eyelashes, the hollow beneath her cheekbone, the corner of her mouth, the pulse beating in her throat.

"I tried to lose myself in one of those landscapes. It should have been easy. It always was in the past."

"You didn't like the Atacama?''

"It's a wild, harsh land. Stone and sand and wind, a sky so empty it makes your soul ache just to look up at it. Dry rivers run down to a cold sea. Desert without end, thousands of square miles where nothing grows. I loved the Atacama.''

His lips returned to her mouth. When he spoke again, his breath washed sweetly over her.

''One day I found a tiny spring no bigger than my fist. The water was cool and pure. A plant with a single flower clung to a crack in the rock around the spring. The flower was so fragile and yet so fierce with life. I sat and watched it. Just watched it.''

He kissed her eyelashes where a few tears still clung.

''When the flower began to wilt beneath the brutal sun, I took off my hat and shaded the petals until the sun went down. Then I walked out of the Atacama and flew back to the only thing I've ever found that was more unexpected and beautiful than that flower. You.''

Gently, completely, Cain found again each texture of Shelley's mouth, each taste of her warmth, the unrestrained sweetness of her tongue caressing his. Her fingers worked through his hair, seeking and finding the heat of his scalp.

''You don't have to go on the road to live with me,'' he said against her lips. ''I came back to stay with you.''

''But I want to see your world. I'm not afraid anymore.''

''What were you afraid of? Me?''

''No. Me. I have a wanderlust just as deep as yours.''

His gray eyes kindled with laughter. "I knew it! But I was afraid you'd never admit it."

"How did you know? More of your killer insight?"

"No. You told me."

"When?"

"When you bought that."

He pointed to the universe of stars she had hung above his bed.

"Look at it," he said. "That painting would have terrified a true homebody."

Shelley looked at the countless, swirling possibilities calling to her, a siren song of the unknown and the unknowable.

Like Cain.

"Yes," she said. "I just couldn't admit it, because I needed security even more than I needed to roam."

"I know. That's why I came back."

"It's different now. You're the only home I need or want."

"Are you sure?"

"Maybe we'll want a home base when the kids are old enough to care. Maybe not. It depends on the kids." She looked away from the painting to the man she loved. "You do want children, don't you?"

He smiled. "What do you think?"

"I think you would have helped me steal Billy."

He whispered her name and his love. Long fingers stroked her neck, her shoulders, her breasts.

"I'd rather make kids of our own," he said. "The world needs more women like you."

Shelley's breath caught. In a shimmering, hot rush

she flowered beneath Cain's loving touch. Her palms slid down his body until he tightened and groaned, moving against the sweet pressure of her hands. His own hands sought and found the hot, unexpected spring within her and felt the fragile, fierce flower bloom for him.

"Show me the landscapes of your soul," she whispered as she joined with the man she loved.

"It will take a lifetime."

"Then I wish we had more than one life to share."

"Maybe we do," he said, gathering her closer with each heartbeat, each shared movement, locked deep and sweet within her. "All those stars, a universe of possibilities. . . ."

Together they explored the most compelling of those possibilities, the shimmering landscape of the soul known as love.

Coming in October 1997

Amber Beach

a story of intrigue, suspense, and
consuming love by the incomparable

Elizabeth Lowell

An Avon Hardcover
First time in print